MINUTES

TO

MIDNIGHT

Midnight Trilogy Book 1

L.M. HATCHELL

3 Minutes to Midnight
Midnight Trilogy Book 1

First published by ALX Publishing 2020

Cover Design by CBC Designs
Editing by Three Point Author Services
& Sian Phillips

Paperback ISBN: 9781916365100

L.M. Hatchell asserts the moral right to be identified as the author of this work.

For Mick, who first spoke the phrase that kickstarted my imagination

Abi is going to kill me!

Phoenix pushed through the throng of arms and legs that flooded towards her in a never-ending sea of bodies. Visibility was almost non-existent thanks to the relentless downpour of rain and her vibrant red hair plastered to her face. More than once she had to duck to avoid the kamikaze pigeons dive-bombing their way through the crowds while giant seagulls circled ominously overhead.

The bitter wind stabbed at her as she navigated her way through the city streets back to Connolly Train Station. Darkness fell around her and she longed for the warm comforts of home: the cosy pub that was her sanctuary as she worked, the easy chatter and friendly banter with customers. Being dry.

She sighed.

What the hell had she been thinking coming into

Dublin, on New Year's Eve of all days? Sure, Abi's incessant party planning was getting on her already frazzled nerves, but she'd just swapped one form of torture for another.

The crowds grew even thicker as she neared the grey stone building. Rowdy cheers and enthusiastic conversations announced the revellers ready to see in the New Year. Weather be damned.

As she pushed through the doors of the station, Phoenix held her breath against the stench of sweat and stale smoke, grateful her sense of smell was only slightly heightened, unlike some species of the Lore.

Occasionally the telltale signature of another Supe tingled across her skin, making her gut clench. Some she recognised – vampire or the occasional fae – others were less familiar. None seemed to pay attention to her, but still her senses remained on high alert, waiting for a strange look or a finger pointed in her direction.

The green digital clock glared at her from the notice board, as if she needed a reminder of just how late she was. *This would be a great time to have teleportation powers,* she thought as she jumped in line for the ticket turnstile.

Not that she'd use them if she did.

A sudden insistent buzzing against her hip made her stomach drop. *Shit, please don't be Abi.*

Inching along with the queue, Phoenix reached into the tight pocket of her leather trousers and pulled out her phone, preparing to apologise profusely. Relief flooded her when she looked at the screen to find Darius's name flashing back.

"Uncle D." She covered her free ear in the slim hope of being able to hear the voice at the end of the phone.

"Did I catch you at a bad time? I wanted to wish you a happy birthday."

Darius's rich tone was warming in its familiarity, and Phoenix smiled. "No, you're fine. I'm just trying to get home before Abi hands me my arse on a plate for being late to my own party."

"It's nice that she wants to celebrate your birthday."

She gave a non-committal grunt. "Are we still good for dinner on Thursday?"

"Of course. I've gotten us a reservation at the new Italian restaurant I mentioned. The table's booked for nine."

Phoenix whistled low to herself. From what she'd heard, it was almost impossible to get a reservation at Bella's. Even with Darius's vast connections, it was impressive he'd managed.

"Nine is good for me," she said.

"Perfect, I'll send a car for you at –"

"No, no, there's no need. I'll meet you there."

"Now, Phoenix, don't be silly."

"Honestly, Uncle D. It'll be easier if I meet you there. Look, I gotta go –"

"Phoenix." His softer tone stopped her in her tracks surer than any argument could. "How are you feeling? Really?"

She paused for a second and debated lying, but this was Darius. He knew her too well. "I don't really know … I don't even know what I'm expecting to feel. Maybe nothing will even happen."

"I know this is hard for you, but you can't bury your head in the sand."

Funny because that's exactly what she planned on doing.

As if reading her mind, Darius's voice turned harder, the familiar impatience evident in his tone. "Your mother settled into her immortality at twenty-five. It stands to reason you will too."

"We don't know that."

"No, we don't. With your unique nature we don't know anything for sure, but ignoring it won't make it go away either."

Her hand clenched around her phone and she closed her eyes against the pounding headache that was beginning to form.

The crackling static of the intercom announced the arrival of her train.

Her words were barely a whisper when she finally spoke. "My train's here, Uncle D. I'll see you on Thursday."

She hung up before he had a chance to respond.

Lost in her thoughts, Phoenix hardly noticed the man-mountain barrelling towards her from the waiting train. He ploughed into her with a force so unexpected that in a blink she was on her arse on the cold ground, watching in shock as his back faded into the distance.

Stunned, it took her a moment to notice the rough hand reaching out to her. She looked up into the rich, brown eyes of another man. His gaze was fixed intently on her, even as his body language was poised for pursuit.

The supernatural energy that thrummed through him was enough to send sparks of electricity skittering across her skin. She backed away from the offered assistance and stumbled, not so gracefully, to her feet. The man regarded her with an odd expression and ran a hand through his dark, tousled hair.

A sudden yell drew his attention in the direction the man-mountain had fled. And with a cheeky grin he was gone, leaving Phoenix staring at the empty space he'd been, heart racing.

The pounding in her head grew stronger and for a moment, her vision blurred. She shook her head, trying to clear the strange mugginess, but her hands started to tremble and heat built in her right palm.

Fear washed over her and she clenched her hand in a fist.

Please don't let me lose control. Not here.

Her fae powers had become increasingly unpredictable of late; any form of stress acted as a potential trigger. With no control over her power and no one to ask, she clung to the only thing she knew how to do. With slow, controlled breaths, she pushed the energy deep down inside and locked it firmly away.

Eventually the heat receded, and her heart slowed its frantic pace. The pounding headache, however, grew worse as she turned to see the train pull away from the platform, and a large crow with strange red eyes watching her from the electricity mast.

2

The party was in full swing by the time Phoenix arrived at the pub, drenched to the bone and far past fashionably late. Music was blasting out of the old-style jukebox, thumping in time to her headache, while the band set up in the corner. The lights were low and the drinks were flowing freely. A comforting sense of home welcomed her as the door closed with a thud, shutting out the miserable night.

A scan of the pub found Abi at her usual spot behind the bar. Phoenix made a beeline in her direction, more than prepared to grovel if necessary.

"Abi, I'm so sorry. I honestly didn't mean to be so late. I missed the train and ..."

Abi glared at her, hands on her hips, lips pursed.

Phoenix's heart dropped, and she said the only thing she could, "I'm sorry for being an ungrateful bitch."

Abi glared for a moment longer before her face finally softened. Her blue eyes sparkled with a hint of laughter as she took in Phoenix's dishevelled appearance. "I'll get you a drink."

Just like that, she was forgiven, and for the first time all day, she felt a bit lighter. Giving Abi a small smile, she slipped behind the bar and upstairs to the apartment they shared.

The headache was just stress, she assured herself. Turning twenty-five wasn't a big deal; Darius was overreacting. There was every chance she'd keep ageing as normal. She needed to get cleaned up and celebrate with her friend.

Anyway, even if she did follow in her mother's footsteps, it didn't mean anything had to change … did it?

"… Five, four, three, two, one!"

Just as the clock struck midnight and the crowd around her cheered at the top of their lungs, the room began to swim and Phoenix's vision blurred. A violent shudder ran down her spine and her hands gripped the edge of the bar, knuckles turning white.

A mere second and the moment passed. Everything came back into sharp focus and Abi's voice reverberated loudly in her ear. "Happy birthday!"

Phoenix shook her head, trying to get her bearings. She returned Abi's embrace and let her friend's ever-contagious enthusiasm wash over her as she pushed back the sense of unease. It was just the drink, that's all.

One arm still locked around her waist, Abi swayed along with the crowd of people, singing a very out of tune "Auld Lang Syne". Phoenix dutifully followed suit, but the niggle of unease refused to leave her.

When the crowd broke into a rowdy rendition of "The Fields of Athenry", Phoenix extricated herself from her friend's grip and slipped away in search of a strong drink. She grabbed an empty glass and made her way to the bar to fetch a fresh bottle.

You can't have a celebration without rum. And that's what this is, isn't it? A celebration.

Pouring a generous measure, she took a breath and knocked it back straight. She waited a moment, expecting the room to spin, or some sign the drink was going to her head.

Nothing happened.

Her vision didn't blur, and the room didn't spin. She tried another large gulp straight from the bottle.

Nothing.

With a sigh, she poured more rum into her glass and topped it with a wedge of lime. Who was she kidding? Her metabolism was far too accelerated for the alcohol to affect her. Maybe she was coming down with the flu. Sure, human diseases didn't normally affect her, but it was possible. All these crazy super bugs going around, who knew?

Clutching the glass, her free hand played with the platinum medallion hanging from her neck. The hard, embossed edges of the sun pressed into the palm of her hand. Her mother's emblem. One of the only things she had left of her.

She never thought of asking her mother what it would feel like when her immortality kicked in. She'd always assumed her parents would be with her when the time came.

Her father had been in his thirties when he was turned. Sure, he had to die for it to happen, but who says her fae side would be more dominant anyway? Just because the fae reached their immortality at twenty-five, didn't mean she would. Maybe she'd need to die before it happened, like her father. Hell, maybe a hybrid wouldn't even become immortal at all …

Looking around, she was filled with an over-whelming sense of gratitude for the life she'd built. Abi had saved her by giving her this job, a place to stay, and a way to escape the Lore. She couldn't ever imagine leaving it behind.

But how many years would she have before people noticed she wasn't aging? How long would it take before

Abi asked questions she couldn't answer? How long before she would have to say goodbye?

No sooner had the thought formed in her head than a shudder ran through her and her vision turned black. The glass slipped from her grasp and smashed to pieces on the tiled floor.

3

"You don't scream for me anymore."

Il Maestro pondered this, tilting his head as he looked at the frail figures curled up on the hard, stone floor. A chain made with thick iron links swung lazily in his left hand as he licked the blood from the fingers of his right.

The smaller of the two forms tensed, no doubt waiting on the inevitable blow. The larger form remained still, unmoving, as it had for a long time now.

"It's started already, you know," Il Maestro continued, pacing slowly around the small, dank cell, in no hurry to make use of the heavy chain. "I felt it as soon as the clock struck midnight. The shift.

"All those years waiting patiently. It will be worth it when the prophecy is fulfilled and I take my rightful place at their side. We will hide in the shadows no more."

He stopped pacing and stared at the torches that lined the wall, their flames flickering hungrily in the dark.

"At least she'll know her life meant something in the end. That must make you proud."

Lifting his arm high, he let the chain fly and felt the satisfying crunch of bone beneath the iron.

Again, his arm raised.

"Let's see if we can make you scream, shall we?"

The tightness in his shoulders had eased significantly by the time he left the chamber. Blood splatter covered the front of his black Armani suit and he made a mental note to get it dry cleaned as he settled behind the large mahogany desk in his office and wiped his hands with the embroidered handkerchief.

"You called for me, Il Maestro?"

Il Maestro looked up at the vampire before him. Even compared to his own impressive height, Raphael was tall. The broad expanse of muscle only served to heighten his intimidating aura; a useful quality to have as head of security.

"I want a full debriefing on the status of all outstanding projects at midnight tonight."

"Yes, Il Maestro." Raphael stood straight with his hands clasped behind his back, a not-so-subtle military air to his posture.

"How are the new recruits coming along?"

"The wolves are reacting well to the new formula. Their aggression has increased significantly but with fewer obedience issues."

Il Maestro nodded, pleased with this development. The mangy dogs had been the most difficult to control. As much as he enjoyed their viciousness – it took very little for them to tear each other's throats out – discipline was paramount.

"Good, it's time we start escalating our preparations. We need to be ready."

He reached for the crystal decanter on his desk and poured a generous measure of the rich, golden liquid into a glass. "Arrange a meeting with the witches and get the newest batch of wolves ready for a field test."

With a swift nod, Raphael turned on his heel and left the office.

The tingling anticipation was starting to build now that preparations were fully underway, but it was important he didn't lose focus.

The clock had finally begun its countdown.

4

Wiping the bar counter absently, Phoenix considered the previous few days. There had been no more blackouts since New Year's Eve, but a sense of dread still lingered insidiously with every waking thought. More than one customer had commented on her distraction, and Abi was regularly throwing concerned glances her way.

Not being able to confide in her friend made it even harder. But what could she say? *Oh hey, did I forget to mention I'm a vampire-fae hybrid? Don't worry I don't suck your blood while you sleep or anything, but I think I might be immortal now and I could really use a shoulder to cry on about all of it.* Probably wouldn't go down too well.

Abi's shout from above pulled her out of her imaginary conversation with a start. "Hey, Fifi, get your butt up here or I'm going to eat all the popcorn by myself."

Phoenix grimaced at the nickname she detested. Looking down, she was surprised to realise the cloth in her hand had turned to tatters; her aggressive cleaning of a single spot causing the threads to wear through. With a sigh she threw the cloth in the bin and rushed upstairs to where Abi was waiting, surrounded by a sea of puffy cushions in the sitting room of their apartment.

The apartment that occupied the upper floor of the pub wasn't the largest, but Abi's unique flair had given it a homely feel not many could have replicated. Quirky pictures hung on the wall, and each room was a strange mish-mash of colours, but it worked somehow. It was the antithesis of the vampire lair where she'd spent so much of her teenage years and Phoenix had loved it from the moment Abi took her in as a lodger.

"So, what did we settle on?" Phoenix asked, dropping into the oversized sofa and grabbing a handful of popcorn from the bowl in Abi's lap.

"Well, Mary – you know the one with the black hair? Well, she was telling me about this TV series called True Blood. It's like Twilight, but for grown-ups, if you know what I mean." Abi's blue eyes twinkled as she wiggled her eyebrows suggestively.

Phoenix choked, a popcorn kernel lodging in her throat at the wrong moment. "I didn't think vampires were your thing," she spluttered, when she could finally speak again.

Abi shrugged. "The main guy is kind of cute. Figured it's worth a look." She grabbed the remote control and pressed play before adding, "Afterwards we can decide what your New Year's resolutions are going to be."

Covering her face with a cushion, Phoenix groaned. Going back to the vampire lair suddenly didn't seem like such a bad idea.

Watching the crowds around him, Ethan shook his head. Even midweek, Temple Bar was heaving with tourists. Lairy stags and cackling hens stumbled from pub to pub, seemingly oblivious to the almost freezing temperatures and cutting wind. The rain-slick cobblestones were proving too much of a challenge for many a high heel, and more than once he winced in sympathy for the ankles that paid the price.

He'd been patrolling the city since the last attack on New Year's Eve, and so far, things had been quiet. But it wouldn't last. It never lasted.

As if to prove his point, a high-pitched scream pulled Ethan roughly from his thoughts. He took off at a run, heading for the shadowed alley the sound had come from. The sense of déjà vu that washed over him was becoming frustratingly common.

What will it be this time?

The putrid smell of rubbish, mixed with the fresh

scent of human excrement, assaulted his senses before he even reached the mouth of the alley. It made him wish, not for the first time, that his senses weren't quite so heightened.

Sticking to the shadows cast by the graffitied brick walls, he could hear the muffled sounds of terror punctuated by low growls in the darkness. But it was the sharp scent of fear that sent Ethan's pulse racing.

He worked hard to control the wolf inside him. He knew his eyes would be glowing yellow from the adrenaline, and the last thing he needed was to scare the woman even more.

A number of industrial bins lined the wall ahead, partially blocking his view. Quietly, he leapt on top of the closest one and took in the scene before him. Rage flared through him at what he saw.

Five large wolves had a woman surrounded. Though they weren't in full wolf form, their beasts were clearly in control; madness visible in their yellow eyes, razor-sharp fangs and fully extended claws.

Well, that explained the fear anyway.

The largest of the pack had the woman pinned to the wall, one huge hand holding her by the throat as he slowly sniffed the length of her neck. Tears flowed freely down her cheeks as she held herself rigid.

The scent of her fear was only driving them wilder and Ethan knew he didn't have long before they would tire of their teasing and attack.

The numbers were against him, and even though none had signatures strong enough to be an Alpha, five-to-one odds were not good. But walking away wasn't an option either. So, he extended his claws and allowed his wolf to come to the fore just enough to give him a fighting chance.

Moving so fast he appeared as little more than a blur, Ethan grabbed the closest wolf from behind and raked his claws clean across his throat.

The element of surprise gave him enough time to turn towards the second wolf before anyone could react. Grabbing him by the throat, he lifted the large frame two foot in the air and slammed his body into the hard concrete, stunning him.

And that was where his luck ran out.

By this time, the remaining three wolves had turned their full attention to him, and the woman, finally coming to her senses, fled to the safety of the street beyond. The snarling wolves surrounded him, their obvious show of logic and organisation posing a strange contrast to their crazed looks and bloodthirsty behaviour.

Ethan braced for the attack.

With his body in a half-crouched position, he was able to quickly shift to the left as one of the wolves lunged at him. The first strike missed him, but it was followed immediately by a second. A sharp claw raked across his bicep, sending a burning sensation down his arm and seriously pissing him off.

Using the offending wolf's momentum against him, Ethan turned and aimed a kick at his ribs, sending the wolf stumbling with a grunt into the large bins.

The next wolf came for him and he dropped low, sweeping the wolf's leg. But as he began to rise, Ethan was caught from behind in a strangling chokehold. His airway was quickly cut off and pressure began to build behind his eyes.

Using all his weight, he shoved back against the wolf and slammed him into the wall behind. Despite the crushing sound of skull hitting brick, the pressure around his throat refused to let up. He pushed back again, weaker this time, as the blood flow to his head slowed and he started getting woozy.

Through his now blurring vision, Ethan could see the largest wolf stalking towards him. Foam dripped from the corner of its mouth and the whites of his crazed eyes were mottled a strange red colour.

Something is seriously not right with these wolves, Ethan thought numbly as he tried in vain to loosen the ironclad grip around his neck.

Suddenly, the wolf stopped his advance. A look of surprise widened the wolf's eyes, and without warning, he slumped forward onto the ground. A large knife protruded from his back.

The wolf holding him growled in confusion, and as he tried to peer around his captive, his grip loosened just enough for Ethan to suck in some air. Taking advantage of the brief reprieve, Ethan launched an elbow into the wolf's gut and twisted out of his grasp. Barely a second later, he heard a guttural yelp and a second knife lodged in the wolf's throat.

"C'mon, big guy. They won't be out for long."

Ethan turned to see Nate's wide grin and the laughter evident in his amber eyes.

Dammit. That was the second time Nate had saved his ass from his own kind. The kid was going to be even more insufferable now.

"What is it with you wolves and all that aggression? Did mammy and daddy not cuddle you enough as pups?"

Ethan took a long sup from his pint, savouring the cool freshness as he ignored Nate's playful ribbing. Now that they were away from the crowds of Temple Bar, he could think a bit clearer, his wolf finally content to take a back seat once the danger had passed.

Cocooned in the cosy darkness of the small pub they'd found, he analysed the scene in his head and tried to pinpoint exactly what it was about the encounter that bothered him so much – aside from the fact he needed saving, of course.

"That wasn't normal wolf behaviour." He sighed, rolling his head from side to side until his neck gave a resounding crack.

Hell, he didn't even know what normal was any more. Ever since he started tracking the vamp that killed Sean, it seemed things were just getting weirder and weirder.

Nate looked at him sceptically, one eyebrow raised. He said nothing, merely took a mouthful of his own pint.

Ethan grimaced. The aches were starting to set in as his body healed itself and he wasn't feeling better for it. "The last time was different –"

"Ye mean the last time I saved your hairy ass?" Nate interjected, and a wide grin conveyed just how pleased he was with himself.

Gritting his teeth, Ethan ignored the taunt. "That was about territory. This was just mindless violence."

"They were controlled though. Organised."

Ethan nodded. "And none of the wolves were Alphas. They shouldn't have been that strong."

As he played with the pint glass in front of him, he didn't miss the flash of concern that passed in Nate's eyes; he was pretty sure it mirrored his own. And not for the first time, he wondered what the hell they'd gotten caught up in.

The two sat in companionable silence for a while, each lost in their own thoughts. All Ethan had wanted was a break from the pack. Some time to be free of everyone's expectations and the constant weight of responsibility. But Sean had to go and follow him. Had to go and get killed.

Ever since, it seemed like things had completely gone to shit.

Tracking the vamp responsible for Sean's death had been a lesson in dead ends. Yet somehow, he kept finding himself in strange situations like the one tonight; it couldn't be a coincidence. More and more innocent people were getting caught in the crossfire of the Lore, and it only appeared to be escalating.

The Lore may not have been known for peace, love, and bunny rabbits, but it was one of their most solemn edicts that humans were to be kept ignorant of their existence. The mistakes of the past had been hard-learned and the Council decreed death to anyone stupid enough to defy them.

"So what, aside from luck, brought you down here tonight?" Ethan eventually asked. He looked sideways at the kid next to him, because that's all he was really, little more than a kid.

Guilt gnawed at Ethan. At barely twenty-one, Nate hadn't even settled into his immortality yet – something that normally happened later for shifters – he shouldn't have been caught up in this mess.

Nate shook his floppy brown hair out of his eyes and

perked up. "I came to find you 'cause it looks like we might've finally gotten a lead."

Ethan's hand froze, pint midway to his mouth. "And you're only telling me now?"

"Well, you seemed a bit preoccupied back there –" Nate ducked just in time to avoid the clip across the ear. "Okay, okay. Lily's gotten some info from a witch friend of hers. Someone with connections to the Dublin coven."

Ethan smiled to himself at the way Nate's voice changed when he mentioned Lily's name, but refrained from interrupting.

"Apparently word on the grapevine is that there's some kind of prophecy at play, and it's causing all this bad juju."

"A prophecy?"

Ethan heard the scepticism in his own tone. The witches were often more clued in than the rest of the Lore. Without the strength and speed benefits of other species, their resilience relied on knowledge. But blaming everything on some random act of fate just seemed too convenient to him.

"Yeah, something about a hybrid and the end of humanity," Nate said, knocking back the remainder of his pint. "All sounds like something from a bad movie if you ask me."

It took a few seconds for the words to register with Ethan, and another few seconds for the shock to follow.

"A hybrid? How in the Lore would a hybrid have been created?"

"Well you know when two people love each other ..." Nate gave a cheeky grin as he highlighted his not so subtle point with even less subtle hand gestures.

Ethan's head was spinning.

Nate was right. If a hybrid existed, there had to have been an inter-species relationship. One that produced an offspring. Not only was that breaking Council edict, another crime punishable by death, but it was also unheard of. Hell, their very nature made it near impossible for members of the same species to procreate – an unfortunate trade-off for being difficult to kill, or nature's culling mechanism, who knew. He couldn't even imagine how challenging it would be for two members of different species.

Something niggled at the back of Ethan's consciousness, a fleeting memory that wouldn't quite solidify. Pulling himself from his own thoughts, he forced himself to focus on one thing at a time.

"So, if the witches know what's causing this, why aren't they doing anything about it?"

Nate shrugged. "That's the million-dollar question, I guess. It all seems pretty sketchy to me, and Lily's friend was pretty nervous talking about it."

"Did the witch give any more details about the prophecy?"

"She was pretty vague according to Lily. But she did say that a hybrid would bring about an 'eternal night and the end of humanity'."

Ethan drummed his fingers on the table, trying to piece it all together. "Is this why we've been seeing so much crazy shit with the Lore lately?"

Nate shrugged again. "Maybe. Either way I'm guessing we're in for a bumpy ride."

5

Phoenix puffed out a cold gust of air and rubbed her hands together briskly as she stepped into the warm cocoon of the restaurant. A low murmur of conversation surrounded her, almost as if the soft candlelight encouraged the patrons to speak in hushed, intimate tones. The occasional clink of glasses added harmony to the almost musical flow of voices.

For the second time in less than a week, she'd left the warm comfort of home to trek into the city. And just like a few days ago, the possibility of her immortality was weighing heavy on her mind. She could only hope Darius would have useful advice for her.

Looking around the lavish space, she tugged self-consciously at her black dress as she searched the room for Darius. Bella's was the newest in a range of high-end restaurants that had been popping up along the quays.

She'd heard it was so in demand that few, other than the stupidly rich and famous, could even hope to get a reservation. Phoenix was neither, and as she stood awkwardly in the doorway, she wished Darius had chosen somewhere a little less impressive for her annual birthday dinner.

A maître d' wearing the obligatory black and white suit came to greet her, pausing for a second to assess her windswept appearance before plastering a welcoming smile on his face.

"Welcome to Bella's. Do you have a reservation?"

It was at that moment she heard Darius's rich, seductive voice, followed closely by a girlish giggle. Seeking the sound with her eyes, she spotted him by a large window that looked out at the picturesque lights of the city.

"I'm here to meet my uncle." Phoenix returned the fake smile and pointed in Darius's direction.

"Oh, of course. You're most welcome, Ms. Crawford." The maître d' flushed as he took her coat.

Not waiting to be shown the way, Phoenix made a beeline for the table where Darius sat. All this yes Ma'am, no Ma'am, can I take your coat Ma'am, just made her feel awkward and out of place. Give her a nice dingy pub any day.

Darius appeared extra suave in his charcoal, tailored suit, most likely made by some designer she'd never heard of. The look perfectly accentuated his thick, black hair and pale, flawless skin. He was clean shaven like always and the epitome of class as he graced the waitress with one of his most charming smiles – fangs retracted, of course.

Phoenix cringed as the woman again dissolved into a fit of girlish giggles, just short of fanning herself with the white cloth she held. She'd love to see the waitress's reaction if she found out she was talking to one of the most powerful vampires in Ireland. Hell, probably in all of Europe. Then again, with the way movies had been romanticising vampires and werewolves lately, it would probably only make the woman worse.

Rolling her eyes, she took the last few steps and moved into Darius's line of sight. He quickly stood from the table, shifting his charming smile to her. His dark eyes were the only thing that showed his amusement as he kissed her on both cheeks in welcome.

The blustering waitress had the grace to look embarrassed as she quickly pulled out Phoenix's chair and offered her a glass of wine. Declining the expensive vinegar, she ordered a rum and coke and shook her head as the woman left the table with a mere fragment of her composure intact.

"You didn't give her a chance at all, did you?" Phoenix attempted to give Darius a disapproving look, but she couldn't stop her lips from quirking up in amused fondness for the man before her.

He really hadn't changed much in all the years she'd known him. Being as old as dust tended to make people set in their ways. The charming sophistication never faltered, and even his expensive fashion tastes had a timeless quality. He didn't have the softest disposition, but he'd stood by her parents when everyone else turned their back. That made him family.

"Oh, Phoenix, darling, I really wasn't trying in the slightest. Merely passing the time." He raised one perfectly manicured eyebrow as if to say, "What can I do if they find me irresistible?"

With a resigned laugh, Phoenix focused her attention on the menu. The reprieve from her troubled thoughts had been brief, and as her amusement faded, she found herself once more distracted by the concerns of recent days. What if Darius couldn't answer her questions? She had no one else to ask. But the memory of their conversation on New Year's Eve was fresh in her mind, and she suddenly found herself reluctant to broach the subject. Instead, she forced herself to focus on the insanely expensive food options.

Once the waitress had taken their order – two steaks, extra rare – they settled into their usual routine. Darius asked about the pub and her friends, and she diverted his prying by asking about his many business ventures. Before long, she was finding it hard to concentrate and he quickly noticed.

"What's wrong, Phoenix?" Darius looked disapprovingly at the half-eaten steak she was pushing around her plate.

"Do all fae become immortal at twenty-five?"

There was a long moment of silence, and Phoenix forced herself to meet his gaze. He regarded her closely, a stillness to him that only vampires could achieve.

"As far as I know, yes." His tone remained neutral, but the intensity of his gaze never wavered.

"Do you know what it feels like? When it happens?"

A furrow creased his brow as he considered her question. "I was turned, Phoenix. As your father was. For us, immortality was a side effect rather than a birthright."

What little she'd eaten of her dinner felt heavy in her stomach. He wasn't telling her anything new, yet she'd hoped he could give her more information. Anything to put her mind at ease.

"Is there something you need to tell me, Phoenix?"

The temptation to lie, to brush it off, was strong. Once she said the words out loud, she couldn't ignore them anymore. If she remained silent, she could stay ignorant and get on with her normal, happy life.

Until she couldn't any longer.

"I've just been feeling a bit strange since my birthday. It could be nothing. Maybe I have the flu."

Darius scoffed. "The flu? What, like a human? Don't be ridiculous."

She frowned, his tone taking her by surprise. Yes, she knew there was very little chance of her getting sick, but Darius actually seemed disgusted by the suggestion.

"It doesn't matter. Like I said, it was probably nothing." She pushed her plate aside, appetite completely gone.

"Maybe, but why don't you tell me what happened?" His face softened as he reached for her hand.

Taking a deep breath, she told him everything: the strange dizziness, the moment of blackness, the edgy feeling she'd had ever since. For a while, he mulled over the information and rolled his wine glass back and forth between his fingers. Eventually, he sat back and looked at her.

"We never did know what to expect with you. Given the two elements that make up your dual nature, it would make sense for your fae side to be dominant. In this respect, at least."

The heavy weight in her stomach dropped, and it was only then that she acknowledged the truth. She'd been hoping he would give her a reason to dismiss her fears.

As far as they knew, she was the first of her kind. The first hybrid. It brought with it a lot of unknowns, and with no one they could ask, each potential milestone was filled with trepidation and an increasing fear of what the change might mean.

"I know you don't want to face this, but I think we

really need to assume you're settling into your immortality," he continued.

A faint buzz started in her head. She rested her forehead in her hands, trying to think past the pressure that was building behind her eyes.

"Is there any way to find out for sure?"

He stared at her.

Sure, she could die and see what happens.

Darius grew grave once more. "Phoenix, if you have reached your immortality, then I think it's time you come home."

"Home?" Confusion distracted her momentarily from the growing headache.

"Back to the lair."

Phoenix froze.

Taking a sip of her drink, she chose her words carefully, though the racing of her heart was no doubt advertising her feelings on the suggestion.

"Why would I need to come back to the lair?"

"Where else will you go once you cut ties with the humans?"

She choked on the sweet, burning liquid that ran down her throat, her eyes watering.

"You know you won't be able to stay with them," Darius said as he pulled a silk handkerchief from his pocket and handed it to her. "And it's not like other members of the Lore will welcome you with open arms.

It's better if you come back to the lair where I can keep you safe."

Her heart stuttered at the very thought.

Go back to the way things were before? To being alone? She'd been a shell of herself, merely surviving. She knew now that wasn't how she wanted to live.

"I can't go back to the dark, Uncle D," she said quietly.

Before he could argue any further, she shook herself off and plastered a smile on her face. "Let's not worry about it for now. We're here to celebrate."

6

"Okay, so what's the plan?" Ethan turned from the panoramic view of the city and looked at the odd assortment of people gathered in his apartment. A vamp, a shifter, and two witches. It almost sounded like the start of a bad joke.

"We're going to do a spell, apparently."

Ethan threw an irritated look at the vampire slouched in the oversized leather sofa next to Nate. Shade's ice blue eyes stared back with the insolent look he seemed to have perfected. A black hoody and baggy jeans only added to the angsty teenage vibe he was projecting, something Ethan strongly felt he should have outgrown at nineteen years of age.

"We're going to search for the hybrid's signature," Annabelle said, swatting Shade with a magazine before she moved to stand by Ethan at the window.

He couldn't help but smile as he pulled the young girl close for a hug. Her small, freckled nose scrunched up as she squeezed him tight and he could almost feel her humming with excitement.

Annabelle's sister, Lily, stood with her back to them in the kitchen, lost in thought as she mixed a variety of strange-smelling concoctions. The sisters looked very similar with their long blonde hair and green eyes, but there was a seriousness to Lily that made her seem older than her eighteen years. Where Annabelle had held tightly to her youthful optimism in the face of their parent's death, Lily had taken on the burden of responsibility and wore it like a visible weight. It hurt his heart to see on someone so young.

"I got that part, but how can we search for it if we don't know what the signature is?" Ethan knew the girls were talented witches, but they were still young and still learning to use their power. This seemed like a big ask, even for an advanced witch.

"Process of elimination," Lily said, finally focusing her attention on the group around her. "We know how a human signature reads. And most of the common supernatural signatures. So, we look for something … other."

Ethan watched as she moved to the dining room table, unfolded a large map, and placed three small bowls beside it. Annabelle left his side to join her sister and a curious silence fell over the room. Nate and Shade both sat forward on the sofa. It was as if the room held its breath.

"You ready?" Lily's voice was quiet as she looked at her sister.

Annabelle exhaled slowly and nodded. With her shoulders relaxed, the excited energy of minutes ago seemed to slip away from her. She calmly took Lily's hands, and the girls began chanting, eyes closed.

The words were unintelligible to Ethan, but a strange sensation tingled over his skin in time with their cadence. It wasn't an unpleasant feeling; nothing like the sickening weight that came with dark magic. This was pure, natural energy, channelled and moulded to their will.

Ethan closed his eyes and let the power flow over him, focusing his thoughts on their intention: find the hybrid.

Unbidden, the vague snippets of a memory flashed through his mind. Green eyes. More vivid than any he had ever seen before. But as he tried to grasp it, remember where he had seen them before, the memory faded in a haze.

When he dragged his attention back to the room, he had no idea how much time had passed. The girls and Nate all stood over the map, talking quietly. Shade watched him from the sofa with an odd expression on his face.

Shaking his head, Ethan pushed away from the window and went to join the others at the table.

"She's somewhere near Dublin, somewhere in the outskirts," Nate said, glancing up as he approached.

"She?"

Lily nodded. "The signature feels … feminine."

Ethan was surprised. He shouldn't have been – hell, plenty of the women in his pack back home were scarier than the men – but he was.

"Can we narrow down her location?"

"We picked up a few hotspots." Lily pointed to marks on the map. "We can't narrow it down further without having something that belongs to her, but I'm sure she's in one of these locations."

"We think if you can get close enough, you'll be able to identify her from her signature," Nate said, making a note of the marked locations on his phone.

Again, the remnants of a thought flitted at the edge of Ethan's subconscious, just out of reach.

"Have we managed to find out what combination the hybrid is?" he asked, directing the question at Nate since he was their go-to for research, but also sparing a glance at Lily in case she'd picked up anything from the signature. Both of them shook their heads.

The question made him curious and anxious at the same time. He'd no idea what kind of traits a hybrid might have – or why she'd be looking to end humanity for that matter – but if she'd gotten the best of two strong species, and coupled it with some psychotic tendencies, they could be in serious trouble.

The increased speed of a vamp.

The strength of a wolf.

Some neat magic tricks courtesy of a witch or fae.

Near impossible to kill.

Shit.

Of course, there was no guarantee she had any of those traits. But who, other than an especially powerful Supe, could have wolves all over the country going feral? Vamps succumbing to bloodlust? An unprecedented uptake in dark magic practices? Because that was what he'd been encountering on a weekly basis ever since he'd left Donegal.

"You have to kill her." Shade's words cut through the silence that had fallen around them, turning everyone's attention to him.

"Shade –"

"No." He shook his head and stood. "I know what you're going to say Ethan. But it's the only way to make sure this stops."

"She could be innocent in all this too," Annabelle said, a look of horror on her face.

"It's one life, Annie," Lily's voice was soft as she stared at the table in front of her. "What about all the innocent people that are getting hurt? What about our parents?"

Annabelle's eyes brightened with tears, but the look on her face remained defiant as she shook her head. "It's not right."

Lily refused to look at her, choosing instead to level her gaze on Ethan. "You said you'd help us find out what happened to them. You'd help us make it right. If she's the cause, you need to fix this."

Ethan's chest constricted at the pain shadowing her young eyes and the truth of her statement. He'd promised to help them, and he was failing. They were all innocent victims in this, each caught up somehow in the events that were unfolding. And they'd placed their trust in him. A trust that wasn't deserved.

Around him, everyone was talking over one another, arguing the morals of murder and the value of one life compared to millions. He couldn't think straight.

"Enough," Ethan growled, not able to listen any longer. "Enough."

He pushed away from the table. They made it sound so simple. Murder the hybrid and everything goes back to normal; they all get on with their lives. Well, life didn't work that way. All actions had consequences. And how many people would be affected by his actions now? Hundreds? Thousands? More? Hell, he'd left his pack to avoid shit like this. Sighing, he grabbed his jacket and headed for the door.

"What are you going to do, man?" Nate called after him, the others watching quietly.

Damned if he knew.

7

Phoenix hummed softly along to the music as she wiped down the bar and restocked the shelves. Aside from a random group of tourists that looked to have set up camp for the night, it had been quiet for a Sunday. Normally she'd have enjoyed the lull, but tonight it gave her too much time to think.

The conversation with Darius earlier that week had been replaying itself on a loop in her head. His assertion that she would need to come back to the lair and leave this life behind was somewhat understandable. Still, the thought alone made her break out in a cold sweat.

He couldn't know how it affected her, spending so much time in the darkness. As a vampire, she craved that very thing. But she wasn't just a vampire, she was also half fae – a sun elemental – and that half of her died a slow death every day she spent away from the sun. Six years had been a very slow death.

That didn't even factor in the consequences for Darius if the Council found out he'd been hiding her. They'd crucify him. Aiding and abetting an inter-species relationship. Harbouring the results of such a relationship. She didn't know much about the Council, but she was pretty sure they'd be pissed.

Darius had taken her in without question when her parents disappeared and she'd be forever grateful to him, but she was older now. It was time to stand on her own two feet.

Lost in her thoughts, she jumped a mile when she turned to find a man standing patiently at the bar behind her with an amused smile on his face. He was vaguely familiar and she was pretty sure he'd come in with the group of tourists. He'd made a few attempts to talk to her earlier in the night, but her head had been too far up her arse to appreciate the attention.

"Sorry, was miles away." Phoenix forced a friendly smile onto her face as her eyes scanned the pub floor for Abi. Her friend stood by the stage with a grin on her face, giving a not-so-subtle two thumbs up.

Phoenix groaned inwardly, "What can I get you?"

"A pint of the black stuff, please."

His Scottish accent seemed to have gotten thicker from earlier in the night and he had a cute dimple when he smiled. He really wasn't bad looking, Phoenix acknowledged, as she grabbed a pint glass and held it under the Guinness tap.

"Any chance I can buy you a drink?" His eyes watched her with unmasked interest as she waited for the pint to settle before topping it up.

"Thanks, but I'm working." Phoenix waved at the half-empty bar around her, giving him a small smile.

The poor guy really had no idea what a loaded question that was. She hadn't let herself feed from anyone in weeks, and the idea of a "drink" sounded pretty appealing. Generally, her fae side was dominant enough to gain sustenance from the sun without the need to take blood regularly. It was one of the few mercies of her hybrid nature, and one of the ways she could maintain the illusion of being normal. But with the stress of the past week, not to mention the serious lack of sun, the urge was making itself known.

"Maybe later." He smiled and looked at her for a moment longer before taking his drink back to his friends.

Maybe ...

Phoenix turned back to her morose thoughts while stocking the shelves. She had no idea how much time had passed when a cold breeze brushed the back of her neck and she heard the creaking of the door. A strange sense of awareness sent a shiver down her spine.

She froze. Arm paused mid-air clutching the bottle of Jack Daniels, she swivelled her head to locate the source of her unease. But all she found was empty space. The door swung closed, bringing with it the icy draught of the winter night beyond.

It was official, she was losing her marbles.

Ever since her birthday, she'd been on edge, feeling eyes on her everywhere she went. She was starting to think becoming immortal wasn't her problem at all. Going crazy was.

"Oh my God, Phoenix, you've *got* to check out this guy that just walked in. Hot is not even the word!" Abi came up behind her, squealing with excitement as she reached around to grab a glass from the back wall.

Phoenix laughed, her earlier irritation forgotten as she turned to watch Abi fill the glass with a pint of Blue Moon. It wasn't unusual for Abi to get excited about a cute guy, but she didn't often reach the girly, high-pitched level she was currently at.

"Now, don't make it too obvious, but he's over in the corner booth beside the stage." Abi placed the pint on the bar and ran her fingers through her long, wavy hair.

"I think you're probably over-exaggerating a bit, there's no way he's that …"

The words trailed off as Phoenix turned to look in the direction Abi indicated, only to find the man staring intensely back at her. The guy from New Year's Eve.

Even across the open space of the bar his dark eyes burned into her; the awareness she'd felt only moments before wrapping around her like a blanket.

"Uh huh, told ye so …"

Abi continued on in the background, but Phoenix was no longer listening. Her head was spinning. What the hell was he doing here? Abi had been right about his looks. Even beneath the black V-neck jumper he wore, Phoenix could see the muscles rippling as he settled back in the seat and ran a hand through his dark tousled hair. His eyes were piercing and a light stubble covered his jaw, just enough to offset the strong lines of his face.

Everything about him screamed male.

And everything about him screamed predator.

Having been sheltered from the Lore most of her life, Phoenix wasn't very good at reading the different signatures of Supes. From this distance, she could tell his energy was strong, much stronger than any human, but nothing like her parents' energy. So, that ruled out vampire or fae. The feral quality of his looks made her guess werewolf, or shifter of some sort, and that meant heightened senses.

Phoenix squirmed and tore her eyes away from him. It was just a coincidence that he'd come into the bar, wasn't it? Sure, Whitethorn wasn't exactly Lore territory, one of the main reasons she'd come here, but it was possible.

It wasn't a big deal anyway. Very few people knew about her true nature. Most Supes would simply mistake her for a vamp, as long as they didn't pay too close attention.

He was paying very close attention …

Ethan watched her from the dark corner where he sat. The small, innocuous pub was the third place he'd tried on the list, and he'd known immediately he was in the right place.

The girl from the train station. The green eyes.

His wolf stirred to attention as soon as it caught a hint of her scent, rich and warm, bringing to mind thoughts of vivid sunsets. Her vibrant red hair only heightened the image. The energy emanating from her was unlike anything he'd ever felt before; familiar enough to mark her as supernatural, but so very unique in its undertones.

He saw recognition flash across her face as her eyes met his. The connection sent a jolt through him, and he couldn't look away. For what seemed like an eternity, her gaze held his. Eventually she turned away and went back to her work. Tension was evident in the stiff set of her shoulders as she busied herself behind the bar.

Ethan found himself fascinated by the sinuous flow of her movements and wondered again what mix of hybrid she was. At a quick glance, he would have dismissed her as a vamp, but her signature was too rich and too full of life.

The more he watched her, the more confused he became. What was she doing working in such a quaint pub in a small suburb? It didn't exactly reek of world-domination ambitions. He hadn't even come across another Supe the whole time he'd been in the area. It was almost like a Lore blackout zone.

The sudden blaring of music from the jukebox broke Ethan out of his reverie. A moment later he found his view of the bar obscured as the group of tourists enthusiastically took to the small dancefloor. Downing his pint, he stood quickly from the table. That was his cue to get back to business. With one last glance in her direction, he slipped out the door and back into the cold January night to wait.

Phoenix put all of her focus into emptying the bins behind the bar. She was more shaken than she'd like to admit by the pull she felt from Mr. Tall, Dark, and Inconvenient. Her pulse thrummed in her ears. An uncomfortable nervousness flitted in her stomach, making her fidgety.

Why the hell is he here?

She'd left the vampire lair behind four years ago, and with it, the Lore and all its bullshit. In that time, she'd largely managed to avoid the hundreds of Supes that called Dublin home. She'd mostly lived a nice, normal life. So why was one landing on her doorstep now? And why was he looking so interested in her?

"Hey –"

Phoenix jumped a mile. The cute tourist from earlier was standing to the side of the bar, hands up in surrender. It took a second for her to realise she'd stepped back into a fighting stance on reflex. Heat crept up her cheeks as she forced herself to relax back into a normal posture.

"Sorry, I didn't mean to startle you … again." He flashed his dimple as he lowered his hands and gestured towards the bags at her feet. "I thought you might like a hand?"

Looking at the four bulging black bags, she was about to dismiss his offer as unnecessary. After all, she could probably lift him and the bags without breaking a sweat. But then the soft thud of his heartbeat echoed in her ears.

Her breath caught sharply. She found herself taking a step back, her mouth watering at the mere thought of the rich, coppery liquid. She stopped that thought in its tracks. There was still the problem of the other Supe. No way could she feed with him around.

A sideways glance towards the stage found her an empty table, complete with an empty pint glass. Surprised, she turned to scan the pub. No sign.

Is he gone?

His signature still tingled over her skin, but faint, like

a scent that lingered after a person had left the room. A sigh of relief escaped her lips, and for the first time since he'd come in, Phoenix's heart rate began to calm.

A loud clearing of the throat drew her attention back to the cute tourist that was now starting to fidget awkwardly. "I'll just leave you to it, will I?"

Phoenix glanced around the pub once more. The Supe definitely seemed to be gone. Abi had the floor covered, and it was pretty quiet; she wouldn't notice if Phoenix snuck out for a quick break. Maybe just a little sip to soothe her nerves …

"I'd love some help." She gave him the first genuine smile of the night as she handed him two bags and followed him out the side exit.

His eyes rolled back when Phoenix slid her fangs gently out of his neck. A look of ecstasy relaxed the lines of his face as he leaned against the wall, dazed and weak from blood loss. He'd have one hell of a hangover tomorrow, but at least she wouldn't have to worry about him remembering anything. The alcohol and blood loss combination nicely made up for her inability to wipe memories.

Pressing against the solid angles of his chest, she licked slowly over the two small puncture wounds. The natural healing property of her saliva was already beginning to remove all trace of the feeding. The masculine groan and obvious feel of his arousal against her hip made her smile.

Glad you had fun too.

She nudged him back through the emergency exit and closed the door so she could have a minute to tidy herself up. It was only then that she noticed the unusual quiet of the night and the rush of air as something moved unnaturally fast behind her.

Before she could react, a large, solid form hit her from behind and pinned her to the wall. A surprised yelp slipped from her lips, and for a moment, all of the self-defence training her father had taught her left her mind completely.

A large hand covered her mouth as a deep voice growled low in her ear, "Don't scream."

Don't scream? Fuck that!

Phoenix began struggling in earnest. She should have been strong enough – she was half vamp, dammit – but she wasn't. No matter how hard she tried, she remained wedged between a solid wall of muscle and the rough brick wall. Anger and frustration threatened to overwhelm her at the sense of weakness, but she fought to push it back down.

The grip holding her lessened for the briefest moment as her attacker removed his hand from her mouth and turned her to face him. She had only a second

51

to recognise the Supe from the bar before a glint of metal drew her attention to a large hunting knife tucked into his belt.

Fear spiked through her as the dim light of the moon flashed off the razor-sharp blade. Her vision blurred and everything went black. When it cleared, she found the Supe from the bar sprawled on the ground looking stunned, and the knife lying far out of reach.

Before she could figure out what had happened, or what to do next, she heard a sound that caused her blood to freeze in her veins.

"Fifi, what in God's name are you doing out here making all that racket?"

8

Ethan watched from his horizontal position on the ground as the human bartender stuck her head out the emergency exit. The shadows hid him from sight, but he remained completely still so as not to attract her attention.

His head was reeling from the blinding flash of light that the hybrid – *Fifi? Really?* – had emitted. The force had thrown him well clear of her and blobs of light now floated in front of his eyes as if he'd looked directly at the sun. At least that clarified the other half of her nature.

The thought of her recent feeding rose unbidden to Ethan's mind, causing blood to rush to places that made his current position even more uncomfortable. He should've been disgusted watching her, but all he could remember was the look of ecstasy on the guy's face. The memory caused a low growl from his wolf and he forced the image from his mind.

Cleary she was half vamp, but as for the rest, there was only one power he knew of like the one she'd used, and only one species with that power. Fae.

But it was night, and it took the strongest of the elemental fae to call on the sun at night. She'd looked as shocked by the power as he was. None of this made sense.

"Oh, I uh tripped over a stupid cat and stubbed my toe. Go inside. I got this."

Her nervous babbling drew his attention back to the scene before him. The hybrid stood with her back to him – *brave move* – blocking him further from sight. Her shoulders were stiff and the tension was pronounced enough that he could see the lines of taut muscle through her tight, black top. The scent of fear oozed from her, stronger now than it had been a moment ago.

"Are you sure you don't need help?" the human asked, her eyebrows raised.

"No, no, I'm good. Go inside before you get cold."

The hybrid urged the other girl through the door and quickly closed it behind her. She slumped against the metal, her chest rising and falling in deep hypnotic movements as she turned to eye him warily.

Ethan knew that he'd gone the wrong way about this if he was hoping for her cooperation, but he still needed answers. He'd just have to make the most of the situation.

"You seem awfully worried about the human for someone who's trying to kill them all." He kept his tone casual and watched her reaction closely for the slightest tick or flinch. Just two old pals talking about getting rid of that pesky human race.

The look of wariness on her face turned to confusion, swiftly followed by anger. "What the hell are you talking about?"

Ethan shifted himself to a seated position, moving his back to the wall. Her confusion appeared genuine; the indignation most definitely was.

"You're not really going to tell me you know nothing about the prophecy are you?"

She looked at him blankly.

"You know," he prompted, "the one where you bring about the end of humanity."

"Are you insane?" Anger gave way to a look of utter disbelief as she gaped at him. "Who the hell are you?"

"You *are* the hybrid, aren't you?"

The quick change of direction caused a shift in her demeanour so slight he would've missed it if he'd blinked.

"It's okay, you don't have to answer that. I already know you are."

"What do you want from me?"

"Well I was hoping we could have a chat, but I'll settle for your name to start. Tell me it's not really Fifi?"

Lucky for him, shooting the sun from your eyes wasn't a real power, because with the glare now fixed on him, he was pretty sure he'd be burned to a crisp.

"No, it's not Fifi," she said through gritted teeth.

He waited, but no other name was forthcoming.

Fifi it is.

"So, Fifi, about this prophecy –"

"How many times do I need to tell you? I don't know anything about a goddamn prophecy! All I want is to be left alone."

"That makes two of us." His laugh held no trace of humour. "But somehow it seems to have become my problem. And from what I hear, you're the one I need to talk to."

"Well, I've no intention of hurting anyone, so your information is obviously wrong." She pushed away from the door, standing straight and defiant.

Ethan looked at her, then down at himself and raised one eyebrow.

"Well you deserved it. You attacked me first." She huffed and crossed her arms over her chest.

Ethan felt his lips quirk at the gesture. This girl fascinated him. Nothing about her reactions felt forced or faked, and all of his instincts were telling him she was being truthful. At least in her mind. If she was to be responsible for ending humanity, he didn't believe it would be intentional. But that didn't rule out unintentional, so where did that leave them?

"Okay, let's say you really don't know anything about this prophecy." Ethan leaned forward and rested his forearms loosely on bent knees. "Do you know of any other hybrids like you?"

For a moment he thought she would refuse to answer, but she sighed and shook her head mutely.

"I don't either." He nodded in acknowledgement of her honesty. "So, let's – for argument's sake – assume you're the hybrid in the prophecy. How might you be involved in bringing about the end of humanity?"

Her jaw dropped and she stared at him dumbfounded for a minute before speaking. "Are you seriously asking me that? What the hell does this so-called prophecy say anyway?"

"Well, the details are a bit vague at the moment –"

"Are you fucking kidding me?"

Her voice reached glass-shattering pitches as she picked up one of the bags of rubbish that had been discarded in favour of feeding and flung it at him.

"You came here to kill me because of some vague, bullshit prophecy you don't even know the details of?"

Ethan held his hands up, palms forward, as he struggled to stand. He was way too much of a sitting duck for flying projectiles if he stayed on the ground.

"Whoa, whoa, whoa! I didn't come here to kill you."

Her hand froze as it reached for the next bag of rubbish and she gaped at him. Opening and closing her mouth repeatedly as if she couldn't form the words, she jabbed her finger towards the ground to the left of him.

He glanced quickly to where she pointed and realisation dawned on him when he caught sight of his hunting knife glinting in the moonlight.

"Oh, that." He grinned sheepishly. "Yeah, I kind of forgot that was there. I always carry it on me."

"What, like a safety blanket?" She snorted her disbelief.

"Things are bad out there." Ethan grew serious. For some inexplicable reason, he needed her to understand.

"What do you expect me to do about it?"

He blew out a breath. How the hell could he get through to her?

"I know you don't want to hear this, and I know I've gone about this the wrong way, but when I say things are bad, I mean they're really bad."

He ran his fingers through his hair, forcing it out of his eyes. "Innocent people are dying, and I can't stop it. I don't know how you fit into all this, but you do. Help me figure it out … please."

She shook her head and took a step back until she was wedged more firmly against the door. "No way. I'm not getting dragged into this. You people wanted nothing to do with me, so I want nothing to do with you people."

With that she grabbed the handle of the door, her forearm tensed to tug it open.

"But it's not us that will suffer, is it? It's the humans. It's people like your friend inside."

She hesitated, and for a minute, Ethan felt hopeful, but then she pulled the door open and rushed inside, leaving him with a resounding thud as the door closed behind her.

Ethan blew out the breath he didn't realise he was holding and bent to pick up his knife.

That really went to plan, didn't it?

Phoenix was still shaking as the door slammed behind her.

How dare he! Coming to her job, attacking her, accusing her of trying to hurt people, and then having the nerve to ask for her help. Where the hell did he get off?

"I hope you gave that cat a piece of your mind."

Phoenix jumped as Abi walked towards her, throwing a towel in her direction, her blue eyes twinkling. She looked at the towel she was now holding and smiled weakly at her friend.

"Hey, you okay?" Abi's smile quickly faded as concern caused her forehead to crease.

"I'm fine, just a bit of a headache."

"Well look, the bar is quiet, why don't you head upstairs and I can finish down here?" Abi began gathering the empty glasses from tables around her, obviously satisfied the matter was settled.

It was only then that Phoenix noticed the lack of music, the jukebox sitting silently in the corner. Most of the customers had gone home for the night and the last few stragglers, the tourists, were preparing themselves to head out into the cold night beyond. The cute guy smiled sleepily and waved as he followed his friends out the door.

She looked back in Abi's direction and her throat constricted. If anything had happened to Abi tonight, Phoenix wasn't sure what she'd have done.

But if what the Supe said was true, then something could happen to her. And it would be all her fault.

And what about everyone else? The people she saw every day? The regulars who would sit at the bar laughing and joking with them while she and Abi worked through the night? Dear old Betty who always had a tale to tell when she came in to help them clean? The other bar staff who helped out when they were busy?

Innocent people are dying. His words repeated in her head. She wanted to cover her ears so she wouldn't continue to hear them.

What could she do? She didn't know anything about a so-called prophecy, never mind how to stop it. How could she be involved in something she knew nothing about? Sure, maybe he was just some unhinged lunatic, and it was pure coincidence that he happened to land on her doorstep. But could she really take that chance? Could she hope everything he said was rubbish and nothing came of it? Hope the people she cared about weren't hurt?

"Abi?" Phoenix heard her voice crack slightly as she

called out. "How about you choose the movie tonight?"

Abi smiled at her and made a shooing motion with her hands.

Still clutching the towel, Phoenix headed to the back of the bar and made her way upstairs. Maybe Darius could do some digging if she asked him. After all, he was the head of the most powerful vampire clan in Ireland, and a Witness on the Council. Surely if something was going on, he'd know about it.

Plus, she'd been avoiding his calls since their dinner on Thursday. If she didn't make contact soon, he'd land on her doorstep too.

Resolving to call him tomorrow, she threw on an oversized hoody and headed into the sitting room. She grabbed the soft, blue throw off the back of the sofa and wrapped it tightly around herself, attempting in vain to stop the shivers while she waited for Abi.

9

"Where the hell have you been?"

Ethan shifted his gaze from his city view to the icy blue eyes glaring at him from the doorway and grinned. "What's wrong, Shade? You miss me?"

"Dammit, man. We didn't know what the hell happened to you." Shade's glare softened only fractionally.

"Yeah, Ethan. Considering how much you've needed saving lately, you could've been getting your ass whooped somewhere." Nate grinned as he pushed past Shade into the large open-plan apartment, Lily and Annabelle hot on his heels.

Dragging himself up from the nice comfortable groove he'd made in the sofa, Ethan sighed and made a mental note to start locking his door. He walked to the large fridge and pulled out a beer, two cans of coke, and a cool bag of O negative fresh from the blood bank, then set the items onto the marble island where the others were now sitting.

After grabbing himself a beer, he twisted the cap off and walked to the large window that ran the length of the open plan room. He looked out over the dimming lights of the docklands and allowed himself to get lost in the hypnotic flow of the water for a few moments.

Nate was closer to the truth than he'd like to admit. He'd fucked up royally with the hybrid and gotten his ass burned in the process. Now, not only did he have to figure out a way to get her onside, but he also had to convince the others it was the right thing to do.

"I found her." The noise from the apartment stopped abruptly at his words. "I didn't kill her if that's what you were expecting."

It was Annabelle that spoke first, her soft voice curious but holding no judgement. "What happened?"

Ethan turned his back to the window and met the stares of the four faces in front of him. "She didn't know anything about the prophecy."

Shade raised a pierced eyebrow in his direction before turning his attention dismissively to the old penknife he was playing with.

When no one commented, Ethan continued, "She was more worried about a human than her own safety. Hell, I don't even think she realised I was there until the last minute."

Taking a swig of his beer, almost to himself he said, "I really can't see her masterminding a doomsday prophecy."

"So, she was hot then." Nate's face remained innocent as he spoke, but laughter danced behind his amber eyes.

"Nate!" Lily swatted at him, glaring.

Ethan complemented her glare with one of his own and his wolf growled softly. "What she looks like is irrelevant. The only question now is how we get her to help us."

"What?" Shade's head snapped up. "Help us? The other day we were talking about killing her. Now we're going to be best buds?"

"No Shade, *you* were talking about killing her. What would you have me do? Murder an innocent woman just because it's the easy option?" The muscles at the side of his cheek jumped as his jaw clenched. "If she's not driving this, then she's as much a victim as the rest of us."

"How do you know you can trust her?" Shade countered, his eyes blazing.

It was a valid question. One Ethan had been asking himself all day. And he still couldn't come up with a good answer. But any time he considered the alternative, his wolf reared its head, ready and willing to defend her. Every instinct he had told him they needed her.

Lily stood suddenly from her stool and slapped her palms down on the counter. "Okay, enough of the testosterone, both of you." Turning to Ethan, she said, "If killing her isn't an option, where does it leave us? What's plan B?"

Taking a deep breath, Ethan walked back to the sofa and dropped into the still warm spot he'd vacated. "Whether intentionally or not, she's involved in this. I'd rather keep her close until when we figure out how."

He gave Shade a warning look, daring him to protest. "I'll keep working on the girl. Convince her to help –" damned if he knew how. "But in the meantime, we need more information. We need to know what we're facing with this prophecy."

"Shouldn't we maybe think about contacting the Council? Let them sort it?" Lily said.

Nate jerked his head up from the laptop in front of him. "Fuck, no. We don't need to attract their attention on top of everything else."

"Nate's right." Ethan nodded. "Lily, can you try your contact again? See if she can give you anything more specific that might help us put a stop to all this."

"I have a friend in the Dublin coven," Annabelle chimed in. "I can get her to do some digging –"

"No way, it's too dangerous, Annie!" Lily softened somewhat as she saw the look of hurt of her younger sister's face. "You can help by searching the wiccan archives. Surely if the covens know about it there must be some other references to the prophecy."

Annabelle nodded a reluctant agreement, her eyes no longer meeting those in the room.

Not having the energy to salve hurt feelings, Ethan turned to the others. "Shade, you and me are on patrol tonight. Nate, see if you can hack into the Gardaí database and find out what spin the humans have been putting on these attacks. They might have spotted a pattern we're missing."

With a wide grin, Nate saluted him, grabbing his laptop as he pushed his chair back from the kitchen island. Shade grunted and followed him out the door without another word.

Ethan rubbed the stubble on his chin and reminded himself again that they were just kids. Hell, hadn't he been as much of a pain in the arse at their age? He grabbed his keys and followed them, ushering Lily and Annabelle out the door ahead of him.

He looked up as he locked the door and was surprised to find Annabelle watching him curiously. Tousling her hair, he asked, "What's up, kid?"

"What was she like? The hybrid?"

Ethan thought for a moment but could only come up with a single answer.

"Unique."

Phoenix had gone to her room with the intention of calling Darius. Instead, she found herself buried among the soft pillows of her bed and staring at the blank screen of her phone.

Doubts started creeping in with the cold light of day, and though she knew he'd be up long before sunset, she held off, reluctant to make the call. He'd use it against her. Use it as proof that his argument was correct; she should return to the lair.

The sudden ringing of her phone jarred her from her thoughts. Her heart pounded when she saw Darius's name flash on the screen. Feeling unnecessarily guilty, she fumbled to answer.

"Uncle D."

"Phoenix, darling. I'm glad I caught you. I was beginning to get worried when I hadn't heard from you in a while."

"Sorry, things have been a bit mad at the bar lately. I've been meaning to call."

She wound the platinum chain of her mother's medallion around her fingers and wondered how she could broach the subject of the Supe without worrying him too much.

"I'm glad to hear business is thriving. I would still very much like to come visit this establishment. Perhaps I could offer some investment options for expansion if it's doing that well?"

Phoenix felt her throat go dry. "I don't think Abi is looking to expand, but the offer is appreciated."

"I suppose she'll have enough on her hands, managing the pub when you leave," Darius said.

"I'm not coming back, Uncle D. I told you that."

She forced her voice to be firm, her decision very clear on the matter. Going back wasn't an option, no matter what else happened. She would stay, or she would find another alternative, anything but that one.

"We talked about this. You can't continue living with the human."

"That human is my friend."

"Phoenix —"

"Have you told anyone about me?" The question left her mouth before she could think it through.

Darius stopped in his tracks, silent for a moment on the other end of the phone. "What's going on, Phoenix?"

"Have you told anyone I'm a hybrid —" She faltered. "I mean, aside from the few vamps that already know?"

"Of course not. Do you think I'd risk your safety like that?"

Shame heated her cheeks. What had she been thinking? Darius had worked tirelessly with her parents to keep her identity secret. Why would that suddenly change now?

"You're right. I'm sorry, Uncle D. It's just, there was a guy in the bar last night. A Supe. He knew what I was. It kind of threw me."

"Do you know who he was?"

There was an edge to Darius's voice that made Phoenix pause. Had she made a mistake mentioning it? Maybe she shouldn't be making such a big deal of it.

"No. I think he may have been a werewolf, but I'm not sure."

More silence.

"Has anything strange been happening lately?" She paused, wondering how much to say. "You know, like, in the Lore?"

Darius released a harsh laugh. "There are always strange things happening in the Lore. Why do you ask?"

"He said there'd been attacks, and that people were being killed. He seemed to think I was involved somehow."

"That's ludicrous."

"I know that, and you know that, but why would he think I was involved?" The question had plagued her all night. She still couldn't think of a reasonable explanation.

"Unless …"

Phoenix sat up straighter, letting the chain fall from her fingers. "Unless what, Uncle D?"

"Unless the Council has heard rumours of your existence. It's possible they might fabricate stories, to act as a … deterrent to others."

"But why would they –" She broke off with a bitter laugh. "Oh, I get it. Make me out to be the Lore equivalent of the bogeyman, so others will be too afraid to follow the same path my parents did."

"It's just a thought, Phoenix. I could be wrong."

A heavy lump settled in her stomach at the harsh reminder of where she fit within the Lore. She was the ultimate symbol of defiance. One of their most sacred edicts broken and unpunished. There was no way they would take her existence lightly if they found out.

"Is there any chance he could have been telling the truth? About the people being killed?" She didn't say what she was really thinking; she didn't dare ask about the humans.

"I would be fairly confident the wolf is not to be trusted, but let me talk to some of my contacts in the Council and see if they've heard anything of concern."

"Thanks, Uncle D."

"Oh, and Phoenix. If this wolf bothers you again, I want you to let me know immediately."

She smiled at his stern tone and hung up the phone.

At least she had one person in the Lore on her side. Funny how it didn't stop the lump in her stomach from getting a little bit heavier.

10

With the door to the frigid morning open in front of her, Phoenix stared at the heavy grey sky. *Figures.*

She sighed and stepped into the miserable, hazy rain before turning left, away from the pub. A steady jog quickly loosened her limbs, and the rhythmic pounding of feet on the pavement became a meditative mantra, clearing her mind of the worries that had plagued her all night.

It wasn't long before the gentle incline carried her to the gate of Whitethorn Park. Instantly, her spirits lifted. She took a deep breath, savouring the freshness of the air and the energy that hummed around her. The park was blissfully quiet with only the occasional jogger or bird braving the elements. Gravel crunched under her feet as water splashed her from above and below, the bare tree branches offering little shelter from the elements.

Consumed by the physicality of her movement, she almost missed him – the Supe from the bar. He sat sprawled on a wooden park bench, his arm resting casually across the back as he watched her. A dusting of dark hair and thick sinuous muscle peeked out from the sleeve of the black V-neck jumper that was starting to soak through.

Geez, doesn't this guy feel the cold at all?

A slow, sexy smile spread across his face as she slowed her pace, and Phoenix felt an almost irresistible urge to slap that smirk right off.

"Are you following me?" She came to a stop with her hands on her hips and discreetly surveyed the park for any nearby humans. She was counting her safety on him not wanting to attract attention.

His grin didn't falter at her cold tone. "I thought maybe we got off on the wrong foot."

"I guess you could call trying to kill me the wrong foot."

An indignant pout replaced the grin as he sat up straight. "I told you that was a misunderstanding. I just wanted to talk."

Having the grace to look sheepish, he relaxed back into the bench. "I may have gone slightly the wrong way about it."

"You think?" Phoenix almost choked in disbelief. *The absolute gall of him!*

She turned, ready to continue her run and leave this madman to his games, when he stood and reached for her wrist.

"Get your hands off me, wolf," she growled, sounding almost wolf-like herself.

To her surprise, he let go, and a brief flash of annoyance crossed his face at her chosen nickname.

"I just want to talk to you, nothing more. I promise."

"We have nothing to talk about," she said, and turned to continue her jog. She noted vaguely that he hadn't corrected her wolf assumption, which ruled out running away. There was no outrunning a wolf's hunting instincts.

He kept pace with her easily. "Are you not even slightly curious about the prophecy?"

"You assume I believe there is a prophecy."

"Don't you?"

Darius's words replayed in her mind, causing her to bite her lip. In a way she would rather believe there was a prophecy. The alternative, that the Council might know of her existence, was terrifying.

"I only have your word to take for it. And considering I don't even know you, why would I believe you?"

"Well, what if I start by introducing myself?" He stopped in front of her, rich brown eyes watching her closely as he held out his hand. "I'm Ethan."

She ignored the offered hand, trying, with difficulty,

not to step back from the intensity of his gaze. "I'd love to say it was a pleasure meeting you, Ethan, but I was brought up not to lie."

He chuckled, a deep rumbling sound. "I guess that's just one more thing that's unique about you."

A thunderous bang from the sky overhead pulled her attention to the heavy black clouds that hung like a thick blanket above them. The previously light haze of rain turned to heavy droplets that splashed against her like miniature puddles and drew her attention to the fact she was getting cold and wet.

"Look, I'm done with this conversation. I'd like to get back to my run now if you don't mind."

For a moment, she thought he was going to keep badgering her, but instead he held out his hand and presented a small, folded piece of paper.

"Just do me a favour and take my number. You never know when you might need it."

A strange sense of unease washed over Phoenix at his words, effectively quelling her urge to tell him where to shove it. Silently, she took the paper and turned towards the park entrance, wanting nothing more than to go home.

11

The silver coin burned as Il Maestro flipped it over each finger, but he ignored it; pain was just a state of mind. Leaning back in the large leather chair, he poured himself a generous measure of whiskey from the crystal decanter on the desk in front of him.

After a few moments, he turned his gaze to the vampire standing to attention by the large mahogany desk. "What's the status?"

"All of the wolves are recovering after the attack, but they were severely injured." Raphael paused and eyed him warily. "It will take time for them to heal."

He gripped the glass tightly. "We don't have time."

"How would you like me to proceed, Il Maestro?"

"Kill them. Get me more test subjects and implement the same formula."

Raphael nodded before turning abruptly on his heel.

"Oh, Raphael."

The vampire stopped with his hand hovering near the door handle. "Yes, Il Maestro?"

"Make sure I don't have to kill this group."

Raphael nodded again and walked out of the office.

Throwing back the glass of whiskey, Il Maestro savoured the burn that slid down his throat as he mused on the condition the wolves had returned in. It would have taken a lot of strength and skill to overpower a group of wolves under normal circumstances, but these wolves were formulated for strength and aggression.

It also wasn't the first time someone had derailed his plans in recent months, and it was starting to become inconvenient. Maybe it was time to escalate matters further.

The air was cool as Il Maestro stepped into the large stone chamber, buried deep beneath the earth. The head of the Dublin witch's coven was already present, standing tall with her arms resting at her sides. Not quite meeting his gaze.

Curious.

"Belinda, so good of you to meet me here on such short notice."

He took one of her hands in his as he bowed to place a light kiss on the back of the smooth hand, noting the ever so subtle stiffening of her body.

"You said it was urgent. I felt it best not to keep you waiting," she said, the aging husky voice belying her youthful complexion.

"Indeed." He turned his back and walked further into the darkness of the chamber. "We are at the precipice of a vital change. It is more important now than ever that our intentions are clear to those we support."

"What would you have of me?"

He raised an eyebrow at her choice of wording. "I think a blood sacrifice might be appropriate, don't you?"

If she was affected by his suggestion, she didn't show it. Then again, he was sure she'd resorted to much worse purely for the sake of vanity alone.

"There's a full moon in three nights," Belinda said, a simple practicality to her tone. "The sacrifice will be more potent then."

"Good." He watched her as he trailed his fingers along the large stone altar that stood in the centre of the room. "It is vital that we keep the favour of the Horsemen. We haven't yet reached the end game and already there have been … interferences."

The change in her posture was so subtle it could easily have been missed, but there was no hiding the ratcheting of her heartbeat. Not from him.

She nodded and moved quickly towards the chamber entrance. "I'll see to the arrangements immediately."

"Belinda."

The softly spoken word stopped her in her tracks.

"Is there something you'd like to tell me?"

She turned, and her eyes defiantly met his for the first time since she'd arrived. "It's nothing you need to worry about."

"Humour me." He waited calmly.

Her right hand slipped into her coat pocket where she no doubt carried a protection charm of some form. Nonetheless, she answered him.

"It appears rumours may have been leaked about the prophecy. The leak did not come from my coven and the details were minimal," she hastened to clarify. "But I have seen to it that the source has been dealt with accordingly."

The smile dropped from his face, and with it, fell any air of friendliness. "There is more."

A brief hesitation, then a nod. "I believe a member of my coven may have also betrayed us recently."

"And what do you intend to do about it?"

A chilling calm settled over the witch's features. "As I said, I have a sacrifice to prepare." With that, she turned and left the chamber.

Il Maestro watched her go while digesting the new information.

The witches were becoming unreliable. Their thirst for power was overly complicated by a tendency towards inconvenient human emotions. It was possible, of course, that this had no relevance to the attack on his wolves, or earlier complications, but he didn't believe in coincidences.

Anger simmered in his veins at the thought of everything being ruined by such simple incompetency. Everything he had worked for. Everything he had waited for. Belinda would rectify the situation or she would find herself the next to be sacrificed.

Needing a release for his anger, he turned to the door that sat, almost invisible, in the stone wall and took the key from his pocket. The heavy metal lock opened and he stepped into the utter blackness of the cell. He smiled serenely as he lifted the blood-stained chain from its hook on the wall and closed the door tightly behind him.

12

As usual, Phoenix felt his presence before he even sat down. The wolf – Ethan – had become such a permanent fixture in the pub over the last few days that she hardly had the energy to get angry anymore. He'd kept things relatively light-hearted in his attempts to speak to her, but she'd be damned if she let him trick her into dropping her guard.

With Abi unloading stock in the back, and the other bar staff not due in until later that evening, she had no choice but to serve him. *Although the less contact he has with Abi the better*, she thought as she remembered Abi's shameless flirting the night before.

"What do you want, wolf?"

"Now is that any way to speak to a paying customer?" He gave her his trademark cheeky grin and rested his forearms on the bar. "I'll have a bottle of Blue Moon please."

Shaking her head at his usual choice of poison, she twisted the top off an ice-cold bottle and plopped it unceremoniously in front of him.

"What, no glass?"

Her hand tightened around a pint glass, and for a moment she considered throwing it at his head. Instead, she placed it calmly on the bar and gave him her sweetest smile.

He put his hand on hers before she could pull it away and watched her with open curiosity. "How have you managed to stay off the radar for so long?"

Phoenix tensed and pulled her hand back. She didn't sense any form of malice or threat behind the words, but his eyes were probing, and his curiosity made her uncomfortable in ways she couldn't explain.

"You know you were less annoying when you were trying to kill me," she said before hurrying to the far end of the bar, and the safety of waiting customers.

Her snarky comment elicited a rich laugh that followed in her wake and sent shivers along her bare arms.

For a while, she worked in peace, chatting and laughing with some of the regular Friday-nighters. She told herself repeatedly that the big lump of testosterone sitting a few seats away was merely a figment of her very annoying imagination. And that worked fine until the big lump of testosterone once again began working his charms on her very human, very breakable friend.

From the other end of the bar she could hear Abi's laughter. Phoenix sighed, and accepting her fate, she trudged back to the corner where Abi stood animatedly chatting to Ethan.

At her approach, Abi turned and grinned. "Hey, Fifi. I was just telling this lovely gentleman about that time I managed to get you really drunk, and we –"

"Abi! I don't think our customers need to hear about how well their bartenders hold their drink." Phoenix glared, all thoughts of safeguarding Abi's wellbeing suddenly replaced with thoughts of throttling her.

"Oh, I think your customers would love to hear all about it." Ethan threw Abi a cheeky wink.

"Why don't you go for your break now, Abi?" Phoenix shifted her glare to Ethan as she gave Abi a not-so-subtle nudge.

"Okay, okay, I can take a hint." With a grin and a wave, Abi sauntered off to the kitchen, the sway of her shapely hips most definitely exaggerated.

"So, *Fifi*, did you want to talk to me about something?" Ethan asked, once he was finished watching the show.

"Nobody except Abi gets to call me that without losing vital body parts." Phoenix reached for a large, serrated kitchen knife and began slicing lemons. The implicit threat earned her little more than a chuckle.

Ethan held up his hands in surrender. "Okay, why don't you tell me your actual name then?"

"And why would I do that?"

"Well, I could always call your cute friend back and ask her." He took a casual swig of his beer.

The thought made her shudder. She really didn't want to witness any more of Abi's blatant drooling. Anyway, why was she even fighting it? He already knew enough to cause her trouble if he wanted to.

"Fine, it's Phoenix."

"Hmm, Phoenix." He rotated the bottle of beer idly in his hands as he seemed to test the sound of her name on his tongue. "I like it."

Oh goody, my life is now complete.

When he didn't elaborate any further regarding his opinion of her name, Phoenix grabbed a cloth and moved to wipe up the pools of condensation along the bar top. Surely she could get back to ignoring him now that she'd been polite for a few minutes?

"You haven't asked me anything more about the prophecy," Ethan said after a brief silence.

Nope, obviously she couldn't ignore him.

Flashing back on the follow-up call she'd had with Darius the day before, she sighed in frustration. As expected, his enquiries with the Council had been fruitless. There were no murmurings of a hybrid, and as he couldn't ask outright without drawing attention, it made questioning difficult. Of course, Darius was a master of wordplay so it didn't stop him digging, but his conclusion was the same as before: either Ethan was lying or the Council had intentionally started the rumour.

The more time that passed, the less option one made sense to her. Why would some random guy seek her out just to tell her lies? Actually, how would some random guy even know she existed to seek her out in the first place?

Which left option two …

Phoenix finally stopped what she was doing and looked at Ethan. "Okay, I'll play ball. Who told you there was a prophecy?"

"We have some connections with the witches."

We?

"And how did you find out about me?"

"The same way."

Shit, now the witches knew about her too?

"That day at the train station, did you know what I was?"

"No. I could sense there was something … unusual about you, but I didn't know."

"So, how did you find me?"

Ethan gave a small smile. "To be honest, I'm not even sure myself."

Ignoring his ambiguity, she hugged her arms around her stomach and asked the question that worried her the most. "How do you know it's true? How do you know this isn't just a rumour the Council started?"

He eyed her quizzically. "Why would they do that?"

She said nothing, but clutched her midsection tighter.

"Look, Phoenix." Ethan leaned forward and lowered his voice. "In the past week alone we've had to prevent six attacks on humans. I'm not talking about your normal day-to-day violence. I'm talking serious shit that would give you nightmares. There's something really wrong out there."

"And how do you think I'd be able to help?"

He raised his eyebrows and a cheeky glint stirred in his eyes before he grew serious once more. "Truth be told, I don't know. But the prophecy refers to a hybrid, so whether you like it or not, someone decided you're involved."

Taking a final swig of his beer, he stood. "You have my number when you're ready to call me. Just don't wait too long." With that, he left the bar, a strange sense of emptiness remaining in his place.

He was right, she did have his number. So why hadn't she given it to Darius?

The cracked leather was rough under her knuckles, the heavy punching bag offering little resistance to her onslaught. Sounds echoed from the stone walls and linoleum floors around her, and sweat and adrenaline permeated the air. Phoenix loved the starkness of the gym; all niceties had been stripped back until the only thing left was determination and drive. Focus. Just what she needed.

She'd been coming to this gym ever since she found herself in Whitethorn, continuing the training her father had started with her before he disappeared. Recently though, she'd been slacking, and something told her it was time to get her act together.

"Not bad for a woman," Ethan's deep, familiar voice teased her from behind.

Without hesitating and driven by sheer frustration, she turned mid-strike and sent a back-fist straight towards his head. He parried at the last second. His look of surprise was quickly replaced with a grin as he moved just out of reach.

"I thought you were going to wait for me to call?" Phoenix dug her fists into her hips to avoid the temptation of a second swing.

Less than two days of peace, that's all she'd gotten – two bloody days!

"I am. I just had some energy to burn and fancied a spot of training."

She stared in disbelief at the impressive v-taper of his back as he strolled towards the large boxing ring in the centre of the gym. Should he even be allowed out on a full moon? Surely there were rules about that kind of thing.

Looking back over his shoulder, he called, "You coming or what?"

What is it with this guy?

Although ... maybe it would be fun to take some of her frustrations out on him. They still had a few hours yet before the moon would be up. Looking around, she took stock of the other people training nearby. There were enough humans that he couldn't really try anything too shady, and she could do with the practice.

With her mind made up, she strolled casually towards him. She folded her arms across her chest and eyed him up and down. "What do I get out of it?"

He appeared to think for a moment, but something about the glint in his eye told her he already had the answer prepared.

"You win, I leave you alone for good. I win ... and I don't."

Her steps faltered.

Tempting offer. But it hinged on one key factor. Could she beat him? Sure, he had the height advantage and was packing significantly more muscle than her. Hell, he was a werewolf; he'd probably chew her up and spit her out without blinking. But she had speed on her side, and with humans present, they'd have to dampen down their Supe abilities anyway.

Was it worth it for the chance to be left alone? Chewing on her lip, she decided the answer was simple – she just needed to make sure she won.

"Deal," she said as she closed the distance between them. Ignoring the hand he held out, Phoenix stepped lithely onto the high platform of the ring and jumped over the ropes.

He followed, slipping off his t-shirt as he went.

When she looked up, she was met with a solid, finely sculpted chest, dusted in hairs the colour of rich chocolate that she imagined would match his wolf's coat when he turned.

He was obviously trying to distract her.

Giving herself a mental shake, Phoenix shifted on the balls of her feet and pushed all distractions from her mind.

"First to pin the other wins." The words were barely out of his mouth before she launched her first attack.

The low roundhouse to the side of the knee knocked him off balance momentarily, but he recovered quickly, blocking her follow up strikes with a speed that belied his size, even when it was obviously being restrained.

They moved in a blur of strikes, parries, twists, turns, and locks. Phoenix struggled to dredge up a very rusty repertoire of moves, but her body quickly settled into a comfortable rhythm; her muscles remembering what her mind had forgotten.

She caught him with a kick to the gut and pressed

her advantage as she turned swiftly into a spinning back kick. Her foot met only with air.

An unexpected low sweep from the side caused her to stumble backwards, and she suddenly found herself pressed up against the corner of the ring. Before she could move, Ethan's imposing form was in front of her, taking advantage of her momentary lapse to pin her in tight.

Her breath caught in her throat and her heart pounded like thunder in her ears as she realised she couldn't move. A memory flashed unbidden into her mind. Fear. Helplessness. A blinding light she couldn't control. Her chest grew tight and she began to struggle in earnest.

But there was nothing holding her.

She blinked in confusion and tried to focus past the pounding bass of her heartbeat. The sounds of the gym slowly filtered back into her consciousness: weights thudding to the floor, fists hitting canvas.

Ethan was standing at arms-length, watching her with concern. He was close enough that she could smell the musky scent of his sweat, but he stood to the side, clearly allowing her a path to move from the corner.

When she didn't move or speak, he turned and walked to the far side of the ring, grabbing his towel to wipe the sweat off his forehead.

"Let's just call that a win for me," he said as he threw her a cheeky grin and jumped over the ropes.

Still shaken, Phoenix pushed herself out of the corner and moved to follow him. "Ethan?"

He stopped and looked at her expectantly.

"Why do you care?"

"Because I can't just sit back while innocent people are hurt."

His words were quiet, but she heard them crystal clear. And she watched quietly while he turned and walked out of the gym, more confused than ever before.

13

Ethan could feel the pull of the moon as he left the gym. It would be completely dark soon, and if he was back home in Donegal, he'd have been preparing to hunt. But this close to the city, he couldn't chance it. Besides, it didn't feel right without his pack. Each month he was away from them, he fought the change – something only the strongest of wolves could do.

It helped that his head was so full of questions about the woman he'd just left. She was fascinating in ways that could only mean trouble for him. There was no point pushing her though, he knew that now. Phoenix had her walls up so high that she didn't even realise they were there. It would take a miracle to get her to trust him. He just hoped they had enough time for that miracle.

The musical tones of "Wild Thing" dragged Ethan's attention back to the present and he made a mental note to kick Nate's arse. The kid was forever changing his ringtone, thinking he was hilarious when he wasn't.

He pulled his phone from his pocket and was surprised to see Annabelle's name flash on the screen. "Hey, kid, what's up?"

Annabelle's voice was unusually low at the other end of the phone. Her fear was almost palpable, as if reaching through the phone to claw at him.

"Ethan, I think I'm in trouble. I don't know what to do."

"Okay, tell me where you are." He forced his voice to stay calm, but his heart ricocheted in his chest.

"I'm in an old warehouse near Celbridge. The witches are doing dark magic. Ethan, I'm trapped."

"Dammit, Annabelle, what the hell were you thinking?"

The words were out before he could stop them, fear for her safety getting the better of him. She wasn't far away, less than five minutes if he floored it, but he needed to be with her *now*.

"I know. I'm sorry. But they have my friend, Ethan." Her voice broke in a whispered sob that gripped his heart. "They're going to sacrifice her."

"Shh, kid. It's okay, it's okay. Just give me the exact address."

She quickly relayed the location to him, and with a promise to stay hidden until he arrived, she hung up the phone. Moving with renewed purpose, Ethan jumped on the oil-slick black Harley he'd taken to the gym. He quickly dialled Nate's number, tapping his hand impatiently against his leg.

No answer.

Dammit, he needed to go. There was no way they'd make it in time anyway. He could only hope he would.

A silence that was almost unnatural hung in the air as Ethan arrived at the address Annabelle had given him. The abandoned warehouses looked like jagged teeth against the dark night sky, and a sense of emptiness pervaded everything in the area.

He'd have known the warehouse he was looking for even without the address. A weight fell over him as soon as he pulled close to the dilapidated structure. The weight of dark magic.

The sensation was almost tangible, like trying to move through a wall of sludge. A cold chill washed over his skin and Ethan felt like he would never be clean again. He kept his mind firmly focused on his goal and pushed through the oppressive feeling. Once he was close enough for an easy escape, he switched off the engine and rolled the bike into the shadows.

Inching along the side of the building, he found a piece of corrugated iron, bottom edge bent upwards. The scent of blood rose up to meet him and his gut clenched – Annabelle's blood.

He tried to calm the adrenaline that pounded through his body and he knelt to take a closer look. A small smear of blood ran along the edge of the sheet; a scratch from when she was crawling through, maybe. His breath left him in an exhale of relief.

If that was the worst of both their injuries tonight, they'd be lucky.

As carefully as he could manage, he bent the iron further, gritting his teeth at the creaking of metal. He was still for a moment as he waited to see if the noise drew any attention. When there was no sign of movement, he squeezed through the tight opening, staying low to the ground.

The warehouse was large and open-plan with metal racks surrounding the perimeter. Old boxes covered in green mould lay discarded on the shelves. The hole he'd squeezed through was behind one of the many shelving racks and, for the moment at least, he was out of sight in the dark shadows.

Without the walls to act as a buffer, the air had grown even murkier with dark magic. Ethan shook his head in an attempt to clear the fuzziness and surveyed the scene around him. He could hear the low chanting of the witches not far from where he stood, but the boxes that kept him from sight also kept them from his. The space along the wall to his left was empty save for a few packages that had fallen over. But to his right was a sight that both eased and sky-rocketed his worry in equal measures: Annabelle, crouched in the corner, hidden by shadows. Visibly trembling, but very much alive.

The relief in her eyes when she looked up and saw him made his gut twist.

We're not out of this yet, kid.

Crouching low, he made his way to her side and held her close when she threw her arms around him, burying her face in his chest. Annabelle quickly pulled herself together, wiping the back of her sleeve across her running nose, and in hushed tones she filled him in on the scene before them.

Through a break in the shelving he could see a young girl, no older than Annabelle. She was crouched on the floor in a white nightdress, tears streaming down her face as she begged and pleaded. The circle of seven witches surrounding her paid no heed as they continued their chanting.

"Okay, Annabelle, I need you to very quietly start moving back the way you came in." He placed his hands on her shoulders, urging her to look at him. "We need to get you out of here. Now."

She shook her head stubbornly. "I can't leave Izzie. They're going to kill her because of what she told me." Her voice broke on the last words.

95

"I'm not going to let anything happen to your friend, kid. I just need you safe first, okay?"

She hesitated long enough to make him worry he'd have to carry her out, but finally, she nodded. With one more glance towards her friend, she edged slowly towards safety.

She made it less than ten feet from him when the chanting began to pick up pace. Ethan's adrenaline surged as he felt his wolf aching to break free. The magic around them was like static shocks prickling at his nerves and he struggled to maintain control.

In the centre of the warehouse, a circle of thick, inky-black candles flared to life, casting an eerie glow on the young girl huddled at their centre. The witches surrounded her, heads thrown back, hands clasped together. Their chanting began to reach a crescendo and one of the witches stepped free of the circle, holding a large ceremonial dagger in her hand. The razor-sharp edge of silver glinted in the candlelight.

Annabelle's forward momentum halted and she turned to peer through a gap in the shelving with a look of horror on her face. Everything seemed to move in slow motion. Before Ethan could do anything, Annabelle instinctively reached out a hand towards her friend, knocking boxes to the ground in the process.

The chanting ceased abruptly and the witches turned as one in her direction.

Realising their time had run out, Ethan's movement became a blur and he pushed over the metal shelving as he hurled himself towards the witches. Their circle broke apart with shrieks of surprise, but Ethan found himself rebounding off an invisible barrier before he could reach them or their young sacrifice.

Stunned, he was only vaguely aware of Annabelle screaming his name. He turned just in time to see the head witch lunge for him. The ceremonial dagger was still in her hand, and her face was contorted in rage. Ethan flung himself to the side, the downward swipe of the blade only just missing him.

As he blocked her next lunge, he allowed his claws to extend and swiped the razor edge cleanly across her throat.

With their leader fallen, a number of the witches fled. The ones that remained took up their chanting again and their words caused the hair on his arms to stand on end.

"Annabelle, a little help here," he called, trying again in vain to reach the girl held within the circle of candles.

"Working on it," she replied, her voice strained. A second later the flames of the black candles flickered out and the chanting came to a sudden halt.

Ethan kicked the candles clear and a whoosh of air passed him as the spell lifted. The girl, however, remained sobbing on the floor.

Dammit, why can't people ever help out when they're being saved.

Just as he reached for the girl, he heard Annabelle yelp behind him. He turned in time to see her flung through the air into a pile of boxes on the floor. One of the remaining witches stalked towards her, the ceremonial dagger now clutched firmly in her hand, having obviously been confiscated from the dead witch.

With a growl rumbling deep in his throat, Ethan leapt at the witch and knocked her clear of Annabelle. Caught off-guard, the witch scrambled for the dagger, but a swift elbow to the jaw stopped her short.

He kicked the dagger well out of reach, but before he could finish her off, a low mumbled chant sounded behind him. The air became leaden as a tangible weight crushed him into the ground.

Using all of his strength, Ethan pushed to standing and searched the warehouse for the source of magic. He found the one remaining witch standing in the shadows with her head thrown back and palms spread wide. Melodic words tumbled from her mouth.

Each step he took towards her almost brought him to his knees. His limbs crumbled under the onslaught of the invisible weight, but he forced himself to move. One limb at a time.

The closer he got to her, the faster the words came. The more each bone in his body felt like it was being crushed. His wolf raged against the attack, giving him a surge of adrenaline that pushed him the final steps. Sweat slid down his forehead as he wrapped his large clawed hand around her throat and squeezed.

With a choke, her words cut off. The weight in the room lifted so suddenly Ethan nearly fell to the floor with relief.

His wolf clawed at its mental restraints, eager to finish the witch off. But just as he prepared to end her worthless life, the air around him crackled with electricity. He turned with the witch in his grasp only to find himself blinded by a fierce blue light that momentarily scrambled his senses.

"Noooo —" Annabelle launched herself in front of him. Her scream abruptly cut off as that same blue light sent a jolt of electricity through her.

In shock, Ethan watched her fall to the ground, her body spasming as the currents ran through her. The witch he'd stunned earlier now stood fully conscious on the far side of Annabelle. Her hands and lips moved frantically as she worked to draw more electricity to her.

Ethan's vision turned red, and in an instant, all conscious thought ceased and his wolf took the reins. With a roar, the hand that held the dangling witch clenched. In one clean motion, he tore out her jugular.

Blood ran down his arm as he stared numbly at Annabelle's crumpled, unmoving form before shifting his attention back to the one remaining witch.

His teeth elongated as he stalked towards her. Rage

and the full moon combined to overpower his usually iron-clad control. Ethan fought the change with what little of his human consciousness remained. Annabelle needed him.

The ball of electricity began to form again in the witch's hand as her chanting grew more frantic. But it wouldn't save her this time.

Ethan waited until she was close to the end of her chant. A brief flash of hope flared in her eyes just before he plunged his fist straight through her chest and gripped her still beating heart in his hand. He crushed it slowly, his wolf looking in fascination at the thick, black blood that ran down his forearm.

A haze filled his vision, and it took all the willpower he had to stumble back to Annabelle on two legs. He fell to his knees beside her, an invisible fist clenching his own heart.

He knew already, but still he checked her pulse.

Nothing.

He could sense no thread of life from her, no small spark to cling to. She was gone.

Her arms hung limp by her sides as he clutched her small frame to his chest, and his wolf howled in anguish. It was his job to protect her. He should have protected her.

A soft whimpering slowly broke through the haze of his grief. Looking up, he found himself staring into the glazed, green eyes of Annabelle's friend, Izzie. As she took in the sight of him covered in blood, canines still elongated, her eyes widened in terror. Scrambling away from him, she let a bloodcurdling scream and ran for the doorway.

Ethan watched her go, too tired to follow. She would have to fend for herself. He rose to his feet and gently cradled Annabelle's body as he walked out into the dark night.

14

Phoenix was just putting out the bins, ready to lock up for the night, when she heard a noise behind her.

Seriously? Again?

This time instead of freezing, she turned, ready and willing to fight. The sight in front of her stopped her short, adrenaline turning to ice in her veins.

Like before, Ethan stood in the alley with her. But unlike before, he was now holding a girl in his arms and dripping blood. His eyes had a haunted look that sent chills through her.

"Is she …" Her breath caught and she couldn't bring herself to finish the question.

Ethan nodded, looking lost as he cradled the small body close to him. "I couldn't save her. I was meant to protect her."

Phoenix stared in shock at the perfect, unblemished

skin of the girl's face, ashen now that the flush of life-giving blood had been stolen. Her eyes were closed and she looked almost peaceful, at rest. But the image was wrong. She wasn't at rest.

The girl was only a child, sixteen at best. What the hell could have happened to her?

Scanning the alley around them, Phoenix noted a large motorbike lying on its side in the shadows, not far from where Ethan stood. She was vaguely aware that there was something strange about the fact he was standing, something about the full moon, but she couldn't focus on anything other than the girl.

"Ethan, tell me what happened," Phoenix said softly, instinctively taking a step towards him.

"The prophecy …" He shook his head, eyes clenched tight as if to shut out the images. "She wanted to help, and they killed her."

He turned on her then, eyes flashing yellow with anger. "She wanted to help."

His words were like a blow. The prophecy? This girl was dead because of the prophecy? Guilt flooded Phoenix in a wave that nearly choked her. All the time she'd spent burying her head in the sand and hoping it would all go away when this young girl had been trying to help.

"I'm sorry. I shouldn't have come here … I only had the bike, I couldn't carry her well, I needed somewhere close …" Ethan shook his head and his arms tightened protectively around the girl. "I needed you to understand."

Phoenix gave herself a shake, suddenly aware of how exposed they were, even in the darkness of the alley. There would be time enough for allocating blame later, but they needed to get inside before someone saw them. Grateful that Abi had already gone to bed, Phoenix ushered Ethan through the side door and into the kitchen at the back of the bar. A small terrified voice in the back of her mind screeched at her the whole time. What the hell was she doing getting involved? She resolutely ignored those thoughts and focused only on the child in Ethan's arms. The girl was the priority.

"The girl is ... was a Supe?" Phoenix pushed past the lump forming in her throat.

"Annabelle. Yes, she ... was a witch." A small smile pulled at the corner of Ethan's mouth as he tenderly brushed a strand of hair from Annabelle's face. "A bloody good one too."

Phoenix noted the pride in his voice but didn't pry further. "Then we need to help her pass?"

Ethan looked up at her, surprise in his eyes. He nodded. "Her soul can't rest without the Ritual."

The Ritual of Passing was one of the few Lore traditions her parents had made certain to pass on to her from a young age. Supes liked to believe they were invincible, but the truth was they could be killed just like everyone else – once you knew their weaknesses. Unlike humans though, a Supe's soul couldn't easily move on when the body was destroyed. Without the Ritual of Passing, the soul would become trapped and never be reborn. It was a thought that filled her with terror.

"I think I have everything we need." She turned on her heel, making her way towards the stairs. "Bathroom's down the hall, get yourself cleaned up."

"Phoenix."

She stopped and looked back at him.

"You don't have to do this."

The smile she gave him was sad but resolved. "Yes, I do."

Taking the stairs two at a time, she slipped quietly into her bedroom and pulled out the small oak box she kept buried at the bottom of her wardrobe. The wood was ornately carved with a sun emblem that matched her medallion; it had been one of the few things her mother had taken with her when she left Faerie.

Opening it to check everything was inside, a sudden thought stopped her in her tracks and made her stomach clench painfully. What about her parents? Would someone have cared enough to do the Ritual for them? She had to assume they were dead after all this time, but it had never occurred to her that they might be stuck and unable to pass on.

Phoenix dug her fingernails deep into the palm of her

hand and forced the thought from her mind. There was nothing she could do to help her parents, but she could help Annabelle.

"Fifi, what're you doing?"

Phoenix froze at the sound of Abi's sleepy voice behind her. Heart pounding furiously in her chest, she willed a relaxed smile onto her face and turned to find her friend standing in the doorway, watching her with a look of curiosity.

"I'm just grabbing my jacket. A friend is stranded so I'm going to pick him up."

"Oh really?" Abi raised her neatly manicured eyebrows, making air quotes as she repeated, "You're going to *pick him up*?"

Crossing her arms, Phoenix glared at her friend. "Yes, Abi. I'm going to *pick him up*."

Abi held up her hands in surrender, but was laughing as she retreated to her bedroom.

Air left Phoenix's lungs in a whoosh as she released the breath she'd been unconsciously holding. She hesitated for a moment longer in case Abi came back, then grabbed the box and a blanket, and ran quietly down the stairs.

Ethan was waiting for her in the kitchen, thankfully looking less like a scene from a horror movie. Maybe no one would even notice that they were carting a dead body around.

She helped him carefully wrap Annabelle's body in the blanket and they slipped out the side door of the bar, moving quietly to her old, imported Mustang, which sat patiently in its parking spot behind the bar.

Phoenix focused on the road ahead, trying hard to give Ethan privacy while he talked to someone named Nate – not an easy thing to do with him sitting mere inches from her. As snippets of the conversation breached her consciousness, she wondered again about Ethan's frequent use of "we". The dead body in the back of her car was proof that others were involved in this prophecy conspiracy, but she had no idea how many, or what she'd signed herself up for.

From the conversation, she knew there was a sister, Lily, that was soon going to receive some of the worst news of her life. There was also reference to someone called Shade – a nickname? – and Nate, the person Ethan was speaking to directly. If there were others, they weren't mentioned and didn't seem relevant to tonight's events.

Ethan kept the details brief and to the point, asking Nate to bring the others to their meeting point so he could break the news himself. Phoenix noted the change in his demeanour with a morbid fascination as he put aside his grief and took charge of the task ahead.

As they drove further from the city, the night grew

darker around them until eventually the only light was from the car headlights and the glow of the moon breaking through the clouds. The shimmering silver light reminded her once more that it was a full moon and her heartbeat ratcheted up a notch as she suddenly remembered another concern even more pressing than the upcoming Ritual.

When Ethan hung up the phone she blurted, "How are you not in wolf form?"

Her question seemed to catch him off guard, and for a moment he looked at his hands in confusion, almost as if wondering himself why they were human. But then he shook his head, regrouping.

"I don't change at the full moon. Not while I'm away from my pack."

Well, that clarified things – not.

Before she could push any further, Ethan pointed at a narrow dirt road swiftly approaching on the left. "Turn here."

Cursing, Phoenix dropped gears and turned just in time. The rear of the car skidded out behind and she had to fight to straighten it, narrowly missing the trees that caged them in on each side.

"Jeez, a bit of notice would be helpful."

Ethan gave her an apologetic smile. "Sorry, it's been a while since I was out this direction."

"Where are we going anyway?"

Phoenix knew it was best to conduct the Ritual where the gateways were weakest, but she'd been following Ethan's directions blindly ever since they left the pub and she was none the wiser as to where they were.

Ethan looked at her for a moment, then turned away as he quietly replied, "The Cathedral."

The car veered as Phoenix turned to him in surprise. "We're going to a church?"

Reaching one hand for the wheel as if to steady her erratic reactions, Ethan shook his head. "No ... well, yes. Kind of. But not in the way you're thinking. It dates back long before the church as you know it now. Back before the church's true meaning was lost."

Phoenix shook her head and added yet one more point to her list of things to be confused about. She really didn't have the energy to play twenty questions. For a while she drove along in silence, leaving Ethan to his thoughts as she concentrated on the narrow winding back roads.

But the longer she stayed quiet, the more anxious she became. Anxious about the werewolf in her car, anxious about the people they were going to meet, anxious about the dead body she was carting around. Until eventually she needed a distraction.

"Tell me about her." Phoenix inclined her head towards the young girl lying across the back seat of her car.

Ethan was quiet, and for a moment she wondered if he'd heard her.

"Annabelle was a sweet kid," he said eventually. "She looked at the world like no one else I've ever met. Just an innocent curiosity, never judging."

"That's a rare quality."

He nodded and the skin around his eyes tightened as he glanced into the back seat. "We all tried so hard to protect her, but we were wrong. We didn't see how strong she was."

"How did you meet?"

Ethan turned back to stare out into the passing night. "I met her and her sister, Lily, about a year ago in Galway. They were on the streets and running scared." He drummed his fingers on the dashboard. "Their parents had been killed, accused of using black magic and sentenced to death by their coven."

Phoenix's throat grew dry at the thought of two young girls wandering the streets alone and scared. Memories clawed their way up from the darkness and she gripped the steering wheel tightly. She'd been the same age as Annabelle. But she'd been alone. Sitting in the dark, waiting for her parents to come back, knowing they'd been gone too long.

She forced her hands to relax on the wheel. "The girls didn't believe it?"

Ethan shook his head. "No, and it wasn't long before

their questions started drawing attention. I helped them out of a spot of bother and they've been with me ever since."

Mulling over the new information, Phoenix tried to reconcile the man sitting beside her with the man that attacked her only a week ago. Sure, he claimed not to have actually attacked her, but he definitely gave a girl mixed signals. That situation seemed so at odds with a man that would help a couple of strangers in trouble; never mind that the man was a werewolf, and the strangers were witches.

Phoenix opened her mouth to ask about the others they were going to meet, but they turned a sharp bend in the road and the charged air around them froze the words in her throat. The hairs on her arms stood on end, but she could see nothing past the dense blockade of trees that lined the road.

"We're here."

15

At Ethan's instruction, Phoenix pulled the car over to a narrow break in the trees and killed the engine. Silence.

The energy she felt in the air had an almost tangible quality to it, drawing her towards the trees and what lay beyond. Still, she stayed in the front seat, suddenly afraid to leave the safety of the car. A buzzing drew her attention back to Ethan, and she watched as the rough stubble on his chin was illuminated by the harsh glare from his phone.

"The others are here."

Phoenix sucked in a breath and tried to calm the sudden carnival in her stomach. She didn't know these people, hadn't even had a chance to ask about them, and now she was going to get a front seat pass to their grief. Nothing about this felt right.

As if sensing her discomfort, Ethan turned to her.

"Maybe it's best if you wait in the car, at least until I speak to them."

She nodded her agreement and tried not to let her relief show.

Ethan took a deep breath and slid out of the car. He disappeared into the night before Phoenix could even blink.

Time seemed to pass in slow motion, and with each minute that flicked by on the screen of her dashboard, Phoenix became more on edge. Needing some air, she let go of the safety blanket that was her car and greeted the sharp cold of the night.

No sooner had the car door closed behind her, than a heart-rending scream of anguish cut through the night, chilling her to her core. The cry was filled with such agony that Phoenix's heart ached, and she wanted nothing more than to get back in her Mustang and leave.

But there was a dead girl lying across the back seat. A dead girl that needed help passing on. So she stayed put, focusing intently on the ground in front of her as she wrapped her arms tightly around her middle.

Phoenix wasn't sure how long she'd been waiting when she heard Ethan clear his throat. She lifted her surprised gaze only to find him standing a couple of feet in front of her. Three others stood in the shadows of the trees.

When did he come back?

"Is she in there?"

The girl, Phoenix could only assume to be Lily, looked vacantly at the car as her quiet, almost toneless voice broke the silence surrounding them.

Feeling awkward and in the way, Phoenix nodded and edged further from the car. "She's in the back seat."

Lily continued to stare blankly as if Phoenix hadn't spoken.

"I brought everything we need for the Ritual but I don't know where ..." Phoenix cleared her throat, unnerved by the watchful gaze of the two male Supes standing on either side of the girl.

As if suddenly becoming aware of the tension around him, Ethan quickly jumped in. "Phoenix, this is Nate, Shade, and Lily, Annabelle's sister."

Smiling weakly, Phoenix lifted her hand in acknowledgement.

Nate barely spared her another glance, having shifted his attention to Lily. He seemed young to her; his messy brown hair and casual clothes gave him a relaxed air that she was sure was misleading based on the concern that marred his features. The energy that came from him was similar to Ethan's, but different somehow, less primal. His features reminded her almost of a fox. A shifter, perhaps?

Shade, on the other hand, kept his icy blue eyes fixed on her. Animosity emanated from him in waves.

Although the scowl looked quite at home on his pale face, Phoenix had a strange feeling this one was especially for her. Having lived around a vampire her whole life, his signature was clearer. He appeared young, eighteen or nineteen perhaps, but that was no real indication of his age, only how old he was when turned.

Lily, Phoenix noticed, looked very much like the young girl lying on the back seat. She had similar long blonde hair and the clear sun-kissed skin she imagined Annabelle would have if death had not taken the flush of life from her. But where Annabelle's features looked youthful even in death, Lily's eyes bore lines of tension that seemed out of place on someone so young.

Without another word, Ethan leaned into the car and carefully lifted out Annabelle's body.

Lily whimpered as she reached a hand toward her sister, but quickly pulled it back as if burned. Her whole body was visibly trembling, but her expression remained a fixed mask of uncomprehending shock.

In silence, they each followed Ethan through the forest until the path ahead opened into a clearing. Trees lined the space, forming a natural amphitheatre, and at the centre stood the most beautiful ruins Phoenix had ever seen.

Solid grey stone stood defiant against time and the elements while clearly outlining what had once been a magnificent building. High walls framed the north and south points, each showcasing three large arched windows that stood as proud now as when they were first built. The east and west sides were edged with a jagged perimeter of varying heights, allowing a clear view of the interior with its moss-covered walls and colourful flowers coating the floor.

The silver light of the moon highlighted their path and cast shadows from the imposing stone structure. Power filled the night, growing stronger and stronger with each step they took.

"So, this is the Cathedral?" Phoenix said breathlessly.

Ethan nodded and stepped over a low section of the wall into the ruins. He moved to the centre and gently laid Annabelle's body on a patch of soft green grass before brushing her hair back from her face.

A little piece of Phoenix's heart broke as she watched him fix the blanket around the young girl, as if worried she might get cold. Immortality had a tendency to make Supes very blasé about life; it wasn't often they were confronted with the pain of loss. The harsh reminder made her think of Abi and what she might stand to lose if her own immortality had definitely come to pass.

Retrieving the wooden box from her bag, Phoenix quietly placed it on the ground beside Ethan. She watched as he lay the sprigs of rosemary, lavender, and sage around Annabelle's resting form with care. Even the cold night air couldn't dampen the soothing fragrance that came from the herbs, and her senses eagerly soaked in the comfort they provided.

The others stood beside them, but no one spoke or made any move to take over. Feeling awkward and unsure, Phoenix busied herself grinding the remaining herbs before bringing the bowl to Ethan's side.

"Help me?" Ethan's voice was soft. His large hand rested on her smaller one as she began to move away. For a brief moment, he allowed her to see the raw pain in his brown eyes.

Phoenix took a deep breath, let go of her insecurities, and knelt beside him. She smudged the herbs between her fingers and rubbed them on Annabelle's energy points: forehead, solar plexus, and just below her naval. With the final preparations complete, she accepted Ethan's offered hand, and picking up the box, stood back to join the others.

The night fell silent around them, the usual rustle of leaves no longer evident as though even the trees held their breath. All that remained was for someone to speak the necessary words. To complete the ritual.

Aware she was the one with the least emotional attachment, Phoenix considered offering. It seemed unfair for a stranger to speak the final words for Annabelle, but if it had been her sister, she couldn't imagine having the strength. Thankfully, her internal debate proved unnecessary.

Ethan placed a large hand on Lily's shoulder and spoke quietly into her ear. Though Phoenix couldn't make out the words, whatever he said seemed to rouse Lily from her catatonic state. She straightened and squared her shoulders as she shook her head in answer to Ethan's question. This seemed to be the response he was hoping for because he smiled and squeezed her shoulder before moving to the side.

With a shuddery breath, Lily picked up a rucksack that lay by her feet. She pulled out a small stuffed unicorn and held it to her chest for a moment as she bowed her head. The unicorn was worn and a little dirty; a much-loved possession. Lily ran her hands tenderly over it once more before gently placing it into her sister's arms. She then turned to Phoenix and held out her hand.

Realising what Lily intended to do, Phoenix handed over the box with its remaining contents. The young girl raised haunted green eyes briefly to meet her gaze before turning to stand by the body of her sister. In a soft, melodic voice, Lily began to speak the words of the Ritual. Verses older than time, written in a language unknown by many, but understood by all.

Phoenix joined the others as they formed a circle around their fallen friend, heads bowed in respect and reverence for the young witch that lay before them. The words grew in strength and filled the air. And with the words, a low keening wail filled the night, making the hairs on Phoenix's arms stand on end. The sound was laced with such sorrow that it spoke to her soul.

A quick glance showed no reaction from the others, but the sound continued until it became a part of her. As the wind began to pick up, so too did the keening wail grow louder in her ears. The calming aroma of herbs overwhelmed her senses, but there was something else. Something Phoenix couldn't place.

Before her eyes, the most extraordinary thing happened: Annabelle's form began to fade. Her extremities dissolved into the currents of air that swirled around them, and Phoenix watched in awe as the body in front of her became little more than a glittering memory carried on the wind.

As suddenly as it began, the wind stopped.

The small stuffed unicorn dropped to the ground, and the night fell quiet. With one final word, Lily crumpled, sobbing as she curled tightly in on herself. Nate rushed to her side and lifted her trembling frame. He cradled her close to his chest, and without sparing the others a second glance, he carried her off into the darkness of the trees.

For a moment, Phoenix, Ethan, and Shade stood inside the Cathedral in silence. Then, with a final glare in her direction, Shade followed Nate, his vampire speed making it seem almost as if he disappeared.

Ethan crouched to pick up the unicorn and placed

his hand on the ground for a brief moment before he stood, staring into the darkness after the others.

The simple truth weighed heavy on Phoenix's shoulders. "They blame me," she said.

Ethan shook his head. "They're just hurting."

"They should …"

He looked at her quizzically, the hint of yellow in his normally brown eyes telling her his wolf had also been present in the clearing with them.

"Blame me …"

"This isn't your fault, Phoenix. I was wrong to make you think that. Annabelle made her choices. We all make our choices."

His voice was firm, conviction evident, but his words from earlier that night replayed in her mind. *I needed you to understand.* He had asked for her help, but she had clung to the safety of her ignorance.

Yes, she'd made a choice. She just wasn't sure if it was the right one anymore.

"Will they trust me enough to let me help?"

The intensity of his gaze burned into her as if trying to see into her soul. "Do you want to help?"

"Yes," she said, letting him see the truth of her words as she looked him in the eyes.

"Then we'll find a way to make them trust you."

16

Leaning back in his office chair, Il Maestro forced his expression to remain neutral as the vampire in front of him finished providing his report.

The witches were dead. And not a single one of them for the purpose of the sacrifice.

His blood boiled.

He picked his glass of whiskey up from the desk and slowly stalked towards the other vampire. "So, you're telling me no one knows who killed the witches?"

The vampire shook his head and visibly stiffened as Il Maestro moved closer to him.

"Belinda?"

"Dead," the vampire responded with his eyes fixed straight ahead.

"The sacrifice?"

A hesitation. "Missing."

Considering this new turn of events, Il Maestro stared at the rich amber liquid as it swirled around the crystal glass. He walked in circles around the vampire and mused on how difficult it was to find good security nowadays.

"Il Maestro, if I might just say –"

The security guard's words were cut off with a gurgle as two sharp fangs pierced his flesh, and in one swift motion, a chunk was torn from his throat.

"No, you may not just say." Il Maestro spat the thick, viscous blood out and wiped his mouth with the silk handkerchief from his pocket.

He stepped over the still-twitching body and reached for the phone on his desk. "Raphael, get me Belinda's second-in-command.

"Oh, and get a cleaner to my office. One of your staff has made something of a mess."

17

Ethan stared out of the car window and into the night beyond. The darkness gradually shifted from almost complete black, to an odd, orange luminescence as they got closer to the city. His mind raced with unanswered questions. Despite what he'd told Phoenix, it was highly likely that the others would blame her, at least indirectly, for Annabelle's death. He had no idea how to convince them to accept her help, but he knew he needed to.

"Did you hear it?"

Phoenix's softly spoken question broke his train of thought and he looked around in confusion, listening intently for any unusual sounds.

"Hear what?"

She kept her eyes straight ahead and adjusted her hands uncomfortably on the leather steering wheel. "The keening … during the Ritual."

Well, that got his attention.

Twisting his body as much as he could within the confined space, he looked at her intently. "What are you talking about?"

"It was so sad. I mean, of course the Ritual was heart-breaking," she quickly clarified, throwing an apologetic glance his way, "but I've never heard a sound filled with such sorrow."

A shiver ran down his spine.

Shit. A banshee's wail?

He blew out a long breath and watched her closely for any sign of awareness. Could she really not know?

"Phoenix, one of your parents is fae, right?"

She hesitated for a moment before nodding. "My mother."

"Did she ever mention anything about the banshee?"

The look she gave him was one of such complete and utter surprise that he could guess the answer even without a response.

"No, she … Are you saying I heard a banshee?"

"Well, I didn't hear anything so I can only guess. But it fits."

"You really didn't hear it?" she asked incredulously.

Ethan shook his head. "The banshee is only connected to particular families, and only members of that family hear her cry."

Phoenix drummed her nails impatiently on the

steering wheel as she pulled to a stop at a red light. "Why did you ask about my mother?" She turned to face him.

"I've only ever heard of the banshee being linked to fae families. Powerful families."

She seemed to mull this information over, not offering any further insights to confirm or deny his observation. When the light turned green, they drove along the quays in silence until they hit another red light and she faced him again.

"Ethan? You're meant to hear the wail of the banshee whenever someone close to you dies, right?"

He nodded.

"I've never heard it before," she whispered.

An odd look of pain crossed her features that he couldn't understand. Surely it was a good thing that she hadn't heard it before?

Ethan directed Phoenix to the old converted warehouse he currently called home, and she drove in subdued silence. Nate's blacked-out Civic was already parked at the side of the building as they pulled up in front, and he could feel her tense beside him. He waited to see if she'd back out, but she got out of the car, closed the door firmly behind her, and followed him up to the top floor without a word.

She'd surprised him tonight. Any sane person would have turned him away. Would have ran a mile screaming, for that matter.

It hadn't even been a conscious decision to go to her, not really. He just remembered cradling Annabelle close to him on the bike, not wanting her to get cold from the bitter wind that slapped at him insistently. Everything had been a blur, until suddenly he was at the pub where Phoenix worked. It had been the closest place to him, but it was more than that. He needed her to understand the cost.

And now, she was at his side as they walked in to find the others waiting in his apartment.

Nate was fussing over Lily, who seemed to have returned to her previous trance, and Shade leaned against the window, staring out into the night while he played with his penknife. The mood was solemn, and Annabelle's absence was painfully obvious.

"What's she doing here?" Shade drove the tip of his penknife into the windowsill as he turned to scowl in their direction.

"I want to help." Phoenix met his gaze steadily until he looked away, directing his anger into the darkness beyond the window.

"You've helped enough," he muttered.

The weariness of the night washed over Ethan, swiftly eroding his patience and all good intentions of diplomacy. "That's enough, Shade. Phoenix is here to help, and you *will* treat her with respect."

Shade pushed away from the window, glaring at him defiantly. "I don't have to do any –"

"Enough!" Lily's voice surprised them all into silence. She was staring intently at Phoenix, green eyes more alert than they'd been all night. "We need all the help we can get. If she wants to help, let her help."

And just like that, it was settled. Phoenix took a seat beside Lily and listened quietly as they filled her in on everything they knew so far. Before long, the night sky began to lighten with the first signs of dawn, and everyone around Ethan looked to be feeling the same bone-deep fatigue he was.

They'd covered a lot of old ground, but really, they were no closer to reaching an answer. A mind-numbing headache was beginning to form behind his eyes and the list of questions were only growing. What were the witches up to? How did Phoenix fit into it all? Could Lily's source have been wrong? He didn't know what to believe anymore.

"Let's call it a night." He stood to stretch his legs and gave his neck a resounding crack.

Nate, Shade, and Lily muttered their goodnights, leaving him alone in the kitchen with Phoenix as they made their way to their respective apartments. A sharp tinge of anxiety clenched his gut as he watched the others walk out the door, and he nearly had to stop himself from calling them back. They were only down the hall.

They're safe.

He busied himself making a pot of coffee and repeated the mantra again in his head. When the coffee was steaming, he poured it into a cup and handed it to Phoenix who stood fidgeting uncomfortably behind him.

"Don't want you crashing on the way home. It's been a long night."

She took the cup from him, her small nose wrinkling in the cutest way as she looked at the black, tarry liquid. "So, you decided to kill me with this instead?"

Her vibrant green eyes sparkled as she smiled, something he hadn't seen her do very often, and he couldn't help his own responding grin.

"You'll come back tonight?" They'd discussed the idea of her going on patrol with them, but still he held his breath, waiting for her to make an excuse and walk away.

Phoenix nodded and her face turned serious as she clutched the warm cup in both hands. "I don't know how much help I'll be, but I'll be here."

"You've already been more help than you realise." His words elicited a surprisingly girly blush from her as she looked away, clearly uncomfortable.

Clearing her throat, she placed the cup down on the counter. "Right … I think it's probably time I make a move. Abi will be getting worried."

Moving aside to give her access to the door, he watched her leave, more curious than ever about the hybrid.

18

"I can assure you, Il Maestro, that Belinda's mistakes won't be mine."

Deep blue eyes met his gaze with an unwavering surety that did, indeed, encourage confidence. The witch's blood red robe made her seem strangely at home in the dark chamber where they stood. Flickering torch flames cast shadows over the stone walls, and her power filled the space, falling like a sweet temptation on his tongue.

"Tell me, Esme, how is it you reached only second in command before Belinda's untimely demise?" Il Maestro tilted his head and watched her with a mild curiosity.

"It was how I preferred it to be … Until I was sure the coven's ambitions aligned with my own." There was no arrogance in her tone, merely fact. Had she wished it, they both knew she would have been head of the coven.

"And now?" he asked, raising a neatly manicured eyebrow.

"Now, it's time for the Dublin coven to reach the greatness it was intended for." Esme's blue eyes flashed fervently even as her face remained expressionless. "Tell me what you need from us and it will be done."

He assessed the woman standing before him. She had an imposing presence and spoke such pretty words. But words were useless to him. Perhaps it was time to test the loyalty she was offering.

"I want you to find a way to speed up the prophecy."

For the briefest moment, surprise registered on her face.

"The clock began to count down when the prophecy was triggered, Il Maestro. Its course will not be easily deterred. Nor will it be easily rerouted –"

"Can it be done?" He wasn't interested in listening to excuses. He was tired of the interruptions.

After a moment, she nodded. "It would require a particular talisman. And a blood connection to the prophecy – the hybrid being preferable," she added thoughtfully, "but yes, I believe so."

"The blood will not be a problem," he said with a dismissive wave of his hand. "Can we obtain the talisman?"

"It is … close. Though I may require assistance to acquire it."

Satisfied, Il Maestro nodded. "You'll have all the assistance you require."

In a blink, she was gone.

19

"And what time did you get home last night?" Abi leaned her elbows on the bar and wiggled her eyebrows suggestively.

Phoenix kept her eyes fixed on the tap she was hooking up, resolutely avoiding her friend's probing gaze. The third degree had been going on all afternoon, and there was no sign of it letting up.

"Aw come on, at least tell me who the guy is," Abi pressed, just to prove the point.

Phoenix sighed and looked up from her crouched position under the bar. "He's just a friend, Abi. You know it *is* possible to have those."

Abi threw her a look that clearly said, "Yeah right!" before walking off to chat with the band setting up on stage.

Phoenix leaned her forehead on the edge of the bar

top in front of her as an uncomfortable feeling settled in the pit of her stomach. She hated lying to Abi. Not that Ethan was more than a friend, if he was even that, but what could she tell her that wouldn't just lead to more lies?

She gave herself a mental kick up the arse and hauled herself up from the floor to set about stacking the glasses. There was enough to worry about without feeling sorry for herself on top of it all. She'd go to Ethan's once she got off work, help him find a way to stop whatever was happening, and go back to her normal life. Simple.

Except it wasn't, because she had no idea how to help. Having avoided that world her whole life, she knew sweet F.A. about the Lore. And having avoided that side of *herself* her whole life, she had little or no understanding of her own powers either. How she was supposed to be involved in the prophecy was a mystery to her. Ethan was crazy to want her on board.

Idly reorganising the bottles of alcohol, she stifled a yawn. Sleep hadn't come easily once she got back from Ethan's that morning. Every time she'd closed her eyes, Annabelle's lifeless form was there, burned into her retinas. And when it wasn't Annabelle, it was her best friend. Reaching for her. Begging for help, as all around her, the world burned. The whole thing was like a nightmare she couldn't wake from.

The shrill ring of her phone made Phoenix yelp in

surprise and she fumbled awkwardly to catch the bottle of Jameson that slipped from her grasp. Already on edge, her heart leapt in her throat as she pulled the phone out of her pocket.

Shit, please not more bad news.

Darius's name flashed on the screen, filling her with relief and apprehension all at once. Did he know something? Surely he couldn't have found out about last night, could he?

The sound of laughter drifted down the bar to her, and her attention was pulled from the vibrating phone back to her current surroundings. Abi was flirting outrageously with the lead singer of the band, her head thrown back as she laughed with pure, genuine delight.

Phoenix hesitated, her finger hovering over the answer button. More sounds of laughter filtered into her consciousness from around the pub: customers chatting animatedly, friends laughing and joking as they put their worries aside for the evening. The life she'd built for herself suddenly seemed unbearably precious. And oh so very fragile.

A fierce need boiled up in her to protect it.

Biting her lip, she put the phone on silent and slipped it back into her pocket, ignoring the persistent vibration. She needed time to think before she spoke to Darius. He'd want to help. She understood that, but she needed to figure this out for herself.

It would've been nice to ease in gently, Phoenix thought wryly as she followed Ethan through Temple Bar in search of witches. Sure, she'd signed up for it, but shouldn't there be an induction or something?

The late hour, coupled with it being a Monday, meant the streets were thankfully quiet. A few straggling tourists loitered about, reluctant to give up even though the pubs were now closed. The occasional homeless person huddled in a doorway as they sought what shelter they could in their sleeping bag. Some unsavoury characters argued amongst themselves over their poison of choice for the night. All were human, and all were of little consequence to their current goal.

Traversing the cobblestones, she was aware of every person and every sound. First night jitters were only compounded by the covert meeting awaiting them. Phoenix gripped the medallion around her neck as she matched Ethan stride for stride.

Lily had been surprisingly active in acquiring an update on the witches in the few hours since her sister's death. She had pretty strong motivation, Phoenix supposed, but it was still impressive considering the grief she must be feeling. With her help, they managed to confirm that the Dublin coven had gone to ground; their

136

second in command had taken the reins since Ethan had killed the previous leader during the attempted sacrifice.

Annabelle's young friend, Izzie, hadn't been seen or heard from since, but Lily did find another witch who was willing to speak to them – under duress. Unsurprisingly, the witch had conditions for the meeting to ensure her safety.

Creepy location in the dead of night: check.

Ridiculous codeword no one would ever guess: check.

Complete lack of backup in case of ambush: check.

Phoenix personally thought they were taking a stupid risk, given the events of the previous day. Yet here she was following Ethan like a lapdog to the agreed meeting point. Some would say she was an idiot. Some would be right.

She blew her unruly hair out of her face and noted a strange shift in the atmosphere as they passed the small square in the centre of Temple Bar. It was like all signs of life suddenly disappeared. The pubs were free of stragglers, and the doorways were empty.

Beside her, Ethan came to an abrupt halt. He looked around and sniffed the air, his body tense. It was only then that she noticed it. Blood.

She'd been so caught up in her own thoughts, and the coppery tang had been so subtle, that her vampire senses had written it off as just another part of their surroundings. But this was fresh.

She looked at Ethan and nodded when he inclined his head towards a side-street just past The Temple Bar pub. Her breath caught in her throat, but she followed him silently as he edged towards the corner.

Empty kegs stood stacked at the side of the pub and the metal shutters were pulled halfway down the windows, making the place appear almost as if it had been abandoned in a hurry. Glasses littered the footpath outside; dregs of beer and spirits were the only remaining sign of their owners. The night around them was quiet.

Ethan pressed Phoenix behind him with a gentle hand before he crouched low and risked a glance around the corner.

"Dammit," he cursed, hurrying towards something not yet visible from her position.

She cast a wary glance around and followed him, only to stop short at the sight that met her.

A woman, largely hidden by the stacked kegs, lay slumped on the ground, her neck twisted at an unnatural angle. She was in her forties, Phoenix guessed. Pretty, but in a forgettable way. A look of fear formed her death mask and a single trickle of fresh blood ran from a cut on her forehead.

Her hand was clenched tightly in a fist, and when Ethan pried it open, a small amulet clattered to the ground. He stood and punched the wall in anger before turning away to pace.

"It's the witch, isn't it?" Realisation hit Phoenix with a dull thud.

Ethan nodded but didn't speak. He just continued to pace and fought to take slow, deep breaths.

"She didn't even make it to the meeting pl –"

A woman's scream tore through the night and ripped away the veil of silence surrounding them.

With a quick glance at each other, they turned and sprinted in the direction of the sound. As they reached the small square once more, they found another woman in a heap on the cobblestones. She sobbed as her partner tried to console her and angry shouts came from the arched stone walkway that led to the quays.

Whatever had happened to this woman, she was in no immediate danger. So, Ethan and Phoenix ran through the archway and followed the shouts down the stone steps and across the road to the Ha'penny Bridge.

At the top of the bridge, Ethan skidded to a stop so suddenly that Phoenix ran straight into his back. She opened her mouth to ask what gives, but the scene in front of them stopped the words before they could leave her throat.

A middle-aged woman, fully equipped in tailored jacket and pencil skirt, stood over an old man. With her stilettos in hand, she rained merciless blows down on his frail form. A maniacal grin covered her face as the man cowered beneath his arms and tried in vain to protect his head. Each strike from the five-inch heels caused him to cry out in pain and only seemed to spur the woman on.

The image was wrong in so many ways that Phoenix couldn't even begin to list them, but more than that, the woman *felt* wrong. There was an energy to her, almost like that of a Supe, but thicker, more tangible and viscous. And her eyes … her eyes were glowing like the flames of Hell.

"Demon," Ethan whispered, his skin visibly pale even in the darkness of the night.

The woman paused mid-strike and her head twisted in their direction. The red of her eyes pulsed and the smile on her face turned to something even more chilling than before. Abandoning her prey, she stalked slowly towards them, her tongue running seductively over bright red lips.

Phoenix shuddered and fought the sudden urge to scrub her skin raw. It didn't make sense. Demons weren't able to cross over. Were they?

"Eh … any bright ideas?" she muttered nervously, not taking her eyes off the woman.

Ethan shook his head. His fists opened and closed convulsively at his sides. "She's just a vessel. We can't hurt her." Which left them shit out of luck since the woman – or demon – looked more than ready to hurt them.

"Hybrid," the demon hissed. Her voice was deep and unnatural coming from the woman's mouth.

Not waiting for her, or it, to get any closer, Ethan

lunged shoulder first into the demon. The vessel didn't budge. Instead, it grabbed Ethan around the torso and lifted his sizable frame before flinging him halfway across the bridge, laughing.

The demon turned its attention back to Phoenix and tilted its head to assess her. Phoenix fought the urge to run as she shifted into a fighting stance. The demon was blocking her view of Ethan, but she heard the thud quite clearly when he landed, and the lack of follow-up attack didn't bode well for him at all. She was on her own.

Her knowledge of demons was limited, but she knew the woman it possessed was innocent, which severely limited her options; she wasn't willing to hurt an innocent human and had zero idea how to separate a demon from its host.

Done with its assessment, the demon abandoned its slow stalking and launched itself towards her. Human hands appeared almost as claws as they grabbed for her face, nails raking across her cheek in burning slashes.

Phoenix blocked the strikes as best she could without resorting to force, but it was useless. The human now possessed the demon's impressive speed, and its strength was overwhelming.

Unable to even restrain the demon, she finally relented and put her morals aside.

Her first punch connected, and Phoenix felt the sickening crunch of a cheekbone beneath her hand. The demon stumbled, and in a moment of utter cruelty, pulled back just enough from the woman it possessed to allow conscious terror and pain to flash behind her eyes. Nausea overwhelmed Phoenix and she had to cover her mouth with her hand to stop from throwing up.

The woman. Oh fuck, she's still aware.

With a cruel grin that looked out of place on the woman's face, the demon regained full control and began to stalk towards her once more. This time it was in no rush, knowing all too well it had effectively crippled her ability to fight back. It pressed Phoenix against the railings of the bridge and ran a chipped red fingernail down her cheek as it sniffed along her neck.

Phoenix held her breath, restraining the knee-jerk reaction to lash out. She couldn't hurt the woman again; there had to be another way. If she could just –

A loud "CAW" sounded before her view of the demon was broken in an explosion of black feathers. Wings beat furiously as a large crow latched its talons on to the demon, its razor-sharp beak striking the soft flesh of the eyes.

The demon roared and moved away from Phoenix as it fought to hold off the unexpected attack. Human limbs and feathers mixed in a confusing blur, but the crow allowed no leeway as it swarmed the demon.

Stunned, Phoenix stood frozen to the spot, unsure of what to do.

A rush of wind from her left was the only indication that Ethan was up and moving before he dived for the demon's legs. Already distracted by the crow's determined attack, the impact knocked the demon off balance and into the railings. Everything moved in slow motion and, for a split second, the demon got the upper hand on the crow as it tore the black wings away.

Furious red eyes met hers. "They're coming," it hissed, and an insane laugh wracked the woman's body.

With that parting sentence, the demon gripped the top of the railing, tore itself free of Ethan's grip, and launched the woman's body into the murky waters of the River Liffey below.

A silent scream froze in Phoenix's throat, but her outstretched hand was met with only air. She ran to Ethan's side and scanned the waters in desperation, but there was no sight of the woman. The water was eerily calm, like a mirror reflecting the night back at them.

Phoenix was shaking as she rested her head against the hard metal of the railings. She closed her eyes to block out the image of the woman's falling body, but it was no use. She'd been aware. The woman had still been alive.

Another "caw" drew her attention back to the bridge, and she turned to find the large crow watching them. From its perch on top of the railings, Phoenix could now appreciate the full size of the bird. Almost two feet in height, it was covered in silky feathers that reflected a miasma of colours back at them. What had initially appeared to be inky black, now shone with ever changing blues, greens, and purples. Eyes like rubies showcased a keen intelligence, and a strange sense of déjà vu washed over Phoenix. She'd seen those eyes before …

With one more squawk, the crow took flight and left Phoenix and Ethan staring in confusion at the now empty railings.

Ethan let out a long breath. "I think we should call it a night."

She wanted nothing more than to agree, but Phoenix suddenly remembered the old man the demon had been attacking. She turned towards the arch of the bridge and her gaze met wide, shocked eyes. Huddled in a pool of urine, the old man clung to the railings for dear life as he stared at them. Phoenix sighed.

20

Ethan paced the length of his living room, unable to sit still with the adrenaline still flowing through his veins.

A fucking demon.

He blew out a breath and looked again at Phoenix to reassure himself she was in one piece. She'd fallen quiet and retreated into herself on the way back to his apartment. The cuts on her face were healing quickly thanks to a balm Lily had applied, and her own healing abilities, but he could tell she was shaken. Hell, he was too.

"And you're sure it was a demon?" Lily asked for the third time as she looked up from the large tome she was scouring.

"As sure as I can be." Ethan ran a hand through his hair, trying to remember any important detail from the night.

"I didn't think demons could cross into this world," Phoenix said, finally breaking her silence.

"They shouldn't be able to," Ethan agreed. "The Council reinforced the barrier between their world and ours in order to maintain the balance. It doesn't make sense."

"Actually …" Nate looked up from his laptop as all eyes turned to him. "It might."

He flipped the laptop around to face the room and pointed to a block of text he'd highlighted. "I've found some references to the prophecy in Council archives –"

"The Council archives, how the hell did you –"

"Don't ask, don't tell." Nate grinned and held up a hand. "Anyway, there's a reference to a tear in the fabric, a kind of 'End of Days'. Seems a little overdramatic, but given current events …"

Shade let out a low whistle.

Phoenix cleared her throat and squirmed in her chair as she raised a hand. "Not to ask a stupid question, but tear in what fabric? You mean the barrier between worlds?"

Nate nodded, all humour gone from his face.

"But that would mean …" Phoenix paled.

"More demons."

Ethan felt the fight leave him in a breath. The demon they'd faced tonight was only a minor demon; if it had been any stronger, it would have taken possession of a

Supe rather than a human. Or worse, it would have been able to take form on its own.

It had taken so little for the demon to overpower him, and even less to stop Phoenix in her tracks. How could they fight something that was stronger and harder to kill than they were?

"Have we any idea how to separate a demon from its host?" Ethan directed his question to Lily, shivering as he remembered the woman's body disappearing into the black depths of the river.

"I've found a spell ..." Lily said.

Green eyes met his, and he knew there was a but coming.

"... but it's not enough to separate the demon. We need to be able to banish it too or it will just find another victim."

Another innocent to leech the life out of. Things had been complicated enough when they just had to protect humans from the Lore. Now this?

"You said the Council played a part in banishing them the first time around?" Phoenix looked at him for confirmation. "Who'd be strong enough to breach the Council's wards?"

Ethan didn't manage to stop the surprise from showing on his face, which earned him an annoyed glare from Phoenix. It was a bloody good question and he wondered why it hadn't occurred to them already.

"The Dublin coven?" Ethan looked at Lily, who shook her head.

"They'd never be strong enough by themselves."

"So, maybe they're not by themselves," Shade said, staring pointedly at Phoenix.

Too tired to go around in circles any longer, Ethan decided it was time to call it a night. He ushered everyone to the door and found himself once more standing alone in the apartment with Phoenix as she held back from the others.

"She was alive, Ethan. The woman. She was still in there. If we could have just restrained her ..." Haunted eyes met his as she pulled her coat tightly around herself.

"We wouldn't have known what to do anyway."

21

Phoenix poured every ounce of frustration and every bit of confusion into the punch, viciously punishing the hard leather for the feelings of weakness and ineptitude that had been dredged up by the previous night's patrol. The punchbag merely clunked on its chain, indifferent to her inner turmoil.

"Don't take it personally, the whole gym's been rigged to withstand our strength." Ethan's tone was teasing as he dropped a 500kg bar back on the rack and strolled over to her. "I'm sure you don't really punch like a girl."

The gym really was impressive, and she'd jumped at the chance to test it out. Comprising the whole bottom floor of the converted warehouse that housed Ethan's apartment, the walls and ceiling were reinforced with thick steel beams to support the heavier weights and frames in the lifting area. Combat weapons of all kinds lined the walls, and one half of the room was dedicated purely to martial arts training. It was Phoenix's idea of heaven.

"C'mon, how about taking some of that frustration out on me?" Ethan started walking towards the training mats without waiting for her answer.

What an arrogant sod, Phoenix thought, stubbornly refusing to follow him and his presumptuous arse. Although, she did feel an irritating need to redeem herself after their first training session. He'd walked away from that fight without a clear win. Sure, he might argue differently, but he hadn't pinned her. The competitor in her needed a clear winner, even if that meant getting her arse handed to her on a plate.

"What do I get out of it?" she echoed the question she'd once asked him, back before life had turned completely upside down.

"Tell you what …" He turned back to look at her appraisingly. "Best of three. Winner of each round gets to ask a question of their choice. Honest answers only."

Well, that made her stop.

He was definitely stronger than her, and a more experienced fighter, but vamp trumped wolf in speed. If she could use that to her advantage …

"Unless you're afraid of losing again?" Ethan's voice was innocent, but his eyes taunted and dared her to prove him wrong.

Screw that! She could lose with the best of them. She smiled a saccharine smile, sashayed to the mat, and threw her towel and water bottle to the side.

"No weapons. External or otherwise," she said, and pointedly looked at Ethan's hands. It had been hard enough explaining the residual scratches from the demon attack to Abi. She didn't want to explain claw marks a second time.

He gave her a boy scout salute, though she doubted he'd ever been one in his life.

They started easy. A light jab here, a snap kick there; testing each other's defences in a harmless warm-up dance. Speed and strength were kept to human levels as they flowed through locks and releases, making no real attempt to attack.

As her muscles loosened and the blood began to flow, Phoenix started testing the limits of her speed. She made Ethan work harder for his strikes and managed to stay just barely ahead of him each step of the way, waiting for an opening.

A feint to the head allowed her the moment of distraction she needed to drop low and sweep his legs from under him. She turned into his stumbling body and wrapped her legs firmly around his upper arm. With a sharp tug, she pulled his arm into a lock that forced him to face-plant the mat.

And led to her winning round one.

She waited until he acknowledged her win with a tap before she released the lock and jumped up, feeling quietly pleased with herself. Accepting her offered hand, Ethan followed her to standing and cracked his neck as he waited expectantly for her first question.

So many thoughts were running through her mind, but there was one that had plagued her ever since their first training session. "How did you get involved with the prophecy?" she asked as she thought back to the change in his demeanour when she'd asked why he cared.

Again, something clouded his eyes that she couldn't quite identify. Ethan grabbed his towel and bottle from the edge of the mat. He wiped the back of his neck and took a large gulp of water before answering.

"It wasn't intentional, believe me." He sighed. "I'd left the pack and was moving around, trying to find my feet. But it seemed like everywhere I went, weird shit followed me."

She raised her eyebrows in feigned disbelief, which caused him to laugh.

"I knew I'd been sheltered by the pack, but what I saw just didn't seem right to me. Surely the Council wouldn't tolerate the level of bloodlust I was seeing in the vamps. And the wolves … their behaviour wasn't normal. So, I started looking into it a bit, asking a few questions."

Phoenix watched silently as he threw his towel

around his neck and rubbed his hair absently with it. There were a million questions going through her mind and she was itching to interrupt, but something about his tone told her to stay quiet.

"At this point I'd been gone a while and my dad wanted me home. He sent our Omega, Sean, to talk sense into me. Only, he never got the chance. The night he caught up with me in Belfast, we stumbled on a vamp feeding." A muscle jumped at the side of his jaw. "The baby couldn't have been more than a few months old. Its mother had been discarded in a heap on the ground, still reaching for her baby even –"

Ethan shuddered, his voice becoming void of emotion. "We fought the vamp, but Sean was killed and the vamp got away. I've been trying to track it since."

"And now, if you walk away from the prophecy, he'll have died for nothing," she said quietly.

He nodded, looking in surprise at the water bottle he held in his hand – now crushed.

Phoenix took a shuddery breath, needing to break the tension. "Okay, you ready to get your arse whooped again?"

He grinned, seeming to shake off the horrors of his story. Without another word, he threw his towel aside and lunged at her, almost knocking her off balance.

Mentally chastising herself, she slipped his grasp and moved behind him before throwing in a sly kidney jab.

With each strike, they grew more familiar with each other's movements. Soon, they were moving at such speed that they would have been a blur to the human eye.

Just as quickly, Ethan got the upper hand and trapped her in a chokehold from behind. Without a second thought, she dropped her weight and flipped the solid lump of muscle over her shoulder. Ethan's surprise at finding himself on his back gave her just enough time to pin him, and she threw in a little wink for good measure.

She slid off him so he could sit up, but decided to save her energy by staying seated on the ground for question two. "What were you running from?"

Ethan's head snapped up. "What?"

"Why did you leave? You said you don't change at the full moon without your pack. It sounds to me like you're punishing yourself for something."

Ethan rested his elbows on his knees and rubbed a hand over his face. "I guess I set the terms, didn't I?" He paused. "My pack is in Donegal. My father is the Alpha. And I'm the first-born."

"So … that would make you next in line for Alpha," she said as she dug deep into the recesses of her mind for the limited knowledge she had on Lore traditions.

He grimaced. "A fact I resented for a very long time. I love my pack, and my family, but growing up, it was always about the responsibility. I guess I just needed a break from it all. So I left."

"I didn't think wolves did well without their pack?" Phoenix eyed him with growing curiosity.

"They don't, generally. Stronger the wolf, easier it is. A relief even. At least for a while."

Before she could probe any further, he jumped to his feet and extended a hand to help her up. "I think it's time for me to reclaim my dignity," he said with a grin.

She snorted and adjusted her hair back into a tight ponytail. "Good luck with that."

Round three began. It was much the same as the previous rounds, with sweat making their skin slick. However, it ended with one important difference: Phoenix found herself flat on her back, not quite sure how she got there, and wondering numbly if the two previous rounds had all been a set up.

Ignoring Ethan's offered hand, she got to her feet and wrapped her arms around herself in a vain attempt to protect from whatever difficult truth he would force her to divulge.

"How have you managed to stay off the radar for so long?"

His question startled her. It was one he'd asked before, back in the bar. Why was it even relevant enough to waste his question?

"My parents were banished by their families for their relationship." She forced her voice to remain neutral. "As you can imagine, they didn't want much to do with the Lore after that. When they found out my mother was pregnant" – she shrugged – "they didn't want to chance my safety."

"So, you've been living amongst humans your whole life?" Ethan's eyebrows raised in surprise as he looked at her.

Phoenix hesitated for a second before shaking her head, reluctant to share too much, but unable to stomach a lie.

"My parents went missing when I was fifteen. I spent some time with a vampire clan until I was old enough to fend for myself."

"Did they know what you were?"

"Only the head of the clan, and a few of his top security. I was kept separate from the others so that no one would suspect anything."

He seemed to digest the information for some time before he finally looked at her again. "It sounds very lonely."

Not able to face his pity, she simply shrugged and walked off the mat. "It was fun sparring with you," she said over her shoulder, not quite sure if it was the truth.

22

The biting wind carried a strong, ever present, threat of rain as Ethan strolled down Grafton Street with Phoenix at his side. The late hour had transformed their surroundings to a pale representation of its daytime persona. Shop fronts were dark and uninviting. The street was empty of music and the life it attracted. Small groups of volunteers had set up makeshift tables and were working tirelessly to dole out the last of their offerings to the homeless. The queue of people in need was an even more depressing sight on the cold winter night.

Beside him, Phoenix's terrifyingly pointy stiletto boots clacked on the cobblestones. The shadows of the night did little to blunt the fiery red of her hair, and her green eyes almost glowed as they adjusted to the dim light. He had to admit that she pulled off the badass look pretty well, though he knew now it was all a front.

Though things had been quiet the past few nights, they continued their patrols, keeping an eye out for any clues or a chance to prevent attacks from rogue Supes. If he was honest, he was also looking for an opportunity to test Phoenix. She'd held her own quite well in hand to hand combat, but he'd yet to see her use her powers aside from the night he'd first met her. It worried him, especially since there had been rumours of further demon possessions.

"Abi's starting to get suspicious about me being out all night," she said, breaking the comfortable silence as they veered down one of the dark side-streets.

Ethan smiled at the mention of the bubbly human bartender. He could well imagine her curiosity being piqued.

Phoenix rolled her eyes. "She's convinced I'm seeing someone."

"So, tell her you're seeing me," he offered, surprised when his wolf took that moment to perk up its ears.

Nudging him with her shoulder, she laughed, "Yeah right, then I'd really never hear the end of it."

He shrugged nonchalantly, wondering in the back of his mind why her response bothered him. "Just thought it might help get her off your back —"

The loud smashing of glass stopped them in their tracks and was quickly followed by a screeching alarm. Phoenix met his look of surprise with one of her own before they set off at a sprint to the end of the street. They made sure to keep close to the shadows as they peered around the corner.

Across the road, just off another dark side-street, they could see two black forms highlighted by a flickering streetlight. Whoever it was stood arguing as a number of other shadowy forms leapt through the broken window of a shopfront.

Angry words drifted to Ethan and Phoenix over the din of the alarm: "Idiot", "Kill us".

Ethan sniffed the air and found the unmistakable scent of incense and herbs. "Witches," he growled.

Phoenix grabbed his arm and pointed to a dark sign above the shop that read *Ulysses Rare Books*. "What would they be doing breaking into an old bookshop?"

"Looking for some light reading?" He edged forward, gesturing for her to follow behind him.

The two witches in front of the shop were so busy arguing that they didn't hear his approach. Ethan grabbed the largest of the two from behind and his arm snaked across the witch's throat, cutting off the man's air supply before the slightest curse could be uttered. A quick glance assured him that Phoenix had the other witch under control, and they dragged the unconscious bodies into the shadows.

Standing this close to the bookshop made his fur prickle as his wolf shifted closely beneath the surface. This was definitely more than just an old bookshop.

Conscious that the alarm would have notified the Gardaí, Ethan stepped carefully over the jagged edges of the window into the shop. The jolt of electricity only lasted a second as he crossed the threshold, but it had him shaking his head to clear the static from his ears.

One look at Phoenix told him she'd felt it too. He waited for a nod to confirm she was all right before he continued forward silently.

The dark of the night, coupled with the flickering streetlight outside, gave the shop an eerie feel. Looming bookcases cast long shadows and seemed to come alive as they stood watchfully on guard.

Aside from the large tomes strewn across the glass-littered floor, the only sign of intrusion was the murmur of voices coming from a room at the back of the shop. A strange glow seeped out from under the closed door and the closer he moved towards it, the heavier the air felt.

His wolf clawed restlessly and tried to take control. Ethan fought the urge. Something was not quite right with the feeling. Instinct told him it would be a bad idea to let his wolf loose.

Without warning, the door at the back of the shop flung open and he was blinded by a scorching white light. Beside him, he heard Phoenix curse, followed by a loud crash.

As the spots began to clear from his vision, someone

barrelled into him from behind. He twisted his body to avoid face-planting the floor, but his shoulder hit the ground with a bone-jarring thud.

The body that landed on top of him was female. Small and unnaturally strong. Her features were twisted and ugly, any sense of humanity long since gone. Pinned beneath her small frame and the floor, Ethan struggled to free his arm. He only just managed to turn his head and miss the dagger she plunged towards his face.

Using the witch's momentum against her, he pushed up through his lower body and threw her off. But just as he tried to rise to his feet, Ethan's legs buckled beneath him.

The loud crack of bone sounded in his ears and, against his will, his body started to shift.

His wolf howled in agony at the unnatural change being forced upon him. Tendons popped as his limbs contorted. Muscles elongated and tore. Sharp fangs pierced his gums and fur sprouted from the backs of his hands.

Through the fog of pain, he heard Phoenix scream his name. Adrenaline surged at the fear in her voice, and he fought to gain control. His eyes searched wildly until they finally found her grappling on the floor with a male witch.

Ethan tried to move towards her, but his knees buckled again and he fell forward onto his hands. His sharp claws dug into the wooden floor as his spine twisted and arched.

Phoenix met his eyes, and in an instant, her expression changed from surprise to steely resolve. With a surge of power, she flipped the witch off her, sending him careening into a wall. She made to move towards him, her hand reaching out, but he pulled back, not trusting his control under the forced change.

"Witch." He ground out the syllables painfully, his now misshapen jaw making speech almost impossible.

The flash of understanding on her face was the last thing he saw before everything went black.

Phoenix's blood ran cold as she watched Ethan collapse to the ground. Every instinct in her screamed to go to him, but she ignored the pull and forced herself to look for the witch responsible.

She found him shrouded by shadows in the corner. He stood tall with his head back and palms wide open as a continuous stream of chanting oozed from his barely moving mouth. For a moment, it seemed as if the witch was oblivious to her presence, but then his head lowered, and Phoenix was met with the whitest eyes she'd ever seen.

Her previously cold blood began to ice over as the witch fixed her with an unwavering stare. She felt her limbs grow heavy, and her body refused all commands to move.

The image of Ethan slumped helpless on the floor flashed into her mind, and anger at the violation flooded her system. Anger not just at the violation of her body, but of his, and his wolf's.

She strained against the invisible bonds that held her and channelled all of her anger. With her eyes fixated on the witch, something snapped, allowing her to move forward.

The witch's strange eyes widened in shock just before Phoenix lengthened her fangs and plunged them deep into his jugular.

A sharp gasp drew her attention back to Ethan. She dropped the now lifeless body and spat out the poisonous blood that tried to slide down the back of her throat. Rushing to his side, she slid down beside him, the fear that gripped her heart only beginning to ease when she could feel the rise and fall of his chest beneath her hand. A sheen of sweat covered his skin as his body slowly, and agonisingly, started to realign itself.

Not knowing what else to do, Phoenix held him close and gave him whatever strength she could while he worked through the pain.

Eventually Ethan lifted his head. His eyes were still strained but they were now a clear brown and showed no sign of his wolf. "The witches?" he asked hoarsely.

His question brought her sharply back to their surroundings as she realised her carelessness. She hadn't even checked if anyone was left alive.

Strangely though, the store appeared to be empty. Even of bodies.

She shook her head and mentally berated herself. "Gone."

23

Ethan listened vaguely to the chatter of voices that filled his apartment. His head was still pounding as he gingerly stretched out each finger and checked for any lasting damage. Phoenix's concerned gaze burned into him. He wanted to reassure her, but he couldn't. In truth, he was shaken, even more than he'd like to admit. Each aching joint reminded him of the violation he'd been helpless to defend against, and the idea made him want to punch something.

How the hell had the witches been able to control his change? Nothing other than the moon and his Alpha should've been able to do that. And he was even strong enough to fight those.

"Do we have any idea what they were after?" Lily paced the length of the living room for what seemed like the hundredth time since joining them.

Ethan looked at the young witch and noticed the stiff set of her shoulders and limp lifelessness of her long blonde hair. She'd latched on to the prophecy and the witches with a determined focus that was growing unhealthy. She hadn't taken time to grieve, and it worried him what would happen when the distraction was gone.

The comforting tempo of Nate's keyboard tapping suddenly stopped, breaking Ethan's train of thought.

"Maybe …" Nate waved Lily over to the table where he sat.

Ethan watched impatiently as the two whispered and pointed at something on Nate's laptop.

"Are you going to share with the rest of us?" he snapped as he stood to continue the pacing where Lily had left off.

"Sorry, we were just looking at something." Lily looked up from the screen, the luminescence highlighting the concerned set of her mouth.

Phoenix and Shade both edged forward on their seats in response to the obvious tension. Ethan stopped his pacing with a sigh. Could it not just be good news for once?

Everyone gathered around the table as Nate turned the laptop to face them. The screen was full of small thumbnails, each with a single line of text underneath. The pictures were difficult to make out, but all showed an object of some type. Most were old, some looked ancient.

"I found our bookshop owner on the dark web," Nate explained. "It seems he specialises in old and extremely powerful relics."

"So, the witches were after one of these relics?" Phoenix asked.

Ethan could see her mentally connecting the dots as she moved closer to the screen with interest.

Lily nodded. "It would seem like a logical assumption."

"Do we know which one?" A bad feeling settled in the pit of Ethan's stomach, and now, even his wolf was pacing.

Nate clicked on one of the thumbnails, enlarging the image so it filled the screen.

"What the hell is that?" Shade asked, a frown etched on to his features.

Ethan felt a similar sense of confusion as he looked more closely. The image showed a small plate of what appeared to be solid gold. There was a symbol carved in the middle and it looked well worn with its edges fading. From what he could make out, the symbol showed some kind of serpent or dragon eating its own tail. It didn't look familiar to him, but something about it made his skin crawl.

"This is the relic we think the witches might have been after." Lily's voice was grave as she directed her answer to them all. "It's a very powerful talisman called an Ouroboros. It was believed to represent the endless cycle of time. Some say that whoever possesses it can gain control of this cycle and bend it to their will."

"Shit," Ethan muttered under his breath.

"Um … that doesn't sound good." Phoenix's worried eyes met his over the laptop and he looked away, yet again unable to reassure her.

His earlier sense of foreboding increased and his wolf shuffled restlessly. What the hell were the witches up to? Blood sacrifices, dark magic, and now this? Although they were a powerful faction within the Lore, witches were never a leading force for change or upheaval. They usually preferred to align themselves with a stronger contender or stay out of the spotlight altogether. That meant they had to be working for someone. And they had to believe that someone had the upper hand.

"So, what's the plan, boss?" Shade had resumed his trademark slouch against the wall and was watching him closely.

Ethan tried to organise his thoughts as he rubbed a rough hand over his face. They needed information, and aside from the witches, there was only one person that could give it to them.

"Take Lily, and go speak to the owner of the bookshop," he said, directing his comment to Nate. "We need him to confirm what was taken. I doubt there's any point checking the police report if he's dealing on the black market."

Nate saluted, shut down the laptop, and packed away a random assortment of gadgets.

Ethan looked at Phoenix, finally able to meet her eyes. Other than the persistent concerned glances she threw his way, her features showed no lasting strain from the night's events. But every time he closed his eyes, he could hear her scream his name.

She'd been left to face the witches alone, and he'd been powerless to help her. The knowledge caused an ugly, painful knot in his gut that wouldn't unravel; it also made him angry.

Despite everything, she still hadn't used her powers. Sure, she'd torn the witch's throat out with her fangs, but physical strength and a bit of extra speed weren't going to keep her alive. Not against other Supes. Or demons.

How could he keep her safe if she wouldn't fight?

Realising the room had gone quiet around him, he looked at the expectant gazes and wondered who else he would fail before this was over.

"Tomorrow," he said, "we train."

Phoenix looked at Ethan standing on the mat across from her. His face said he meant business. His yellow eyes said his wolf did too.

As soon as Nate and Lily had confirmed their suspicions with the shop owner, Ethan had ordered them all to the gym to train at the break of dawn. Even as a half-vampire who thrived at night, the lack of sleep was starting to wear on her.

"We need to up your training." Ethan gestured impatiently for her to move towards the middle of the mat. "We don't have time to take it easy anymore."

"Hey! I saved your ass, remember?" Sure, she'd been scared as hell, but she'd held her own and that had to count for something.

"What's that, boss?" Nate turned from the target that was playing victim to his knife skills with a wide grin on his face. "You're getting your ass saved by girls now too?"

Irritation clouded Ethan's face, and Phoenix noticed with amusement the rhythmic twitch in the muscle of his jaw. Curiosity tempted her to ask for clarification, but a low growl from his direction made her rethink, and she moved to the centre of the mat with a sigh.

"You were lucky last night," Ethan cut straight to the chase. "The witches won't let you get that close next time. You need to start using your other powers."

She felt herself tense. Her body became utterly still as she fought to slow her breathing and control the involuntary reaction to his words. This wasn't the first time he'd broached the subject, but something about his tone said he wasn't going to let it drop this time.

170

"I told you before, I don't have any. That light thing was just a weird fluke. I can't do it again." Phoenix dug her fingernails into the palm of her hand. He was expecting too much of her. She couldn't do it. *Wouldn't* do it.

"It's okay." Ethan held his hands out in a placating gesture. "We're going to start slow. But we *are* going to start, Phoenix."

Without warning, he leapt for her, giving her no chance to prepare or gather her defences. For the first time since they'd begun training together, she sensed a difference in his intensity. His eyes glowed yellow and he moved with an animalistic grace. More than ever, his energy screamed predator.

She fought with everything she had. Her vampire speed, she used. Her vampire strength, she most definitely used. Hell, her fangs even made an involuntary appearance at one stage. Still, it wasn't enough.

Ethan pushed her relentlessly and nothing she did satisfied him. The harder she fought, the more frustrated he seemed to become. Obviously convinced that she was holding out, the expectant look in his feral eyes pleaded silently with her.

Eventually, her endurance failed, and with a final tackle, Ethan pinned her beneath him. His body was firm against hers, yellow eyes searching her own for … something.

An uncomfortable silence filled the gym around them, and Phoenix was suddenly very aware of Ethan's hips pressed tightly against hers. Squirming under the unseen scrutiny of the others, she wriggled out from under him and tried to ignore the unintentional friction it caused.

He followed her up from the ground, eyes no longer meeting hers as he grabbed his towel from the side of the mat.

"Let's leave it there for now," he called over his shoulder on his way to the door. "I want everyone back here tonight for more training."

Phoenix scrubbed her hand over her face. *What the hell just happened?*

Needing some air, she turned to find the gym empty of all but Shade.

"It's not going to work, you know." The animosity was clear in his expression as he stalked towards her.

"I don't know what you're talking about." Phoenix sighed wearily and tried to step around him. Her body was already aching from the training session with Ethan and she was in no mood for a confrontation.

Shade moved to block her retreat, pressing himself close as he let her see the full force of hatred behind his icy blue eyes. "Ethan might not see you for what you are, but I do."

Tiredness, frustration, and confusion all caught up

on her at once, eroding any patience she might have had for the situation.

"I don't give a fuck what you think of me, Shade. Just get out of my way and let me go home." She squared her shoulders and looked him dead in the eye, not willing to be intimidated by his attitude.

Tension filled the air between them, causing the hairs on her arms to raise. Could she take him on if she needed to? She'd never really seen him fight, but as a full vamp he would likely be faster than her at the very least.

Just when Phoenix thought she might have to test the theory, Shade stepped to the side and opened his arm in a wide sweep towards the door. She hesitated for a moment before walking past him.

"He'll never feel the same about you."

Her feet faltered just as she made to step through the door.

"We don't want you here, Phoenix," Shade said softly. "Why don't you go back to your cushy little life and stop pretending to be a hero? You'll never be one of us."

And with that parting blow, he pushed past her and disappeared from sight.

Phoenix shoved open the heavy door of the pub and took a deep breath, letting the familiar scent of home wash over her. She'd broken the speed limit the whole way back in an attempt to get as much distance as she could from Shade and his words, but still they rang in her head.

He'd made it sound like she was the one trying to push into their lives, trying to be part of their little makeshift pack. But it was the other way around. They'd forced themselves into her life! All she was trying to do was get the mess cleared up so she could go back to her "cushy life" as he'd so scathingly put it.

Grateful that it was still too early for the cleaner to be in, Phoenix slipped quietly towards the back of the bar. She was hoping to catch a few hours' sleep before she had to face people again.

Fate seemed to have other ideas, however.

As she stepped through the door at the back, she ran straight into Abi. Her friend stood wrapped in a fluffy purple dressing gown that engulfed her petite frame. Her arms were crossed as she leaned against the stairs that led to their apartment.

"I heard you go out early. I was worried."

Phoenix looked away as the guilt temporarily wiped all other thoughts from her mind. "I couldn't sleep. Thought maybe I'd go for a run."

"Bullshit."

The softly spoken word pulled her attention back to Abi in surprise. Concerned blue eyes watched her expectantly and for the first time ever, she didn't know what to say to her best friend.

"I'm worried about you, Phoenix." Abi unfolded her arms with a sigh. "You haven't been yourself … not since this guy came on the scene."

"It's not like that, I –"

Abi held up a hand to stop her protests

"If you don't want to talk to me about it, that's fine," she said, although the hurt expression in her eyes stated otherwise. "But don't insult our friendship by lying to me."

A lump formed in Phoenix's throat that caused a dull ache and made it difficult to swallow. She wanted to deny Abi's words, but how could she when they were true? Silence stretched between them and unspoken words caused a void that Phoenix didn't know how to cross.

"I'm calling Paul in to cover the bar. Take the night off and get some rest. You look like shit." Her friend turned her back without another word and started up the stairs.

At the top, she looked back over her shoulder one last time. "I love you, Phoenix. I'm here when you're ready to talk."

24

Il Maestro regarded the silver coin as it burned an imprint into the palm of his hand. It was funny how such small, innocuous things could cause so much pain. The searing ache of silver had not subsided over the years. He merely found he'd come to enjoy the challenge it posed and the focus the pain demanded. It was now a useful reminder of the hardship that must be endured in order to achieve greatness.

Some things did not need to be endured, however, and he'd reached the end of his patience with the constant interference in his operations. There was too much on the line; he'd waited too long for this.

"Tell me again what happened at the bookshop," he ordered his head of security. He needed to get the scene straight in his head.

In quick, concise detail, Raphael recounted the

botched robbery, including a list of casualties. "Esme has confirmed the talisman is now safely in her possession, however."

Il Maestro waved the comment away, troubled by something else entirely. "What could the witches tell us about the attackers?"

"Not much. The ones that got away were either more concerned with the talisman, or were feeling somewhat forgetful thanks to their injuries." Scorn laced Raphael's tone, making it all too clear what he thought of the witches' weakness.

"They've confirmed that one of the attackers bore the signature of a wolf. The other signature was … unclear."

It was an odd choice of words. The witches were barely a generation away from being human, but even their inferior skills should have been able to identify the signature.

"It seems strange, don't you think, that we have once again run into setbacks as a result of a mangy dog." Il Maestro spoke mostly to himself as his eyes followed the path of the coin over the back of his hand.

Raphael placed enlarged images on the desk in front of him. "We managed to pull these from CCTV footage in the area of the robbery. And this" – he placed another image on the desk, grainier but still legible – "was taken from Temple Bar on the night that the test subjects were attacked."

Even in the poor quality black and white images, the similarities were evident. "So, we're dealing with the same subject."

"We believe so."

The confirmation didn't surprise him; it was as he expected. Much of their recent testing had focused on werewolves, it was possible they'd inadvertently drawn attention to themselves as a result. Still, another thought was beginning to take shape in the back of his mind.

As he looked back at the images from the night of the robbery, it was the second subject that drew his attention. Encased in shadows, the figure was little more than a silhouette in the print, but there was one very definable feature that stood out to him.

"Subject two was a woman?" He looked to Raphael for confirmation.

"None of the cameras picked her up clearly, but based on the shape, and the witches limited information, that would seem to be the case."

A somewhat disconcerting smile settled over Raphael's face. "Quite a fit one too if the silhouette is anything to go by."

Not for the first time, Il Maestro was reminded why this vampire was his right-hand man. A vision of control and efficient practicality, but beneath the surface lay a level of depravity that rivalled any other he'd encountered. Generally, he could appreciate, and encourage, such proclivities, but for now, they needed to tread carefully.

He debated his decision for a moment before giving the order. "I think it's time we fetch our hybrid."

Raphael's mouth split into a wide grin, displaying his razor-sharp fangs and transforming his face into a thing of nightmares.

25

Phoenix felt an unexpected sense of comfort and relief being back in her own gym. The smells, the noises, the familiar faces, and a convenient ban on supernatural powers. It seemed like an ideal place to satisfy Ethan's desire to train but keep his incessant nagging at bay. So she'd thought at least.

"Dammit, wolf, what's your problem?"

She blew sweat-soaked hair out of her eyes. Had he decided pummelling her to death was the best way to stop the prophecy?

Ethan merely grunted and flung a towel at her as he turned for the changing rooms. "Get dressed. Abi will be expecting you."

Phoenix sighed and wiped her face with the towel. It had been so tempting not to answer her phone after the last training session. So tempting to just stay home and forget it all. She'd even cancelled her round of patrol the following night by claiming the bar was short-staffed and she needed to work. However, it didn't take long for guilt to get the better of her.

As it turned out, Ethan had fallen off the radar himself for a few days, so no one seemed too concerned about her absence; a fact that only reinforced Shade's words. Questions to his whereabouts had been met with vague responses, but he was definitely crankier since returning. If she didn't know better, she'd swear it was the full moon again already.

Once at the showers, Phoenix struggled out of her now-drenched sports top, wrestling to free herself of the clingy material. Every muscle in her body ached, and even her bones were making their protest known.

The presence of humans hadn't given her the upper hand in the slightest. If anything, he'd gone harder on her since he couldn't push the issue of her non-existent powers. She was still glad she'd made him train on her terms for once, though. The distance from the others, Shade in particular, gave her a bit of the perspective she'd been needing.

By the time the scalding water finished its pounding dance over her skin, she was even feeling somewhat understanding of the stress Ethan was under. Somewhat.

She took a couple of minutes to blow dry her hair – death by pneumonia would be very anti-climactic –

before grabbing her jacket and heading outside to find Ethan under the dim glow of a streetlight.

The sight made Phoenix stop. It was odd for him to place himself in such a visible, open position; he was usually more careful than that. Her concern grew as she noted the stiff set of his stance and the strain showing around his eyes.

What the hell is up with him?

Before she could comment, he shifted his weight from the lamppost and motioned for her to start walking.

She pulled her jacket tightly around herself and followed him in silence. Her breath misted in front of her face as the chilling air hit her lungs. The cold didn't seem to bother Ethan at all, and Phoenix found herself envious of the naturally high body temperature that was typical of wolves and shifters.

The streets were deserted as they walked in the direction of the pub. The near freezing temperatures and heavy threat of rain encouraged anyone with sense to curl up in front of a warm fire for the night.

"Why did you want to train here?" Ethan asked, breaking the silence that sat heavily between them.

She hesitated, wondering how honest to be. In the end, she opted for his tactic: keep it vague. "I just needed to be close to home for a while."

"Shade said you weren't around for training while I was gone."

Phoenix tensed. What else had Shade being saying to him when she wasn't around? "I'm sure he didn't miss me too much."

Clearly noticing the edge to her tone, Ethan gave her a mildly reprimanding look. She fought the urge to stick her tongue out at him and focused instead on the path in front of her.

"I know he's not an easy person to get on with, but Shade's a good guy once you get past the exterior."

"Sure."

"His Sire abandoned him before he'd even finished turning. He was all alone, yet he managed not to give in to blood lust."

Ethan's words stopped Phoenix short, just as he knew they would. Young vampires were extremely susceptible to blood lust; it was why the Council imposed such strict rules around siring. For a newly turned vampire to wake alone and control those urges was astounding.

"His Sire just left him to turn?"

Ethan nodded. "He has no memories from before he was turned. At least that's what he says."

She chewed this information over as they lapsed back into silence. Had she been too quick to judge Shade? Sure, he had a shitty attitude, but waking up dead and alone had to leave you with some issues. Rather than making her feel more charitable, the thought just made her more irritated. Shade had been a complete dick to her since she'd met him. And for what? All she was doing was trying to help.

She blew out a long breath and forced herself to let go of the silent argument that was brewing in her head. It would do no good wasting precious energy being pissed; best to just forget it.

As they passed Whitethorn Park, Phoenix's thoughts turned to the strange makeshift pack Ethan had formed. He'd surrounded himself with a member of nearly every race of the Lore and seemed oblivious to how strange that was. What would he do when it was all over?

"Will you go back to your pack? When everything is over with the prophecy?"

He looked at her in surprise, a puzzled expression settling on his face. "I hadn't really thought about it. I guess so. There'd be no real reason for me to stick around."

"Do you not think the others would miss you?"

More confusion. "Why would they?"

Phoenix let out a short laugh of disbelief. "You're their leader. They look up to you."

At her words, his expression closed down completely, only the telltale muscle tick in his jaw telling her she'd hit a nerve.

"I'm nobody's leader," he said tightly, and turned away from her.

More than ready to call bullshit, Phoenix stopped

walking and stood with her hands on her hips. "Really? Well, it doesn't stop you from bossing everyone around!"

He gave her a warning glare but didn't respond.

"Oh, come on, Ethan. Lie to yourself all you want, but you're an Alpha through and through. You can't hide from what you are."

He turned on her in an instant, his eyes flashing angrily. "Really? You're one to talk, Phoenix."

She reeled, the sting of his anger catching her completely by surprise. "Me?"

"Yes, you, Phoenix! You've spent your whole life trying to run from who you are, and now you're going to judge me?"

Phoenix stood frozen to the spot. Her gut clenched as if his words had been a solid right hook. All the anger and frustration of recent weeks began to rise like bile in her throat, burning open countless old wounds.

"I don't have a problem with who I am," she spat back, digging her nails into the palm of her hands to stop them trembling. "It's everyone else that seems to have a problem with that."

"Oh, cry me a fucking river, Phoenix. You've had a hard life? Well, guess what? Everyone has. Maybe if you started accepting who you are, everyone else would too."

"I do accept who I am," she shouted, no longer feeling understanding or conciliatory in the slightest.

"Then why do you hold your powers back?" Ethan

yelled, equally as loud.

Without thinking, she took a step back and a look of triumph flashed in his eyes. Anger was quickly replaced with numbness as the walls she'd perfected her whole life were thrown up to block the pain caused by his words. Funny, she hadn't even realised they had come down to start with.

Without another word, she turned and walked away. The deafening thud of her heart the only sound that followed her.

Phoenix was shaking as she strode purposefully in the direction of the bar. Adrenaline flooded her system, making her feel sick to her stomach, and she pointedly ignored the strange burning in her throat that indicated the embarrassing potential for tears.

Who the hell does he think he is? He better not even think about following me …

Actually, why the hell wasn't he following her? He should be rushing to apologise; he'd been completely out of line!

Where had that outburst even come from? She'd obviously hit a sore spot, but that didn't mean he had to lash out at her. She was working her arse off trying to help; it wasn't her fault if she wasn't living up to his expectations –

Her mental ramblings were swiftly cut off by a snarl as a dead weight hit her, dropping her to the cold, unforgiving concrete.

Her head hit the ground with a solid *thud*, and the flash of pain caused her vision to swim. A heavy weight pinned her and made it impossible to move. Her lungs struggled to expand beneath the restriction.

She tried to get a look at her assailant, but a large hand shoved her face unceremoniously back towards the ground. Her senses screamed vampire, but the blow to her head, coupled with reducing oxygen levels, made it hard to think straight. Whoever her attacker was, he wasn't human.

The hard grit of the ground rubbed against her cheek, and she could feel his warm breath on the back of her neck. Large hands moved from her shoulders to run suggestively down along her sides. The movement caused her heart rate to ricochet and her vision to clear abruptly.

With considerable effort, she forced herself to slow her breathing and let her body become soft and compliant. The pressure on her back eased a little, and a deep, masculine voice chuckled softly in her ear. The sound made her skin crawl; it was all she could do not to scratch her skin off.

She waited until he was preoccupied with his uninhibited groping before she snapped her head back with as much force as she could muster from her limited vantage point. Her efforts were rewarded with a satisfying crunch of bone and an angry grunt as blood splattered the ground around her.

His hold on her didn't give, however. Instead, it tightened as he hauled her to her feet like a ragdoll. She struggled against him as every cell in her body screamed to get away from his touch. A heavy heat began to build in the palms of her hands.

"Uh uh, no you don't," he growled as he slammed her against a nearby wall.

His voice. There was something strangely familiar about it. A niggling memory tugged at her consciousness, but before she could think on it further, she felt a sharp prick in her neck and all strength left her body in an instant.

Fear spiked through her as she watched the needle fall to the ground. Her thoughts became hazy, and she was dimly aware of the cold air hitting her stomach as her attacker roughly pushed a hand under her top. His calloused skin grasped her breast as he shoved her legs apart.

"Il Maestro never said anything about me having a bit of fun before I brought you in. I've wanted to do this for a very long time." The low-spoken words were filled with such malice that, even through the haze, it chilled her to her very soul.

A voice, deep in the back of her mind, screamed for

her to fight back. But she couldn't move. Her limbs were heavier than they'd ever felt before. She wanted to sob, to scream out in frustration at her ineptitude.

Slowly, her vision began to fade, filling with a white light that seemed to grow stronger and stronger. Numbly, she was aware that her body was shaking and a heat was building once again. Only this time, it was building not just in her hands, but throughout her entire body. It grew hotter and hotter as the white light grew stronger.

"Argh, you bitch!" Her attacker roared in pain and slammed her against the wall again before sinking a pair of razor-sharp fangs deep into her throat.

In an instant the light was gone, and all that was left was pain.

Blinding pain.

Phoenix screamed.

26

Dammit that woman drives me insane!

Ethan fumed as he stared in the now empty direction Phoenix had stalked off. She had no right lecturing him about accepting who he was when she was the one who insisted on ignoring everything that made her special.

As if being unique was a bad thing.

He blew out a breath and tried to calm the part of him that was itching to continue the argument. He'd thought going home for a few days would help clear his head. It hadn't. If anything, it just made things worse. Having to face everybody, knowing Sean's killer was still walking free …

Guilt started to seep in, slowly and insidiously. The feeling of righteousness from only moments ago was replaced with a horrible sinking feeling in the pit of his stomach.

Had he taken it all out on her?

She was oblivious to her own potential and it frustrated the hell out of him, but would he have fared better without someone to guide him? He wasn't so sure.

With a sigh, he looked again at the empty road ahead of him. He should probably follow her and apologise. A soft growl and gentle nudge from his wolf very clearly conveyed the animal's agreement. He tucked his hands into his pockets and walked briskly in the direction of the pub.

The night around him seemed unnaturally quiet. There were no cars passing, no rustle of leaves, just an icy silence. It was almost as if the night itself was pissed at him.

As he reached the main street, a sharp scent flowed to him from beyond the now dark shopfronts: fear.

He forced himself to remain still and listened closely, allowing his stronger senses to take over. A slight scuffling sound came from somewhere to the left. After a moment, the sound became louder and more frantic. Careful to remain silent, Ethan moved in the direction of the noise. The scent of fear grew sharper with each step he took.

An odd glow seemed to lighten the night beyond the row of shops, silhouetting the buildings against the backdrop of the heavily clouded sky. He'd barely gotten ten feet when the night was ripped apart by a violent scream.

Phoenix.

All thought of remaining silent was quickly forgotten as he sprinted to the end of the street. His claws elongated, and his canines ruptured from his gums. He knew his eyes would be yellow because his wolf was tearing at its binds to be released. But he didn't care. His only thought was reaching her.

The sight that met him in the dark shadows almost made him lose what little control he had left. Phoenix was pressed against the wall of the building. Her head was thrown back in fear and agony as a large dark-haired vampire tore into her throat with his fangs.

The coppery tang of her blood filled the air and made his wolf howl. His vision sharpened like a laser on its target and he lost all sense of humanity, lunging with every bit of power his body possessed.

In the deep recesses of his mind, he was dimly aware they needed answers, they needed the vampire alive. But his wolf didn't care. His wolf wanted blood.

Even in his heightened state, he was careful not to hurt Phoenix. He attacked the vampire, taking advantage of the momentary chaos to turn the tables and latch his own teeth into the vampire's throat. With a roar, the vampire released Phoenix and tried to fling him off, but Ethan held fast.

The shift in position gave him his first proper view of the vampire, and he found himself staring into the empty black eyes that had haunted his dreams. It was him. It was the vampire that killed Sean.

Rage overpowered rational thought and the world around him became red. The vampire's strength was phenomenal, but he was no match for the fury that coursed through Ethan. The more the vampire fought, the more Ethan tore at him.

Claws slashed. Fangs pierced.

The blood that coated his mouth was vile and poisonous. Still, he continued. Possessed. Tearing through flesh, sinew, and bone.

It was only the weakening thud of Phoenix's erratic heartbeat that pulled him back to his senses. She lay slumped on the ground, unmoving. The slow beat of her heart was like a percussive death knell.

Fear gripped him. Had she reached her immortality? He had no idea.

In the periphery of his awareness, he noticed the vampire had stopped struggling beneath him and was shaking. It took Ethan a second to realise the vampire was laughing. A deep, shuddering laugh.

The vampire's words, when they came, struck the heart of both man and wolf. "You can't save her, you know."

In an instant his vision clouded red again and with a furious roar, he ripped the vampire's head clean off his body. Lifeless blood dropped to the concrete and slowly began to fade.

As Ethan stood panting and struggling to regain control of his wolf, he heard a whimper behind him. The simple sound made his heart clench violently.

Phoenix's eyes opened wide as she surveyed the scene in front of her, unable to stop the low moan that sent a flash of pain through her throat.

A pair of blue, lifeless eyes stared at her from their position on the ground barely three feet away. A somewhat hysterical laugh bubbled up in her chest as she realised the eyes belonged to a head that seemed, strangely, to be missing a body.

She watched as the head began to disintegrate in front of her eyes. Some vague thought pushed insistently at her consciousness, something important she couldn't quite grasp through the haze of pain. As the gruesome image gradually disappeared, it was replaced by a large black crow, its red eyes glowing as it stared at her. A soft, keening lament drifted on the night, not too dissimilar to the wailing she heard at the Ritual, but quieter, more gentle.

And then it didn't matter because Ethan's yellow-brown eyes appeared and his concerned face filled her view. Except his concerned face was covered in thick, dark blood and looked every bit as gruesome as the disembodied head.

He was speaking to her. She could see his lips moving, nearly hypnotised by the sight, but she couldn't hear a thing. And then everything went black.

Phoenix didn't know how long she was out for, but when she came to, the world around her seemed to be moving. Her stomach felt queasy and she scrunched her eyes tightly together against passing flashes of light. She felt a comforting hand smooth the hair back from her forehead as the world began to drift away again to blackness.

27

Phoenix shot up with a gasp. Blood rushed to her brain, making her head explode as spots formed in front of her eyes and the strange room began to spin violently. In an instant, Ethan was by her side making soothing noises and encouraging her to lie back down. But she couldn't lie back down because he needed to know. She needed to tell him what she remembered.

She knocked his hands away and frantically tried to get the words out, but all that came from her throat was a raw croak. She tried again, but only managed a dry rasp.

Finally, recognising her distress, Ethan disappeared and quickly returned with a glass of water. He gently helped her raise the glass to her lips and slowed her movements when she would have gladly gulped it in one go.

The water felt like a solid lump trying to painfully

pass through her throat, but still she gasped for more. Eventually, the cool liquid eased the burning pain enough that she could speak.

"I knew him."

Ethan froze, and a strange expression passed over his face.

"The vampire. I knew him," she repeated insistently, grabbing the sleeve of his jumper. He needed to understand how important this was.

Ethan sat down on the bed beside her – wait, how did she end up in a bed? – and took her hands in his. His thumbs rubbed soothingly across her palms to calm her frantic fidgeting.

"It's okay, it's okay. You're safe now. Just tell me what happened."

A sob threatened to escape as the memories came flooding back to her like flashes from a horror movie. The sharp piercing of fangs. The violation. The lifeless blue eyes. She forced her breath to slow. Breathe in and out. In and out.

Stick to the facts, you can do this.

"He attacked me from behind. I tried to fight back but" – her breath caught – "he was too strong."

Ethan's grip on her hands increased painfully, and for a moment she thought she saw his eyes flash yellow. But when she looked again, all she saw was warm brown eyes full of concern.

"Something happened when he attacked me," she continued, trying to pick through the haze of memories. "I felt a strange heat build up … Then he bit me, and there was just pain."

Ethan stiffened slightly at her words, and Phoenix wondered vaguely whether it was the mention of the heat or the biting that got his attention.

"You said you recognised him?" he prompted.

She nodded and the sense of relief at being able to move her neck outweighed the aching stiffness that was setting in.

"His voice was familiar, but I didn't get a proper look at him. Not until I came to and saw the –" Bile rose up in her throat and she swallowed with effort. "He's the head of security for the Dublin clan. He works for my … uncle of sorts."

Ethan's jaw dropped in unmasked astonishment. "Your uncle sent someone to kill you?"

"No, no way." Phoenix sat up so quickly that the room began to spin again.

Ethan steadied her, propping pillows behind her for support.

"None of this makes sense." She scrunched her fists into her eyes and wanted to scream her frustration. "Uncle D would never hurt me."

She tried to organise the million questions that were crowding her thoughts. "Raphael, he said something. I don't think he was meant to kill me. I think he was meant to bring me somewhere."

"Phoenix, that was the vamp that killed Sean." Ethan's voice was low and shaking with barely restrained anger. "Whatever his intentions, they weren't good."

Her breath left her in a whoosh. Raphael killed Ethan's friend? Did Darius know? Surely not.

An uneasy silence fell between them, and Phoenix's thoughts turned to her surroundings. The room around her was masculine but lacking personality. Navy and cream provided clean, efficient décor, but it was lacking personal touches. There were no photos or knick-knacks to provide clues to the owner.

Was she in Ethan's apartment? His bedroom?

She lay on a king-size bed surrounded by soft pillows and a thin blanket covered her from the chest down. A large white t-shirt was the only thing separating her skin from the covers, and she tugged the blanket up to her chin self-consciously. While she was extremely grateful not to be caked in blood anymore – particularly her own – she cringed in embarrassment, wondering at what point she'd been divested of her clothes.

As if sensing her shift in focus, Ethan stood quickly and distanced himself from the bed, busying himself with a mess only he could see.

"I called Nate to pick us up. I didn't think you'd want Abi to see you hurt. And Lily had stuff here to help with the healing." Ethan seemed to realise he was rambling and stopped talking abruptly.

So, they were in Ethan's apartment then.

The wild musky scent she'd come to associate with him was flooding her senses, which meant she was most likely wearing his t-shirt too. The thought made blood rush to her cheeks. Realising he was looking at her for reassurance, she smiled weakly and nodded her thanks.

He cleared his throat and looked uncomfortable. "The others are here to discuss what happened when you're feeling up to it. I've left some clothes at the end of the bed for you. Figured you might want to freshen up before you see them."

Again she nodded, feeling awkward from the strange intimacy of finding herself in Ethan's bed, wearing his clothes.

"The bathroom's through there." He indicated to a door to her left and turned to leave.

At the thought of being left alone, panic wiped away all concerns of where she was or who had seen her naked. She pushed it back angrily, but with it came another thought. A memory that left her cold.

That sound – a soft keening lament as she lay on the cold ground.

"Ethan?"

He stopped with his hand on the door and looked at her in question.

"How badly was I hurt?"

As she voiced the words, she already knew the answer. She knew what the sound had been, and what it meant. But still she had to ask.

Ethan's expression turned guarded. "Badly." A muscle at the side of his jaw ticked. "If you hadn't already reached your immortality, you'd have been dead."

It took Phoenix a long time to drag herself out of the luxurious shower. Waterfall showerheads and scalding water did little to chase away the chill of Ethan's parting words, but the pounding beat lulled her into a gentle trance that allowed her to stop thinking. At least for a few minutes.

When she walked into the living room, everyone was assembled in their usual places. Lily and Nate were at the breakfast bar, and Nate's head was buried in his laptop. Shade slouched by the window, flipping his penknife open and closed as he stared sullenly into the darkening sky. And Ethan sat pensively on the sofa, his foot tapping as he surveyed the door she was exiting.

A deafening silence fell as soon as she appeared. She tugged self-consciously at the sleeves of the baggy jumper Ethan had left her. All eyes turned in her direction, and Ethan leapt from his seat to usher her to the sofa.

"If you're feeling up to it, I thought we could talk

about what happened yesterday?" he said, handing her a steaming cup of black coffee.

Phoenix took the cup gratefully and let the rich aroma fill her senses before taking a sip. It took a moment for Ethan's words to register, but when they did, the scalding liquid caught in her throat, nearly choking her.

"Yesterday?" she wheezed out between coughs.

"You were badly hurt. You needed to heal." Ethan watched her with concern. "Lily gave you an herbal remedy to keep you asleep while your body repaired."

All things considered, losing a day of her life was really the least of her worries, but this new information only made her feel worse.

Shit, Abi!

Phoenix didn't even realise she'd jumped up until Ethan gently pressed her back down into the sofa.

"It's okay, it's okay," he said as he took the half-spilled coffee from her hands and placed it on the table. "I texted Abi. Told her you had a family emergency and you'd be gone for a day or two."

Sinking into the soft cushions, Phoenix added that text to the ever-growing list of lies she needed to keep straight. It would be a miracle if Abi was even speaking to her by the end of all this.

"Ethan said you knew the vampire that attacked you?" Lily's question drew everyone's attention back to the matter at hand.

"Figures," Shade muttered, ignoring Ethan's reprimanding look as he scowled out the window.

Phoenix sighed – good to see a near death experience didn't change anything – and nodded, but confusion made her head pound. Why would Raphael have attacked her? Growing up in the Dublin clan, she'd always avoided the large man that worked as Darius's head of security; he'd creeped her out in a way she couldn't quite put into words.

But he worked for Darius. He knew who she was, and that she was under Darius's protection. What would make him go against his Master's orders? Was he working for someone else? She tried to remember his words as he attacked her, shuddering at the memory of his hands groping her and his large body crushing hers. He had said something … a name …

"Il Maestro," she said, speaking her thoughts out loud. "That was the name he used. The person that had given him the orders."

Nate glanced up from his laptop, gave a quick nod of acknowledgement, and resumed his furious typing.

Phoenix picked up what was left of her coffee and took a large gulp. The bitter liquid burned a path down her throat as she debated what to tell them. With nothing left to lose, she started from the beginning.

"My parents disappeared when I was fifteen. Uncle D – Darius – took me in. My parents' families both disowned them before I was even born. Darius is the only one that stood by them. He's the only other family I've ever known."

"The vamps accepted you?" Shade waved his hand vaguely in her direction, looking at her with renewed curiosity.

"Most of them didn't know about me, only his closest advisors. He kept me hidden to protect me. I left when I was twenty-one. They'd have no reason to hurt me ..."

As her words trailed off, the memories assaulted her. The night her parents went missing, waiting, knowing in her heart that something wasn't right. Going to live with the Dublin clan. The realisation, even from such a young age, that she must hide who she was if she were to survive. And the darkness. Most of all the darkness.

"What clan did you say this was?" Nate asked from behind his screen, breaking the tense silence that had fallen.

Phoenix cleared her throat and tried to keep her tone matter of fact despite the emotion that threatened to break free of her tight grasp. "The Dublin clan."

Nate nodded, chewing on his lip in concentration.

"Did you ever find out what happened to your parents?" Lily's voice was soft and childlike as she looked at Phoenix. Her green eyes begged for a happy ending to the story.

Phoenix just shook her head and looked down at the table in front of her. She couldn't talk about this, not now.

"Got it!" Once again Nate broke the building tension with his sudden declaration. "Okay, let me see … Uh huh … yep … okay …"

"Nate, are you going to share anything useful here, or just keep making a lot of annoying noises?" Ethan spoke for the first time since she'd begun her story. He glared at Nate with his arms crossed over his chest.

Nate looked up sheepishly, a crooked grin on his face.

"Sorry," he said, and flipped his laptop screen around so everyone could see. "It looks like an investment firm has made a number of payments to the Dublin witches coven recently."

From the satisfied look on his face, Phoenix could already guess where this was leading. Empty of everything except the black coffee – which now threatened to make a reappearance – her gut clenched and she had to swallow back the feeling of nausea.

After throwing an apologetic glance her way, Nate continued, "The investment firm is called IM Investments. It appears to be owned by the Dublin vampire clan."

"Which means –"

"Which means the attack on Phoenix may not have

been a coincidence," Ethan finished, eyes flashing yellow.

He turned to her. "When was the last time you spoke to your uncle?"

A loud buzzing filled Phoenix's head as she tried to make sense of what she was hearing and what it might mean. "Not for a while, I've been avoiding his calls."

She sat up straight. Was that it? Had Darius grown worried when he couldn't reach her? Maybe he'd sent Raphael to get her, not realising his head of security couldn't be trusted. As she opened her mouth to voice the thought, she looked around the room and found herself met with sympathetic stares.

Of course, they all thought he was involved, why shouldn't they? But she knew Darius. He'd never hurt her. There had to be some other explanation.

Maybe if she just spoke to him …

28

Phoenix slipped quietly into her bedroom, grateful to have avoided Abi. Now that she was immortal, her healing abilities, helped along nicely by Lily's remedies, were impressive, but the damage to her neck had been substantial, and it would be a while before she could pass off the scarring as an over-enthusiastic hickey. No doubt her friend would have questions.

She pulled out her phone and scrolled through her contact list to Darius's name. The information Nate found weighed heavily on her mind, despite the confident brush-off she'd given Ethan and the others. Uncle D had too tight a rein on his clan and its business ventures not to know if there was something going on with the witches. Yet he claimed ignorance about the disturbances in the Lore. Disturbances which the Dublin coven were heavily involved in.

The only logical explanation she could think of was that he'd been lying to protect her. He'd sheltered her from the Lore all her life, it'd stand to reason he would try to do it now. But she wasn't a child anymore.

She took a deep breath and made the call, her phone gripped tightly in her hand.

One ring. Two rings.

"Phoenix! Where the hell have you been? I haven't been able to reach you for weeks."

A sob caught in her throat at the concern in Darius's voice. This was the man she'd grown up with, the man that looked after her as if she was his own child. The others were wrong about him. They had to be.

"Hi, Uncle D," she answered after taking a moment to get a grip on her emotions. "Sorry it's been a while. Time just kind of got away from me."

"Are you okay, Phoenix? You don't sound yourself."

She hesitated, realising she hadn't really thought the conversation through before ringing. Did she just come straight out and ask why he'd sent Raphael after her? Ask why he was funding a homicidal gaggle of witches?

"It's been a crazy few days." Fuck was that an understatement.

"How about we meet for dinner and you tell me –"

"Uncle D? Do you remember the wolf I told you about? What he said about the attacks and me being involved somehow?"

"Yes?"

"Did you ever find out any more from your contacts? Is there anything I should be worried about?"

"Phoenix, what's going on?"

He didn't answer the question.

Phoenix gripped the phone tighter and mentally willed Darius to say something to ease the ever-growing knot that settled in her stomach.

"I remembered something else he said. It's been playing on my mind. He mentioned a prophecy, said something about the witches being involved …"

Silence.

"The wolf was lying, Phoenix," Darius said, finally. "If there was any such prophecy, the Council would know about it."

"But the witches –"

"Are under the same rule as the rest of us. If their activities have been in any way questionable, the Council will deal with it. You're worrying for nothing, Phoenix," his tone softened.

She reached up and gently ran her fingers along the bandage that covered the side of her neck. "I have to go," she whispered, and hung up before he could respond.

Ethan was surprised to receive Phoenix's call so soon after she left. It made sense that she would need time to process everything they'd learned. He was even more surprised at her words.

"Are you sure you want to do this? Break into the lair?" he asked for the third time.

They were all gathered back in his living room, and Phoenix sat across from him fidgeting restlessly with the medallion around her neck.

She nodded, her expression remaining emotionless despite her obvious unease.

His breath came out in a whoosh. Were they really going to break into the lair of the most powerful vampire clan in Ireland?

Beside him, Nate was rubbing his hands together gleefully and already firing up the laptop, ready to do what he did best. Lily sat beside Phoenix with a slightly shocked look on her face as if she thought they were all nuts. Shade slouched against the breakfast bar; his single raised eyebrow telegraphed more interest than Ethan had ever seen from him.

"Okay, first things first." Ethan looked back to Phoenix. "We need the exact location of the lair."

Vampire clans were among the most secretive races of the Lore when it came to protecting their resting place, and for good reason. Although the stronger members of a clan could often withstand a degree of sunlight, there were still many that were particularly vulnerable during daylight hours. Open knowledge of their lair location would be a security nightmare, and vamps were anything but stupid.

Phoenix brought up a picture on her phone and set the device on the table so they could all see. Lily's face mirrored Ethan's own surprise, nicely highlighted by Nate's low whistle, and an "I'll be damned," from Shade.

"The lair is in the American Ambassador's residence?" Ethan asked, staring at the image of an imposing white building with grand pillars framing the entranceway.

Phoenix gave a wry smile. "Best place to hide is in plain sight."

"Nate, can you pull up the schematics for the lair?"

A couple of taps later, "Negative." Nate shook his head, pushing unruly brown hair out of his eyes. "The plans listed only show the upper storeys." And it went without saying that the official lair was buried deep beneath the earth, away from the sun and prying eyes.

Ethan chewed this over, running through and discarding the various options that might be available to them.

"I can get you in," Phoenix cut off his thought process. Her voice was quiet but determined as her unwavering, green eyes met his.

He thought about arguing. He wanted to make it easier on her, but this was her demon to face – his desire to protect her didn't come in to it.

"I used to sneak out sometimes when the darkness got to be too much for me," she continued when no argument was forthcoming. "There are some old, abandoned service passages that made it easier to get around. They're our best bet."

Her words were clipped and he could see her working to keep her emotions in check, but she sat tall, shoulders firmly set, and Ethan found himself proud of the strength she displayed.

"Not to put a dampener on things," Shade interjected, very clearly intending to do exactly that, "but how do we get in without being noticed by a lair full of vampires?"

"*We* don't," Ethan said firmly, and cut off all arguments with a commanding look. "The more of us that go in, the more likely we'll be detected. You guys can help from a distance, but Phoenix and I will be going in alone."

The lair was large and housed hundreds of vampires; they'd have no chance of escaping alive if they were detected. He could only hope Darius really did have Phoenix's best interests at heart because they'd be staking their lives on it if they were caught.

"We need to pick a time when there'll be as few vamps as possible. Anyone have any ideas?" Ethan looked around the room and his lips quirked into a smile when Nate raised his hand with a smug grin on his face. "Yes?"

"It just so happens there's a very exclusive gala ball being held in the ambassador's residence. Only one problem." Nate hesitated. "It's tonight."

"Okay, what other options –"

"No" – Phoenix held up a hand to stop him – "it's perfect. When there's an event held, the vampires are either in attendance or ordered to make themselves scarce. Security below ground would be as low as we could hope for."

"I could probably help with that side of things." Nate grinned as he rooted around in a rucksack that was leaning against his chair. He pulled out a small flash drive and held it up for them to see. "If you can get near enough to their servers to plug this in, I *should* be able to get access to their security systems and cause a few distractions."

Ethan took the drive from him and put it in his pocket. He still wasn't sure this was a good idea. If they got too close to any of the vamps, their signatures would be picked up. Phoenix might be able to mask hers enough, but he definitely couldn't.

Lily obviously had the same thought as him. "There's a spell that might be able to help change your signatures temporarily," she said as she worried at her nails. "But I'm not sure if I'm strong enough to cast it."

"It's okay." Phoenix patted Lily's shoulder awkwardly. "The bottom levels are warded. Uncle D had it done when I came to live with him to help keep my presence a secret. The wards act as a kind of buffer for our signatures, almost like sound proofing I guess."

Ethan watched her closely, waiting to see if she'd realise the significance of her words, but she seemed to be lost in the memory of her past.

"Who set the wards?" Lily's intelligent eyes met his across the room.

"The witc …" Phoenix trailed off, all manner of emotions crossing her face as realisation dawned on her.

For that brief moment she looked lost, and Ethan found himself wanting to hurt the person that put that look in her eyes. Then she pulled herself together and a steely resolve removed all trace of emotion from her face.

"Tonight."

"Can you get everything set in time?" He looked questioningly at Nate, knowing his expertise would be vital to get past what would no doubt be an impressive security set-up.

With a grin and salute from Nate, the decision was made.

29

Phoenix watched the city lights flash by, vibrant colours blurring together hypnotically. The late hour allowed Ethan's Audi to keep an impressive pace as they drove along the quays, hampered only by the occasional drunk that stumbled into the road.

She'd never been comfortable in big cities. The grey buildings felt cold and soulless to her, and the hordes of people made her feel even more alone. For the first time in many years, she longed for the rolling green hills that had surrounded her childhood home.

It didn't take them long to reach the lair. Nestled in the heart of the Phoenix Park, impenetrable walls surrounded a building that was both grand and understated in equal measure. White, with large arched windows and a long winding driveway, the ambassador's residence was lit by low lighting that cast eerie shadows onto the lush, manicured lawn.

That night, the tall wrought-iron gates stood open to the honoured guests of the gala, many of whom were blissfully oblivious of the truth hidden within the depths beyond.

"Keep driving for another kilometre," she directed. "There's an old service road on the left."

The tension in the car was palpable and her pulse thrummed in her veins. She hadn't been back here since the day she left four years ago, but she'd spent a lot of time within those walls, learning the secrets they held. She could only hope that everything was as she remembered it.

It wasn't long before they reached the road she was looking for. The trees and bushes had become even more unruly in the passing years and it was a struggle to get the car through. Ethan winced every time a branch scratched the side of his Audi, and Phoenix almost laughed at the forlorn look on his face. Although, she was extremely glad they hadn't taken her Mustang.

When they could go no further, they abandoned the car, pulling into a gap in the trees so it would be hidden from view if anyone happened to follow them. A frigid breeze ruffled the branches around them, grating in the otherwise quiet night. Phoenix's nerves were on edge. Every crunch of leaves and every gust of air across the back of her neck wound her tighter and tighter.

She led the way through the soft mud and explained in a low voice, "There's an old service tunnel ahead that leads to the boiler room in the basement of the house."

As a young girl in the lair, she'd kept herself busy by finding forgotten passages that allowed her to explore her underground prison without detection. She'd pretend she was on a secret mission and her task was to outsmart the vampires.

The isolation had been for her own safety, of course. Darius had risked his reputation by sheltering her. To the Council, she was a symbol of weakness; one of their most sacred edicts broken and allowed to go unpunished. An inter-species pairing that was allowed to continue and produce offspring. All it would take was a single vampire to speak of her existence and everything would fall to pieces.

So, she was kept apart and alone. Only Darius and his most trusted vampires were aware of her presence among them. All for her own safety. But things were different now. She had a life she loved, and she needed answers so she could get back to it.

Finally, they reached the entrance to the tunnel, which was largely obscured by rocks and overgrown bramble. Ethan took out his hunting knife, the one that had terrified her when they first met, and began to hack away at the thorny branches until there was just enough room for them to squeeze through. With that done, Nate handed him a small black pouch and Ethan gave a nod to confirm they were ready.

She took a deep breath and stepped into the tunnel, her clothes snagging momentarily on the remaining thorns. Ethan followed close behind her, and his warm presence helped to calm the frantic beating of her heart.

The air was stale and the smell of packed earth was heavy around them. With each step they took, the darkness became more complete, almost like they were walking into the black, gaping mouth of the beast. She'd taken this same route many times when she was younger; her yearning to see the sun had been too strong to ignore. The same clawing fear that she felt then, the fear of being caught, caused adrenaline to thrum through her veins now.

At the end of the tunnel they waited, listening intently for any noise on the far side of the old metal door. The only sounds that reached them were the whirring of machinery and the clunking of the large boiler that serviced the house.

Phoenix was uncomfortably aware of Ethan's close proximity at her back and she had a strange urge to push him away. This little trip down memory lane was leaving her raw and exposed in ways she never imagined.

With a final glance of agreement, Ethan put his shoulder against the heavy door and pushed. The loud creaking of rusted hinges made Phoenix cringe back into the shadows. Heat from the boiler hit them like a solid wall in contrast to the cold air of the tunnel, but other than that, she registered no movement within the room.

Moving silently, they edged forward and wove between the heavy-duty machinery that filled the space. Large pipes covered the ceiling in a tangled maze above their heads, adding to the claustrophobic feeling and making Phoenix's chest feel tight.

The next door led to a long, empty corridor. Concrete floors and starkly painted walls echoed even the slightest sound. Phoenix inhaled a slow breath and paused for a second to compose herself. They were in the basement of the main residence, not yet low enough to hit the lair, but that didn't mean they were safe.

The main server sat on this floor; it linked to sub-servers above and below ground. It would be guarded, but if they were to have any hope of getting into the lair unnoticed, they would need to go there first.

At Ethan's nod, she led the way, stopping them just short of the server room.

Scuffling sounds and the occasional snort confirmed the presence of a guard beyond the final corner. Phoenix felt a sudden urge to backtrack and forget about their crazy plan. But Ethan didn't give her a chance. He handed her the small package from Nate and in the blink of an eye, he was gone, leaving her alone and exposed in the corridor.

For a whole minute it felt as if her heart had stopped beating and her lungs had forgotten how to expand. Then she heard a banging in the distance and her heart stuttered back to business.

A low curse sounded and heavy footsteps faded into the distance. Phoenix counted to ten before crouching low to peer around the corner.

Empty.

She ran towards the server room, fumbled with the package in her hand, and pulled out a small black scanner. After connecting it to the pin pad at the door just as Nate had instructed, she waited, watching while numbers flashed on the small screen in a blur of red.

It seemed to take forever, and every second that passed felt like a ticking time bomb. When the screen finally flashed green and gave a soft beep, she nearly yelped with surprise.

She yanked the door open and slid quickly inside before pulling it tight behind her. A cold breeze from the air conditioning system caused goose bumps to prickle along her skin, and she rubbed her arms briskly against the chill.

Lights, cables, black boxes. It looked like a scene from the future when computers had officially come to take over the earth.

"Nate … Nate? Can you hear me?" She pressed the small earpiece, willing him to answer.

"I've got you." Nate's answer came back through a burst of static. "Okay, I need you to find the main server. It'll probably be the one with the most cables in the coldest part of the room."

Phoenix looked around, quickly discounting the smaller boxes and monitors.

There!

Towards the back of the room, a large cabinet stood with floor to ceiling black boxes and flashing lights. Cables ran from it like tentacles ready to crush anyone that came near.

"Once you find the server," Nate continued in her ear, "plug the hard drive into any free USB port. I'll do the rest."

Doing as she was instructed, Phoenix plugged in the hard drive and waited nervously. Where the hell was Ethan? What if he'd been caught?

Despite the icy cold air coming from above her, sweat dripped down her spine and her hands felt clammy. Every buzz from the machines or new flashing light made her heart ricochet, and when the door to the server room opened suddenly, she nearly pissed her pants altogether.

"Phoenix?" Ethan's voice whispered from the far side of the room.

Stepping out from behind the server – with difficulty since the cable tentacles had become tangled around her legs – Phoenix called softly, "Over here."

"Where's the guard?" she asked when he came into view.

"He's otherwise occupied." Ethan grinned, looking very pleased with himself. "How are we getting on?"

"Nearly … there …" Nate's voice came through the earpiece to both of them at just that moment. "Okay, I'm in."

And just to prove his point, the distant sound of alarms reached their ears and emergency lights began flashing red in time with the sirens.

The trip via stairwell to the lower depths of the lair was thankfully uneventful. Whatever distraction Nate had managed to concoct seemed to be working, and his newly acquired access to the security system allowed him to keep them updated of the guards' position at the far side of the building. Their luck was holding out. Temporarily at least.

When they reached the fifth floor where the lair's security team was housed, they stopped and tentatively peered through the small glass panel in the door. A lone guard sat in front of a bank of monitors, swivelling on a black leather chair as he used a sharp hunting knife to clean dirt from under his nails.

They could take him out if they needed to, but would it be worth leaving a trail? Phoenix wasn't convinced they'd find anything of use in Raphael's quarters, and the thought of getting anywhere close to the scent of him again made her sick to her very stomach.

Ethan waited patiently, giving her space to make the decision, and following her without a word when she took a breath and continued further down the stairs.

Level six: her old living quarters. She hesitated, waiting for the barrage of memories, but none came. The truth was, this place held no real memories for her, just an overwhelming sense of sadness. That realisation allowed her to walk past the door on the sixth floor and continue down to the final level. No time, or need, for a trip down memory lane when there was no lane to walk.

The seventh and final level housed Darius's living quarters and personal office. Phoenix had visited him there many times while she lived in the lair. She could vividly remember the large, solid mahogany desk and the bookcases filled with ancient tomes she longed to touch. It was one of the few places she hadn't felt alone.

What they were doing now felt like a complete betrayal of everything Darius had done for her, but there was information here they needed. Darius kept detailed files on every vampire in his clan. If there was information to be found on Il Maestro, it would be here.

Although there were no security cameras for them to contend with on this floor, access rights were even more restricted than the other levels. Relying once more on the

223

pocket-sized wonder of technology from Nate, they waited impatiently for the right code to get them through the stairwell door.

When the pin pad flashed green, Ethan pulled the door open and ushered her into the hallway beyond.

Mahogany panels lined the rich wine-coloured walls, mirroring the décor of Darius's office. The lighting was muted, coming only from intricate candles placed in alcoves at equal intervals along the hall.

The stairwell had barely disappeared from view when a noise dead ahead stopped them in their tracks. Voices drifted down the hall, though the words were muted by the hushed tones. Phoenix's heart tap-danced in her throat as she recognised Darius's voice.

Ethan grabbed her hand and tugged her into an unlit alcove a few feet ahead of them. As they huddled in the shadows, she tried desperately to calm her heartbeat. Surely any vampire within a twenty-mile radius could hear the blood racing through her veins.

From her new vantage point, the voices became clearer, certain words jumping out vividly: Raphael, update, ritual.

She took a slow, deep breath and eased herself to the edge of the alcove to peer carefully beyond the wall. Two large figures stood, barely visible, at a bend in the corridor, just out of reach of the flickering candlelight. Darius's shape was as familiar to her as her own, but the second figure she couldn't quite make out. It was neither figure that caught her attention, however. It was what they were standing in front of.

A door.

What the ... There shouldn't be a door there ...

Just as the thought crossed her mind, the door closed and the two figures walked briskly in the direction of their hiding spot. Ethan pulled her close to him, pressing her back against the wall as he shielded her body with his. The musky scent of him, coupled with the adrenaline flooding her veins, made her head swim. Phoenix could feel his muscles tense in preparation for a fight, but his breathing remained calm as he forced her to meet his eyes. She focused on the steadiness she saw there, using it to help her to relax.

The voices drew closer and Phoenix wracked her brain desperately for a way out of the situation. She was seriously contemplating jumping out and yelling, "Surprise!" when the footsteps suddenly stopped. Ethan raised an eyebrow but didn't move, his body remaining unnaturally still.

Realisation dawned on Phoenix when she heard the chime of a lift, and she nearly dropped to the floor with relief. The voices cut off abruptly with the closing of the doors, and she finally allowed herself to release the breath she'd been holding. A wide grin split her face, but the happiness was short-lived.

"Come on. We might not have long," Ethan said, stepping out of the alcove once it had been quiet for a minute.

Phoenix followed him down the corridor, but halted abruptly when she came to the spot where the two figures had stood.

"Where's the door?" She looked at the space in confusion, not seeing any sign of the door but knowing it must be there.

Ethan placed both hands on the wall and moved them systematically across the wall until eventually he nodded. "It's well hidden, but it's here. I can feel the edges."

"So, how do we get it open?"

He didn't answer, but continued his careful exploration with a look of deep concentration. Eventually, a low click sounded and the wall swung outward, forcing them to jump back.

Her heart pounded in her chest as she stared into the gaping darkness that appeared before them. Gone were the plush floor coverings and richly panelled walls. In their place was cold, hard stone with steps leading deep into the earth.

"You know where it leads?"

Ethan's question broke through her thoughts and she shook her head. "I had no idea it even existed. It feels … wrong."

She shivered, something about the darkness making her want to run in the opposite direction, to scrub herself raw until she finally felt clean again.

"Dark magic."

She looked up in surprise and was met with a grave expression.

"What you're feeling is dark magic."

30

Ethan's words repeated themselves on a loop in Phoenix's head as they slowly descended into the darkness, the only light coming from a candle Ethan had grabbed from a nearby alcove.

Why would she be feeling the weight of dark magic? It didn't make any sense.

Her confusion was only heightened by the trajectory of their steps: downwards. Never in all of her years had she heard mention of an eighth level to the lair, yet here they were, very obviously descending deeper underground.

Without even realising he'd stopped, Phoenix found herself running into the solid mass of Ethan's back. She reached out for the wall to steady herself, but quickly pulled her hand back as a bone-deep chill, unlike anything she'd ever felt before, shot through her.

Everything about this felt wrong to her, and as she craned her neck around Ethan to view the large stone chamber that had opened before them, she felt no more comforted by what she saw.

In the centre of the room stood a large stone altar surrounded by thick black candles. Even in the dim light, Phoenix could make out dark stains covering its surface, and she refused to let herself think too deeply on what may have caused them.

As she turned a slow circle to take in their surroundings, Ethan walked around the chamber with a grim expression on his face. Following his lead, she stepped further into the strange room, grimacing as the unclean feeling intensified and settled over her limbs like a palpable weight.

A single lap of the chamber was enough to leave her feeling sick to her stomach. Weapons of a sort she had never seen before adorned the walls, their metal covered in thick stains not dissimilar to the altar. Intricate symbols were carved at random intervals and pulsed with energy as she passed them.

"We should probably get out of here before someone comes back," Ethan said, his face somewhat paler, even in the dim candlelight.

Phoenix rubbed her arms, trying in vain to chase away the chill that had settled into her bones. Her instincts were screaming at her that they were missing something, but for the life of her she couldn't figure out what it was.

She turned in another slow circle from her new vantage point by the altar to take in the room one last time. As she reached the end of her rotation, something caught her eye on the far wall of the chamber – a small patch that seemed different to the area surrounding it. It was so subtle that she wasn't quite sure if her imagination was playing tricks on her.

Holding her breath, she walked towards the wall. Her eyes struggled to determine what had caught her attention. As she drew closer, the dark shadow began to take form; it was small and so dark that it almost blended into the stonework. She reached her hand forward and was surprised to feel the cold touch of metal, even though part of her expected it.

"It's a handle," she called back to Ethan, impatiently urging him to come closer with the candle.

Phoenix groped around on the rough stone until her hands found the grooves of a doorframe, set so tightly into the wall that it was almost invisible, just like the entrance to the chamber had been. A solid and imposing lock sat below the handle and Phoenix gave it a tug, not really expecting it to open.

"Can you break it?" She looked at Ethan hopefully, willing to admit he was the stronger Supe if it meant gaining access to whatever was behind the door.

He reached out a hand to examine the lock, but pulled it back as if he'd been burned. He shook his head ruefully. "There's silver built into the lock. I won't be able to break it. Our only hope is to find the key. Or …"

"Or what?" Phoenix tapped her foot impatiently, in no mood to play psychic.

"Or you could try to melt it."

That made her pause. The memory of the heat was fresh in her mind from the attack by Raphael mere days ago. It might not have been enough to stop his attack, but it had been there. And for once, it had been useful. A fae power.

Could it really hurt to try now?

There was only one problem: she had no idea how to do it, at least not on purpose. Would she even be able to call on the power of the sun so far below ground? At night?

Grinding her teeth, she mumbled self-consciously, "I don't know how to start."

Ethan placed a hand on her shoulder and looked at her with an intensity that made her squirm. "I'll help you, just trust me."

The sincerity in his warm, brown eyes calmed her, and she realised suddenly that she did trust him. So, she nodded, expecting to fail, but willing to at least try.

"Close your eyes."

He waited until she obeyed before continuing. "Place

your hands on either side of the lock. Good. Now, try to picture a warm light building between your hands. Feel the heat pulling from the centre of your chest. Feel it growing with every breath …"

She was about to tell him to cut the mumbo jumbo and speak English, when suddenly her palms became warmer. Her eyes opened in surprise, jaw dropping when a small, white spark ignited between them.

Clinging to that small spark for all it was worth, she concentrated on the warmth radiating from it and imagined it growing stronger. It flickered, and in a panic she fumbled, desperate not to lose the light. Ethan squeezed her shoulder gently and she felt grounded once more. Phoenix closed her eyes and focused on her breathing. Each exhale pulled the warmth from her centre, and slowly, she felt the heat grow between her palms as it gained life.

She wasn't sure how long she stood there before a loud clunk shocked her from her trance and pulled her awareness abruptly back to the room. A lump of metal lay on the ground at her feet, and she stared at it in shock. When she looked up, Ethan had a wide grin on his face and his eyes shone with something almost resembling pride.

Together, they turned to face the door and a strange sense of dread replaced the heat in the centre of Phoenix's chest. With the lock no longer impeding the way, it was a simple matter of pulling the heavy door open to see what secrets it hid. She watched with her breath held as Ethan inched it open. Her heart hammered louder and louder with every creak.

The first thing that struck her was the smell. It was so overwhelming it almost formed a physical barrier to the small, stone room that appeared in front of them.

No, not a room, a cell.

Human excrement left a stench so putrid it was palpable, and almost, but not quite, masked the metallic tang of blood. The air was thick with decay and cloyed at the back of Phoenix's throat as she tried not to breathe through her nose.

Ethan moved into the cell first, almost disappearing in the darkness. Every instinct in her body wanted her to turn and run. Leave this place and scrub herself clean of its memory.

Instead, she followed him.

Even her heightened senses struggled to adjust to the darkness, but when they did, her stomach heaved at the sight that met her eyes. The cell was tiny, no more than ten feet wide. Sharp metal instruments of all shapes and sizes hung from one wall, and a drain sat in the centre of the floor. Dark stains covered the instruments and coated the surrounding walls.

But what troubled her most was the shadows that filled the corner furthest from the door.

Two bodies lay huddled in the corner, covered only by rags. Chains hung from limbs that were little more than bone, and they were surrounded by the remains of human waste.

Beside her, Ethan growled low in his throat as he too noticed the frail forms. In the darkness his eyes flashed yellow, and something about his uncontrolled anger made the hair stand up on the back of her neck.

Steeling herself against the sight before her, she inched forward with trepidation.

Just as Ethan reached out a hand to stop her, one of the bodies moved. As if in slow motion, she watched the head rise. Long hair hung limply, coated in dirt, framing a face that was little more than a skeleton.

Frozen, Phoenix watched in horror as the head turned, and she was met with the anguished gaze of vivid green eyes.

Eyes that were almost identical to her own.

And she screamed.

31

Phoenix's scream cut through Ethan like a knife. He had known what they would find when they stepped into the small stone cell; the familiar threads of her unique signature had filled his senses before the truth could even register with her.

Moving quickly, he clamped a hand over her mouth and urgently whispered soothing words to calm her. If they drew attention to themselves now, they'd all be dead.

Ethan couldn't pull his gaze away from the green eyes that were so like Phoenix's. They reflected an untold pain back at him, but also disbelieving wonder as they stared in awe at what could only be their daughter.

As soon as he was confident Phoenix would stay quiet, he released his hold, freeing her to run to her mother. His chest clenched as he watched her reach out with trembling hands. It was obvious she wanted so much to touch the woman, but it was hard to imagine how even the slightest touch wouldn't bring pain to the frail form.

Shifting his gaze to the other form that lay huddled in the corner, his fists clenched in anger. The naturally pale skin of who he assumed to be Phoenix's father, was now almost translucent as the man lay unmoving at the feet of her mother. Even in the man's unconscious state, what was left of his muscles appeared to be clenched tight in agony, and Ethan could guess all too well what tortures had been inflicted upon him.

As Phoenix sobbed quietly with her mother, he looked around the cramped space for a way to break the chains that held her parents. It took him only seconds to spot the keys – hanging on the wall barely more than an arm's reach from the two prisoners.

Ethan's wolf growled and he had to fight back the rage that boiled up in his chest. The level of cruelty was not surprising considering the physical torture that had obviously been inflicted, but the thought of freedom being so tantalisingly close – for ten long years – was soul-destroying.

Not wasting a second more, he grabbed the keys and unlocked the chains, careful to avoid the silver coating the vampire's manacles.

"Daddy?" Phoenix's voice cracked as his movements drew her attention to the still form of her father.

When she looked up at Ethan, her tear-stained face

was filled with horror. "How are we going to get them out of here?"

Ethan could feel another, similar pair of green eyes staring at him intently, beseeching him. He knew what those eyes were asking, and it went against everything in his nature. But he couldn't refuse.

Meeting the eyes of Phoenix's mother, he gave a small nod of acknowledgement and gently moved Phoenix from where she was now huddled over her father. Before he had time to think further, he allowed his claws to extend and sliced along his forearm.

His wolf squirmed uneasily, but stayed silent in agreement. He forced his arm against the vampire's mouth, angling it as best he could to ensure the blood would make contact.

At first the body remained unresponsive and Ethan feared they'd reached the vampire too late. But then suddenly, like an electric shock, the body jolted, and a pair of razor-sharp fangs latched onto his arm like a vice.

The pain he expected never came. Instead, as the blood was sucked eagerly from his vein, the rhythmic pull lulled Ethan into a calm daydream; the ebb and flow of his blood formed a hypnotic wave of motion for him to float upon as his muscles relaxed with each passing minute.

His wolf growled.

The sound was the nudge he needed, a reminder that

he needed to stay conscious of their surroundings. They'd been underground too long already, and though his body would quickly replenish the lost blood, he couldn't afford to be light-headed if he was to get them all out in one piece.

With that thought in mind, Ethan moved to pry the vampire's fangs from his arm, expecting a fight for the much-needed food source. Instead, he found himself meeting a pair of warm, brown eyes. Fangs swiftly – and willingly – retracted from his arm.

For a moment, he just stared at the vampire before him, filled with an awed respect for Phoenix's father. It was glaringly obvious that he'd been starved for a very long time. The strength it would have taken for him to willingly relinquish the blood was beyond comprehension.

A split second later, Phoenix flung herself at her father, tears streaming down her face as she met Ethan's eyes over her father's shoulder. What Ethan saw in her eyes made him more uncomfortable than even the feeding, and he turned away from the gratitude he didn't deserve.

Giving them as much space as he could within the cramped room, Ethan pressed his earpiece. "Nate?"

Nothing.

"Nate? You there?"

Silence. *Shit.*

Quickly assessing their options, he turned to Phoenix's father. "Can you walk?"

In truth, even with the Supe'd up blood, the man still looked like a corpse with limbs so thin and fragile they looked liable to snap, and a face little more than a skull covered in skin. But there was an awareness to the eyes that hadn't been there before, clearly reflecting the healing power of the werewolf blood. And a determination that said the man would fight to his last breath. So Ethan wasn't surprised when he nodded.

As Phoenix helped her father gingerly to his feet, Ethan turned once again to meet the bright, green eyes that reminded him so much of Phoenix's.

"I have nothing that will give you strength, but I have more than enough strength to carry you if you'll allow me to?" Reluctant to take all choice away from a woman who had very clearly been refused her dignity for a long time, he kept his tone patient and respectful, despite the niggling feeling that time was against them.

The smile he received in return was like sunshine itself, and there was nothing but gratitude in the woman's eyes as he bent to lift her small frame.

Phoenix's head was a dizzying mix of questions and disbelieving shock as they made their way back towards the boiler room. Her father's arm rested limply across her

239

shoulder, its meagre weight very clearly confirming he was real. Yet she couldn't quite bring herself to believe it.

They had been here all this time.

She choked on a sob, but forced herself to put one step before the other. While her and Ethan might have found an excuse for being in the lair beforehand, the presence of her parents would quickly rule out any false pretences of a surprise visit. It would be a death sentence, or worse, if they were caught.

The comms had stayed silent from the time Ethan tried to contact Nate. But more worryingly, the lair was silent too. Unnaturally so.

Phoenix knew Nate's original distraction wouldn't have lasted this long. She could tell by the tension around Ethan's eyes as he carried her mother that he'd come to the same conclusion. So, they moved quickly, praying to a god they didn't believe in that the clever shifter had somehow bought them more time.

It was with surprise that she registered the sound of the boiler in the distance. They'd somehow made it back to their entry level without incident. If they could just –

"Stop!"

Ethan's soft curse told her all she needed to know before she turned around. A single vampire stood in the hallway behind them, dressed in the non-descript black of the lair's security uniform. He had no visible weapons, but being a vamp, he didn't really need any.

"Did you have a nice nap?" Ethan asked, voice friendly and stance relaxed.

The vamp growled – actually growled – and Phoenix very quickly surmised that he must have been the vamp guarding the server room.

"Phoenix," Ethan said quietly, keeping his eyes on the guard. "Why don't you take your mother and head on home? I think I have some apologising to do here."

He shifted his weight to pass her the frail form of her mother, and at the same time, her father pulled his supported weight from her shoulder with obvious effort.

Phoenix hesitated.

Ethan was a good fighter, and he was damn strong, but she couldn't leave him alone in the middle of a vampire lair. It would be a death sentence.

As if sensing her reluctance, Ethan turned serious brown eyes to meet hers. "Phoenix, you need to get your parents out of here."

Dammit! There has to be another way.

And just to prove that fate can be a cruel bitch sometimes, two more vampire guards took that moment to step around the corner and into the hallway, grinning.

Ethan didn't give her any more time to argue. Pushing her mother into her arms, he turned and launched himself at the vampires, claws extending even as he moved.

She didn't want to leave him, but the feel of her

mother, so light in her arms, made her turn towards freedom. The sounds of fighting followed them with every step as they moved closer to the boiler room, and it took all of Phoenix's willpower not to turn back.

Ahead of her, her father stumbled, but kept one hand on the wall for support as he continued forward with focused determination.

A strange clunk was the only warning they had. Suddenly the hallway filled with smoke, completely obscuring their view. Flashes of blue flame were the only break in the smoke, and the flames were so bright in their intensity that they were almost blinding.

Amongst the chaos, Phoenix could make out the sound of a woman chanting. Male voices shouted over one another, and the sound of footsteps running towards her made Phoenix huddle close to the wall, turning her body to protect her mother as best she could.

"Phoenix," a muffled voice said, close to her ear, "put this on."

A large black mask was shoved in front of her face, and before she knew what was happening, her mother was taken from her arms.

Her only thought was to stop them. There was no way they were taking her parents from her again. But then a hand landed on her shoulder, and Ethan's large frame was beside her. His scent filled her senses even through the haze of smoke and the acrid smell of burning.

"It's okay. We've got her," he assured, taking the mask and quickly fixing it around her face.

The difference was instantaneous.

Phoenix hadn't even realised she was having trouble breathing until all of a sudden she wasn't struggling anymore. Her view, though still hazy, cleared significantly, and even with the black masks covering their faces, she could now make out the forms of Lily, Shade, and Nate standing not more than five feet away. Her mother was held safely in Nate's arms, and her father slumped against the wall beside them.

The chanting and flames were coming from Lily in an impressive light show that was quite effectively holding back any vampire guards attempting to join the party. However, it was obvious from her slumped shoulders that she was weakening and wouldn't be able to keep up the onslaught much longer.

When Ethan urged her towards the boiler room, Phoenix ran to help her father. Just as she bent to lift him, determined to carry him out of the lair, Shade was there beside her. Without meeting her eyes, Shade lifted her father and was gone in a blur of speed towards the tunnel. Nate wasn't far behind as he carried her mother to safety.

Phoenix followed their lead, dragging Lily with her as Ethan pulled up the rear. The thunderous sound of footsteps and snarls echoed in her ears as she ran. They weren't going to make it.

Smoke was replaced by the thick, earthy smell of the tunnel, followed seconds later by a brief glimmer of light. They'd barely cleared the exit when a loud explosion rang and Phoenix was flung through the air.

She landed unceremoniously amongst the trees, her ears practically vibrating from the ringing that sounded in them. Ethan lay on the ground beside her, shaking his head as he pulled off his mask. Phoenix followed suit and turned to look back in the direction they'd come. All that was left of the tunnel entrance was a pile of rubble. Nate stood nearby, mask removed with a huge grin on his face, holding a small black handheld computer. Her mother was by his side, being tended to by Lily.

It took her a moment to realise that the night sky around them was no longer dark. While they had been in the lair, the subtle light of daylight had begun to fill the world around them, chasing away the shelter of the night.

Fuck, where's dad?

He was a powerful vampire, and at full strength could easily withstand the weak morning sun. But he wasn't at full strength. He wasn't at any strength at all. Even the slightest hint of sun would kill him.

Phoenix scrambled, frantically trying to get her feet under her as she looked around. The world tilted viciously and she fought back the urge to throw up. She had to confirm he was safe. Ethan was by her side in a split second, steadying her. He was mouthing something at her, but Phoenix could hear nothing other than the ringing in her ears.

Shade. That's what he was saying. Shade had taken her father to safety. Her heart both calmed and clenched tight at the reassurance. Shade, as a pure vampire, was faster than the rest of them, but did she trust him with her father's safety?

Unable to do anything more than hope, she rushed to her mother's side.

The light touch of her mother's hand against her face made Phoenix suddenly aware of the tears streaming down her cheeks. There was so much love in the green eyes staring back at her that Phoenix had to swallow past the sob threatening to choke her. Gently, she lifted her mother into her arms and followed Ethan back to the car, clinging for dear life to the precious weight she carried.

32

As soon as Ethan's apartment came into view, Phoenix flung the car door wide, completely ignoring the spray of gravel as the car skidded to an abrupt halt.

Please tell me they made it okay.

The relief when she found her father's pale sleeping form in one of the blacked-out bedrooms brought her to her knees. He was so still it would have been easy to assume he was dead, but she could feel the weak threads of his signature, as familiar to her as her own even after all this time.

He would sleep until darkness fell again; his body was far too weak to fight the daylight hours, even here, hidden from the sun's touch. And while he slept, he would heal. Physically at least.

As Phoenix stared at the man she thought lost to her forever, she tried in vain to wrap her head around everything. They'd been alive this whole time. Her parents had been mere floors from her, suffering, and she'd done nothing to help them.

Her thoughts continued on along this vein, swamping her in guilt, until Ethan's scent filled her nose and pulled her out of the useless ramblings of her mind.

"Your mother would like to talk to you." His brown eyes were full of concern as he helped her up from her kneeling position.

"Aria," Phoenix responded automatically.

Ethan's look of concern turned to confusion.

She shook her head to clear her thoughts. "I never told you her name," she clarified. "My mother, her name is Aria."

"Aria." He nodded, as if the name somehow fit for him. He glanced towards the still form of her father in question.

"Marcus."

Her chest constricted as she remembered back to the lair, back to Ethan feeding her father his blood. He'd saved her father's life. Emotions choked her and she fought to find words that might begin to express how grateful she was.

"Ethan ... I can never thank –"

"Shh." He stopped her words and pulled her close for a brief hug before pushing her towards the door of the bedroom. "Go to your mother. She's on the rooftop. I'll

247

keep watch over your father."

Phoenix found her mother sitting on a soft blanket on the flat roof of the warehouse apartment. From her position, she had a perfect view of the morning sky with the most beautiful mix of reds and oranges splashed like watercolours across a backdrop of the city.

Aria wore a look of pure bliss on her face as she angled it towards the emerging sunlight. Her hair was tied in a knot at the back of her head, but the orange and blonde strands still flared like flames as the sun's rays hit them.

With the dirt now gone, her mother's skin once again looked flawless. But the natural glow Phoenix had envied so much as a child was missing. In its place, a pale, thin frame that acted as a stark reminder of the truth behind the peaceful scene in front of her. She knew it was an illusion, and it made her heart ache.

But, illusion or not, Phoenix was reluctant to disturb it. So, she merely watched. Her keen eyes noted the slow return of colour to her mother's cheeks; the healing power of the sun swift and astounding to behold when the fae was finally returned to her natural element.

Eventually, Aria smiled, pushing a loose strand of hair over a pointed ear as she turned towards Phoenix. "You turned out more beautiful than I ever could have imagined."

Suddenly self-conscious, Phoenix attempted to smooth the clothes that were now beyond ruin after the night's adventures. She made her way to her mother's side and sat hesitantly on the blanket, wondering where to even begin.

Before Phoenix could say anything, Aria reached out a trembling hand towards her. The hand lightly touched the medallion that hung around Phoenix's neck, as tears glistened in her mother's eyes.

"You kept it." The words were barely more than a whisper.

Phoenix looked down to watch as delicate fingers traced the embossed sun emblem. She swallowed hard and nodded. At fifteen, she'd understood enough to know her parents wouldn't leave her willingly. She'd known when she left her childhood home that she wouldn't be returning, and she'd needed to take some part of them with her. She chose her mother's medallion and, hidden in the depths of her wardrobe, her father's sword.

More reluctantly than she'd have liked to admit, Phoenix moved to take the medallion from around her neck. She intended to return it to its rightful owner, but her mother stopped her with a shake of her head and a loving smile. Phoenix looked at the still youthful face in front of her. Even having lived it, it was so hard to believe ten long years had passed since she last saw that smile. Ten years lost forever.

And just like that, reality hit like a frying pan to the face.

"Have you been there this whole time?" Phoenix asked.

The thought alone almost broke her and she clenched her teeth against the burning pain in her throat. The smile wavered on Aria's face and a sad understanding filled her green eyes as she nodded. Phoenix hugged her knees tight to her chest and focused all of her attention on keeping her breathing steady.

"We all trusted him, sweetheart." Aria's words were soft, and tinged with an unspoken pain as she laid a comforting hand on Phoenix's shoulder.

Darius had been their friend for many centuries before Phoenix was even born. He'd stood by them when their families banished them. He'd encouraged their relationship. He'd been family.

Covering her mother's hand with her own, Phoenix took a deep breath. "Tell me."

Aria gazed out at the city, saying nothing for a very long time. "How much do you remember?" she asked finally.

Phoenix gave this some serious thought. The feelings were so clear to her, even ten years later: the unsettled niggling in her belly, the feeling that time had slowed to a complete halt as she waited. But the details had blurred over time. Small images had become symbols for the whole, while the bigger picture was only the hazy memory of a child.

"I remember … you coming home. You were upset." Phoenix nodded to herself. "You and Dad were talking about something, but you wouldn't tell me what was going on. You just said you had to go out and that you'd be back soon …"

Aria's face remained expressionless, but her grip on Phoenix's shoulder tightened for a brief moment before relaxing. "I was out shopping that day, and a woman bumped into me, accidentally, I think. Anyway, the woman was a Seer —"

Phoenix nodded her understanding of the term at her mother's questioning look. A pang of sadness hit her as she thought of all the hours spent in Darius's library, learning things from a book that she should have learned from her parents.

"The woman," Aria continued, "started speaking in tongues. She spoke of a prophecy, and a hybrid that would bring an end to humanity."

At the mention of the prophecy, Phoenix froze. Her mother gave her a knowing look.

"Needless to say, I was upset. Your father and I had been so far removed from the Lore by that stage that we had no way of knowing if she spoke the truth. And we knew of only one hybrid …"

"So, you went to Darius."

251

Aria sighed, a sound filled with so much regret it made Phoenix want to weep. "So, we went to Darius. As it turns out, he was all too familiar with the prophecy. I don't know what he used, but somehow he drugged our wine, and when we woke up, we were in the cell where you found us."

Phoenix's thoughts were in turmoil as her mother grew silent. She'd seen the evidence of Darius's betrayal, had seen the truth of her mother's story, but she still couldn't wrap her head around it. How could she reconcile such evil with the man she'd loved like family?

"But then who is Il Maestro?" Phoenix asked, desperately clawing through her mind for another explanation, one that might actually make sense.

Aria looked at her, confused. "Where did you hear that name?"

"Raphael. He said Il Maestro had given him his orders."

"Il Maestro was Darius's Sire. He was notoriously psychotic. If we'd known earlier of Darius's true origins …"

Aria shook her head. "Il Maestro can't have given Raphael his orders. He's dead. Darius killed him many centuries ago."

So that was it. There was no other mysterious bad guy waiting in the wings, laughing to himself as they all ran around blaming the wrong person. No answer that would make the truth any more palatable.

"Why?"

It was the only thing Phoenix could think of, the one word that kept repeating itself in her head.

In an instant, her mother's face hardened, her eyes almost glowing with the anger that radiated through them. She grabbed both of Phoenix's hands in hers and squeezed so tightly it hurt.

"He's evil, Phoenix. Everything you know about him is a lie, an act. You must remember that."

"What did he do to you, Mam?"

Overhead, the sun dimmed and a fierce wind began to blow. A shiver ran down Phoenix's spine.

"What he did to me is nothing." Aria's voice was as cold as the ice that settled in her green eyes. "What he did to your father ... he will die for."

33

"Woah, careful!"

Phoenix was so caught up in her own thoughts that she had somehow completely missed the mountain of wolf standing on the stairs in front of her. As a result, she found herself face to face with Ethan's bare chest, his hands on her shoulders to steady her.

Even distracted, it was hard not to appreciate the broad expanse of muscle only inches from her. Dark hair covered Ethan's chest, adding to the animalistic aura that came off him in waves. A light tan showed no signs of stopping as it followed the impressive v-taper of his waist into the well-worn jeans that hung low on his waist. All helpfully accented by a teasing trail of hair that led downwards.

Phoenix shook herself and looked up to meet a quirked eyebrow and teasing grin, both of which faded when Ethan took in the haggard look on her face.

"How did the talk with your mother go?"

Phoenix sighed and slumped down onto the step as she leaned her head against the wall. "As expected, I guess. She's so angry."

"It's not really surprising." Ethan sat down beside her and his body heat pushed away some of the chill that seemed to have settled permanently within her.

She shook her head. "I know, but this seems different. She's not angry about what was done to her. She's angry about my dad. Only she won't tell me what happened to him."

Beside her, Ethan went still.

"You know?" Her tone was accusing. She didn't mean it to be, but why should he know when no one would tell her?

Ethan shook his head. "No, not for sure, but I have an idea."

He held up a hand to stop her before she could interrupt. "I'm not going to tell you what I think. Suffice it to say that if it was my mate, I would kill him too."

She wanted to argue, but the look that clouded his features stopped her and his ferocity sent a shiver down her spine.

"Did Aria tell you why he took them?" he asked, quickly moving the subject along.

"The prophecy ..." That stupid word seemed to echo

on repeat in her head. No matter what she did, she couldn't seem to escape it. "Darius has been encouraging it all along."

There was no surprise on Ethan's face, and she guessed it was logical given the events that led to this point. But as Phoenix recounted her mother's story, she just felt numb, as if she was talking about someone else's life entirely.

"I don't understand how I could have been so wrong about him."

Her shoulders sagged, and she put her head in her hands. It was as if the uncle she loved had died. Only, she couldn't mourn him, because in his place stood a monster that made a mockery of every memory she ever had of him.

Ethan was quiet for a moment before wrapping an arm around her, pulling her close. "We've all been wrong about people before."

"Repeat that." Darius strode into his office and closed the door firmly behind him. He kept his expression calm, but his blood was simmering at a temperature that would rival an erupting volcano.

The vampire standing in front of him tried valiantly to maintain eye contact, but a stain on the desk in front of him was too fascinating to ignore. "It appears they hacked into our security systems, Il Maestro. The guards on duty were tending to a code one alert when –"

A hand silenced the vampire. Darius wasn't interested in hearing any more about the incompetency of his security team. They would be dealt with later.

"Raphael?"

"Has not returned, and we haven't been able to trace his phone."

Darius said nothing, merely nodding his dismissal of the vampire as he picked up the ballpoint pen on his desk and twisted it absently around his fingers. Raphael, for all his twisted inclinations, was Darius's most trusted vampire. If his head of security hadn't returned, there could be only one explanation.

Stabbing the pen into the mahogany desk, Darius stood.

As he made his way through the winding corridors of the lair, vampires moved swiftly out of his trajectory; their natural survival instincts wisely warned them against any form of engagement.

Reaching the hidden doorway to the underground chamber, he paused. There were no obvious signs of disturbance, but every instinct told him something was amiss.

Not stopping to light any of the torches lining the wall, he strode down the stone steps, easily finding his way despite the complete darkness.

The broken lock on the floor was the first clue that his instincts were correct.

The empty cell was the second.

Chains hung impotently against the wall, mocking him with their vacant shackles. His bellow of rage shook the very foundations around him as he ripped the heavy door from its frame and flung it across the room.

As he stalked from the chamber, he mentally assessed the situation. His leverage was gone, and his head of security most likely dead. It was safe to assume Phoenix was now aware of his true role in events and wouldn't be quite so amicable going forward.

He needed to move quickly. The witches had better be ready.

34

"It'd be suicide to face him ourselves. We need to let the Council deal with this." The words came out of Ethan's mouth, but they didn't sit well with him.

Night had begun to fall once more, and he'd called everyone for a meeting in his living room to agree a plan of action. Their venture into the lair hadn't gone unnoticed, and it would only be a matter of time before they had vampires breathing down their necks. They needed to be prepared before that happened.

"Ethan's right." Marcus's voice was quiet as he shuffled slowly into the living area, supported by Aria.

Phoenix jumped up from her seat on the sofa and rushed to his side. The healing sleep, combined with supernatural blood, had worked wonders in healing Marcus's wounds, but his skin remained paler than death and his movements were stilted; pain caused him to wince as he was moved to the sofa where Phoenix propped up cushions behind him.

"Darius is very old," Marcus continued, "and more cunning than you ever could imagine."

The words were spoken without inflection, and without emotion, but Ethan could tell the pain they caused. The anger on Aria's face didn't go unnoticed either; it was obvious the thought of giving up her revenge didn't sit well with her.

"Why would the Council help us? Or believe us for that matter?" she said, green eyes flashing. "Darius sits as one of their Witnesses. We are nothing more than lawbreakers in their eyes."

Ethan nodded his acknowledgement of her words and forced himself to ignore the flinch it elicited from Phoenix. It would do them no good to deny the truth. "That may be, but Darius risks exposing us all with his actions. The Council won't take that chance."

"How do we know the Council aren't in it up to their necks?" Shade pushed away from the kitchen table and made a beeline for the fridge. He pulled out two fresh bags of O negative blood and handed one to Marcus before tearing the other open with a slice of a fang.

"He has a point," Phoenix said, obviously reluctant to agree with Shade about anything.

Ethan heard the weariness in her voice, noticed how she gripped her father's hand a little bit tighter, and wished he could make it easier on her somehow. But the Council wouldn't take his word as truth; they'd need proof. They'd need to see the hybrid.

"The Council's edicts go against everything Darius is trying to do. They created the barriers that protect our world and they have no reason to see that effort undone." Ethan could see scepticism on a number of the faces staring back at him. He could even understand why they felt that way, but he needed to believe what he said was true. If the Council had turned their back on their own edicts, they didn't stand a chance.

He focused his attention on Aria and appealed to her the only way he could. "You've just gotten your family back. Is revenge worth losing them again?"

He could see her anger fight to hold firm against the truth of his words, the battle raging visibly on her delicate features. Finally, her shoulders slumped and she shook her head.

"Are we all in agreement then?" Ethan asked as he held up his mobile, a strange mix of numbers and symbols visible on the screen.

A weighted silence was the only answer, and Ethan felt no victory as he made the call.

Phoenix tugged nervously at the sleeve of her leather jacket, idly noting the strands of thread that had come loose as a result of the bad habit. The room around her was filled with the hum of conversation, a multitude of languages and accents blurring in an excited babble of voices.

"Remind me again why we're doing this," she said as she glanced sideways at Ethan.

"The only way we'll get to the Council is by going through the Council Liaison Office first. If we can prove to their rep that we're telling the truth, we can be assured the Council will get our message."

Ethan leaned casually against the large glass window, seeming completely unimpressed by the panoramic view of Dublin that spanned out into the night beyond.

"I get that, but why here?"

Nate had explained the role of the C.L.O. to her while Ethan was on the phone stating their case. Bowing to the demands of the Council's guard dogs irritated the snot out of Phoenix, but she accepted the necessity. What no one had explained, was why she now found herself standing on the seventh floor of the Guinness Storehouse, twiddling her thumbs while night covered the city and the vampires undoubtedly began their hunt.

"I agreed to meet their rep, so long as it was on our terms. I won't risk your safety any more than I have to." The intensity in Ethan's brown eyes was at complete odds with the relaxed slouch he'd adopted, and something about the juxtaposition made Phoenix shiver.

Needing to focus on anything other than their upcoming meeting, Phoenix stared out at the lights of the city, becoming mesmerised as they blurred together in a kaleidoscope of colour. Even in the glass enclosure of the Gravity Bar, the sickening smell of the hops filled her nostrils, over-powering the various aromas of perfume and aftershave surrounding her. Abi had never understood why Phoenix disliked the smell of the Guinness brewery so much, but it always reminded Phoenix of an odd mixture of vomit and chipper chips.

Thinking of Abi now, she wished her friend was here to complain to about such trivial concerns. It felt like an age since she'd last been back to the pub. The hourly texts from Abi filled her with guilt as she responded with assurances that everything was fine and she'd be home very soon. It killed her to lie to her friend.

"The hybrid, I presume?"

The man's voice broke clearly through her thoughts, and Phoenix turned to find herself face to face with the C.L.O. representative. A well-tailored grey suit clothed an average-height body, and clean cut brown hair framed a reasonably handsome, but largely non-descript, face. Everything about the man was forgettable. Even his signature seemed vague and intangible to her.

His question was directed towards Ethan, and the smile on his face didn't quite reach his grey eyes. The man held out his hand – again directed solely towards Ethan –

in a gesture that seemed to hold a lot more weight than a mere greeting.

Ethan looked at the offered hand and then back at the rep, his face expressionless. "The hybrid's name is Phoenix," he responded coldly.

The man's smile faded marginally and he dropped the ignored hand. He turned reluctantly towards her and nodded in acknowledgement. "Indeed."

A brief grimace was quickly replaced by a politician's smile as the rep gestured to the single empty table beside them. "Shall we?"

With a sigh, Phoenix pulled up a chair next to Ethan. She'd known it would be like this. How could a representative of the Council not view her with disdain? But she thought he might at least try to hide it better.

"Maybe I should begin by introducing myself. My name is Vicktor, and I'm the head of the Council Liaison Office."

The head of the C.L.O. came himself? I thought this was just a formality?

"I act as a liaison to the Council on highly sensitive cases, such as this one," Vicktor continued, glancing pointedly in her direction.

As he droned on about how unique their situation was and how it must be handled with the utmost care, Phoenix found herself growing impatient. Every minute they wasted was one more minute Darius had to track her and her parents.

"Look," she interrupted, sitting forward in her chair, "Ethan already told you everything we know. You've seen the illusive hybrid for yourself and verified my existence. Now can you please put us in touch with the Council so we can get this matter resolved and go about our lives?"

"Ah." Vicktor leaned back and rested his chin on steepled fingers. "I'm afraid it's not quite that simple now is it?"

"What do you mean?" Phoenix asked as a sense of trepidation caused her stomach to flip.

"Well, you're correct that I have indeed verified your existence – your signature is unlike anything I have ever encountered before. However," he paused, "I have not yet verified the story regarding your parents' fate."

Ethan placed a hand on her arm, stopping her before she could respond.

"I made it clear on the phone that Aria and Marcus would not be presenting themselves before you or the Council. Not unless you can guarantee that past transgressions would be exempt from punishment."

Vicktor shifted his attention fully to Ethan, sitting forward in an obvious challenge to the heated energy flowing his way. "You're saying that Aria and Marcus have parted company?"

"What? Of course not!" Phoenix leaned forward to

break up the pissing contest that was no doubt about to start between the two men. They didn't have time for this.

"So, they would not be past transgressions we are speaking of, would they?" Vicktor sat back in his chair once more, a small, victorious smile settling on his face.

She stopped in her tracks, realising too late the trap she'd walked into. Ethan had been adamant her parents stay behind, and she'd agreed it was safer. But she hadn't understood, not really.

Phoenix stood, knowing Ethan would follow her lead without argument. "This meeting is over. Thank you for your time, Vicktor." And with that, she turned and walked towards the lift.

It wasn't until the doors of the lift closed that she released the breath she was holding. She slumped against the mirrored walls and tried to force herself not to panic. What had she just done? They needed the Council to stop Darius. What if Vicktor refused to help them now?

"We'll find another way," Ethan said, as if reading her thoughts.

Plucking at the threads on her jacket, she bit her lip. "He can't keep the information to himself, can he? Surely he'd at least have to notify the Council that there's a security concern."

Ethan nodded and rubbed her arm comfortingly. "It would be a big risk not to. And I'll speak to my father, he'll help us get a message to the Council, just in case

Vicktor doesn't." The last words were almost a growl. Ethan's opinion of the C.L.O. rep was clear by the very mention of his name.

When the lift reached the ground floor, they made their way through the throngs of tourists in silence and out beyond the large, black gates to the waiting night. Heavy clouds hung overhead like ink stains in the sky, and the damp pavement served as a reminder that rain was never far away.

"It's not going to be safe for you once the Council knows," Ethan said. He stared ahead and avoided her eyes.

"Was it ever safe for me?" She laughed wryly.

He gave her a small smile in acknowledgement before shoving his hands into his jacket pockets. "No, probably not. But –"

"But you think the Council will come for me now too?"

Ethan sighed as he finally turned to her. "I honestly don't know. Technically you haven't broken any edicts, but your parents have, and the Council will want their pound of flesh."

"They avoided the Council before, they can do it again."

He watched her closely.

It took a moment to click. Having spent so long alone, Phoenix had forgotten what it was like for her life to be closely linked with anyone else's fate. The realisation hit her like a ton of bricks.

"And if they've to run … I've to run," she said quietly, wrapping her arms around herself.

35

"What can I get you?" the petite female behind the bar asked with a smile.

"I'll have your finest whiskey and the pleasure of your company for a drink," Darius said, allowing his natural persuasion to seep into the words.

Her blue eyes sparkled, but she took only a single glass from the counter.

Stretching to the highest shelf behind her, she grabbed an old bottle, causing Darius to raise a neatly manicured eyebrow. She knew her whiskey. It almost made him feel bad about his plans to torture her ... Almost.

"I haven't seen you around before." She poured the rich golden liquid into a glass and slid it towards him.

"I travel a lot for business," he replied as he noted her appreciative glance at the black Armani suit he'd chosen.

"It's not often I get to appreciate the benefits the area has to offer. It appears I've been missing out."

The female snorted and gave him a look that very clearly said "cut the bull".

Swiftly changing tactic, Darius leaned back and rested his arm along the back of his chair. "You own this place?"

She nodded and he looked around, wondering what it was that Phoenix had loved so much about the small, dingy pub. Although, the whiskey *was* good, he conceded as he took a sip of his drink, savouring the rich burn as it slid effortlessly down the back of his throat.

"It's impressive," he said out loud. "Could I be so bold as to ask the name of the owner?"

She shook her head with a wry smile. "I'm Abi. Might I be so bold as to ask your name?"

"A lady as beautiful as you may be as bold as you like." He inclined his head and took another sip of his whiskey. "I'm Darius."

With introductions complete, his prey relaxed noticeably; her smile came more quickly to his carefully placed compliments, and her pupils dilated ever so slightly as he ran his tongue over his bottom lip.

He allowed the conversation to flow, imagining creative ways to make her pale skin bleed as he smiled and laughed along at the appropriate moments. Eventually though, he grew tired of the small talk and decided to cut to the chase.

"What time do you get off work?" he asked, subtly brushing against the fingers she'd been moving subconsciously closer to him.

Abi gave a quick glance around the bar, then smiled at him. "Any time I want. I'm the boss."

"Let me buy you dinner."

She hesitated.

Darius took her hand in his as he stood and met her uncertain gaze with his most seductive smile. "I'm sure your barman can manage without you for an hour. You wouldn't leave a man to eat alone, now would you?"

She looked around the bar once more. Only a handful of tables were occupied, and the few customers at the bar were happily nursing their pints.

"Feck it, why not." Abi's smile grew bigger and her eyes sparkled. "Let me tell Paul I'm going and leave a note in case my friend comes back."

The smile that watched her back as she hurried away was his first genuine one of the night.

36

Even with the benefit of Ethan's motorbike, the journey
took forever. Ethan had wanted to go straight back to his
apartment, but though Phoenix knew it was dangerous,
she needed to see Abi. She needed to say goodbye.

The angry growl of the engine only highlighted the
crushing weight of things unsaid, and her heart was heavy
as they pulled up in front of the pub. Phoenix braced
herself for what she needed to do. It wouldn't be forever.
As soon as the whole mess was fixed, she'd come back.

With a deep breath, she paused at the door and
turned to Ethan. "Can you wait here for me?"

"Phoenix –"

"Please, Ethan. This is hard enough."

She could see the battle rage across his face. He
wanted so much to protect her, and this was the easiest
place for Darius to find them. But she knew her friend;

Abi would think she was being pressured into leaving and that Ethan was the bad guy.

Eventually, he sighed and nodded. "Make it quick, Phoenix. It's not safe here."

As she turned towards the door of the pub, he reached out a hand to stop her. "I called my father before we came out tonight, just in case things didn't go to plan with the Council. He's agreed to give you and your parents refuge with the pack until everything blows over."

Ethan watched her closely, as if trying to gauge her reaction. "You'll be safe there. I'll make sure of it."

A strange feeling tightened Phoenix's chest and all she could do was nod her gratitude. She pulled open the heavy door and was hit with a blast of warm air along with the familiar scent of home. Low music formed the background soundtrack to the hum of conversation and occasional laughter.

She looked around apprehensively as she made her way through the pub, but there was no sign of Abi. Grateful that Paul, their part-time barman, was preoccupied with customers, Phoenix gave a small wave and slipped behind the bar, running upstairs to find her friend.

The dark silence that met her at the top of the stairs caused her steps to falter. There was a strange feeling of abandonment to the apartment. The darkness muted all the bright colours that usually brought it to life, and shadows hinted at ominous possibilities.

"Abi?" Phoenix called, trying to ignore the niggling sense of unease that was tapping its way along her spine. As she made her way down the hallway to check Abi's room, she chastised herself for being so jumpy. It'd been a long few days and she needed sleep.

Abi's room was empty and the bed neatly made. A subtle hint of musk permeated the air. Phoenix instantly recognised the scent of Abi's 'good' perfume.

She debated whether or not to call Abi's mobile as she made her way back to the kitchen, but when she got there, she noticed a small sheet of white paper stuck to the fridge with her name on it. Abi's bubbly script was immediately recognisable and her shoulders loosened their rigid hold with a sigh of relief as she pulled it from the door. Trust Abi to resort to stone age communication on the off-chance Phoenix returned while she was gone.

A smile began to form as she read, almost able to hear her friend's enthusiastic voice describing the tall, dark, handsome man that had come into the bar and insisted she join him for dinner or his life would not be complete. She shook her head, laughing, clearly able to picture the scene in her mind. Abi loved flirting with the customers, but she also liked to make them work for it.

As she reached the end of the note, the laughter died abruptly in her throat. The words leapt off the page at her, turning her blood to ice in her veins.

You better get home soon. I need my roomie back. Wish me luck with Darius! X

Time froze around her, and the words blurred on the page. She clutched desperately for any other explanation; a random coincidence of names, a spelling mistake. Anything.

It was with an oddly calm sense of detachment that she pulled the phone out of her pocket and scrolled through her contacts. The roar of her heart beat was all she could hear as she pressed the call button and raised the phone to her ear.

"Phoenix, darling, I've been waiting for your call."

Darius's voice was rich and warm on the other end of the phone, but now she could hear something in his tone she'd never heard before – a cruel mocking; subtle but very present.

"Where is she?" Phoenix was surprised at the steadiness of her voice and amazed that her hands remained still, even as a crushing weight bore down on her chest.

Laughter rolled through the phone, sending chills through her. "What? No time for small talk? But we have so much to catch up on."

"Don't play games with me, Darius."

Darius's voice turned cold, devoid of its feigned warmth. "I don't play games, Phoenix. You should know that."

For the first time, Phoenix realised she was hearing Darius for who he really was, and a little part of her heart – the part that still held a childish hope – broke.

"What do you want from me?" she asked softly, gripping the phone so tight it was a miracle it didn't snap in half.

"It's time we had a little heart to heart. Come to the lair. Alone. If I even sense your little werewolf friend, I will kill the human. And then I will take much pleasure in killing him too."

The thump of her pulse grew louder and louder until it was like thunder pounding through her head. She knew the question she needed to ask, but the words stuck in her throat like razor blades.

"How do I know Abi is alive?" she said finally, and braced herself with resolve.

The line was quiet for a moment before the silence was shattered by a muffled scream.

Phoenix's heart stopped short, and fear for her friend threatened to overwhelm her completely. "I swear, Darius, if you hurt her –"

"Now is not the time for idle threats, Phoenix. If I were you, I'd get here quickly. It wouldn't be a good idea to leave me alone too long with such a fragile toy."

With a click, the phone went dead and Phoenix let it slide limply from her hand. She stood frozen, her mind desperately grasping for any options available to her. But really, she had none.

He would kill her. Despite her difficulties comprehending this new reality, she was under no illusions about that point. It didn't matter though, she wouldn't leave her friend at his mercy. Whatever happened, she would get Abi out.

A satisfied smile spread over Darius's face as he let the phone fall to the ground and crushed it under the heel of his shoe. She would come. There was no way she'd leave her friend to suffer. Always such a bleeding heart.

As his thoughts returned to the human, he assessed the small frame hanging from chains fixed to the wall of the main chamber. She was a curious sight, so small and fragile, her blue eyes wide with terror. Yet, a strange defiance remained, and even with her fear, she continued to look him square in the eye.

It would be fun to try to break her while he waited for Phoenix to arrive.

He moved closer to her and ghosted his hand slowly down her jaw. Her heartbeat quickened, but still she refused to look away. Driven by her defiance, he let his finger trail down the front of her throat, moving ever lower until it hit the opening of her loose blouse and brushed against the pale mound of her breasts. Her fists clenched tightly as she tensed against his touch, eliciting a rich laugh from him.

Turning to the metal table that had been set up to the left of the shackles, he ran his hands over the various toys he'd laid out. Soft leather lay in stark contrast to hard, cold steel. Each object held tantalising possibilities.

Which to choose, which to choose …

He picked up the heavy iron scissors, enjoying the weight of the metal in his hand. With slow, deliberate movements he made his way back to the girl, twisting his hand so that the flickering candlelight glinted off the blood-stained blades.

Following the same path his finger had taken, he slid the tip of the scissors gently along her jaw and down the front of her throat. With careful precision, he allowed the razor-sharp blades to continue down before slicing through the soft material of her blouse like it was tissue paper. He paused only when he reached the soft, vulnerable skin of her stomach.

Sweat beaded on her forehead and she held her breath, as if she could make herself invisible by remaining completely still.

With a swift upward slice, he tore through the gag covering her mouth. He'd expected her to beg and plead, but was surprised when, instead of doing either, she reared back her head as far as the restraints would allow and spat in his face.

Warm saliva slid a mocking trail down his cheek and he clenched his jaw in fury. Turning once more to the table, he wiped his cheek and put down the scissors. In its place, he chose the soft leather whip that was his toy of choice for pretty ladies.

As he faced the human, Darius allowed his fangs to extend. And this time, as the candlelight glinted off the silver spikes that graced the end of the whip, the screaming started in earnest.

37

Ethan paced restlessly in front of the pub. It wasn't safe for them to be here. How had he let her talk him into coming?

The night around him was quiet and the streets were empty as midnight drew closer. There'd been no sign of the vampires, and no trouble since they'd made their getaway from the lair. That fact alone worried him.

Needing to do something productive while he waited, he pulled out his phone and called Nate.

"Is Aria with you?"

A huffy response regarding his lack of manners, and some muffled noises preceded Aria's breathless voice.

"Is Phoenix okay?"

"Yes, yes, everything's fine," he quickly assured her, realising too late the thoughts that must be going through her head.

He kept one eye on his surroundings and one on the

door of the pub as he quickly relayed the details of their meeting with the C.L.O. rep.

"It's not safe for us to stay here any longer is it?" Aria said after a long pause, her voice heavy with resignation.

He resisted the urge to apologise, knowing his words wouldn't change the reality she'd faced ever since meeting Marcus.

"I think it's best that we head to Donegal tonight," he replied instead, focusing on the ways that he *could* help.

"We'll be ready. Just bring my baby girl back safe, Ethan." And with that she hung up, leaving him staring once more at the door of the pub, wondering how long Phoenix had been gone.

His wolf paced restlessly, something about Aria's words setting his animal instincts on edge. Phoenix would be furious at him for interrupting a heart to heart with Abi, and he wanted to give her time to say goodbye, but they'd been lucky until now. That luck wouldn't last forever.

With a sigh, he pushed his way through the heavy door and was met with a blast of warm air. Dimmed lights and hushed conversations gave an intimate feel that seemed suitably matched to the cold winter night beyond the pub's confines. Ethan gave the room a quick scan, not really expecting to find Abi or Phoenix in the main part of the bar. He waited until the barman was busy cleaning tables before he slipped quietly to the back of the bar and through the door that led to the living quarters. He took the stairs two at a time, noting vaguely the cool draft as he stepped into the apartment.

Phoenix's scent clung to every surface of the small space, but the bright, artistic décor seemed to him the complete antithesis of her personality. Any other time he'd have smiled trying to picture her here with Abi, surrounded by so many colours and soft furnishings. But the silence of the apartment distracted him from any other thoughts of colour charts.

Phoenix's scent was fresh, confirming she'd come up to the apartment. So where was she?

He looked around each room, but saw no signs of struggle and no obvious cause for concern, yet something was setting alarm bells trembling in his head. The cold blast of air when he opened the door to the kitchen explained the draft he'd been feeling. And the open window at the far side of the room sent those alarm bells screaming at full force.

She wouldn't have ...

In his rush to the window, Ethan struck something with his foot, sending it sliding across the tiled floor with a clatter. The soft glow of moonlight filtering in from the open window glinted off the object and caused his heart to leap in his chest.

Phoenix's phone lay abandoned on the floor, cracked screen causing the shine that had drawn his attention.

With a new sense of urgency, he picked it up, temporarily grateful for her negligible sense of security as he easily flicked to her call list without a pin code.

He knew what he'd find before he saw it – Darius's name at the top of the list, mocking him. What he didn't know, or understand, was why she'd call him. Was she that desperate for revenge?

He forced himself to stay calm as he continued towards the open window. Her scent was particularly strong there, and as he looked down on the alley at the back of the pub, he cursed his incompetence for letting her go in alone.

Wanting to roar in frustration, he slammed his fist down on the kitchen counter.

Another quick scan of the room showed nothing out of place, aside from a crumpled piece of paper that looked odd for no other reason than the relative cleanliness of the room. After pocketing Phoenix's phone, he unfolded the paper. Bubbly script covered the page before him, and as he quickly scanned the words everything became clear.

If there was one thing he'd learned about Phoenix, it was that she was unfailingly loyal. She may not be stupid enough to face Darius for revenge alone, but if he had Abi, she wouldn't hesitate to offer herself up as a sacrifice.

Without wasting another second, he left the apartment, pulling his own phone from his pocket as he went.

"Nate, we have a problem."

38

The trip back to the lair was the longest of Phoenix's life. Her heart had twisted in her chest as she snuck out the back and slipped away into the night in her trusty Mustang. Ethan would be crushed by her betrayal, but there was no other choice.

Ahead of her, familiar imposing walls loomed, blocking her view of the large, white mansion that lay at the end of the winding driveway. Thick, metal security gates opened silently as she approached, and she drove solemnly into the mouth of the beast. She could feel unseen eyes watching her every move as she pulled up in front of the lair and stepped out of the car.

The night around her was completely silent, devoid of all signs of life, and shivers ran down her spine that had little to do with the chilling wind. The unnatural silence and the feeling of being watched followed her as she entered the large mansion that housed Darius's vampires.

A single vampire stepped into the hallway in front of her, and Phoenix tensed. She didn't recognise the man, but his black uniform clearly identified him as security, and his seemingly calm demeanour was no indication of his orders. The vampire merely sneered in acknowledgement of her obvious fear and held out a large hand with his palm up.

Her weapons. He'd been sent to collect her weapons.

Phoenix almost laughed out loud, realising they'd given her far more credit than they should have. Fear for Abi had overwhelmed her so much that all she'd been able to think about was sneaking out of the pub without Ethan noticing. The large carving knife stuck down the side of her boot wouldn't have been much help against a lair full of vampires anyway, so it cost her little to hand it over.

Unsatisfied with her pathetic offering, the vampire flung the knife; it lodged deep into the door behind her with a thud. It took all of her restraint not to lash out, but one quick frisk later and she was free to pass.

Phoenix wasted no time moving through the halls, more convinced now that Darius wouldn't allow his vamps to hurt her. At least not before he could. Regardless, adrenaline thrummed through her as she kept a close eye on her surroundings, all the while grasping desperately for a plan that might get Abi out alive.

In the space of what seemed like a heartbeat, she

found herself once more standing in front of the entrance to the underground chamber. The door stood open, and the darkness beyond beckoned her forward for the final descent.

She faltered only for a moment, knowing that once she took the final step through the door, there would be no going back. Hell, maybe there'd never been a way back for her. Maybe she'd been screwed from the moment she found out about the prophecy.

As she crossed the threshold into the darkness, the same feeling of wrongness she'd felt previously enveloped her. It was stronger now, an almost palpable weight that made her every movement sluggish. She clenched her fists, and took slow, deep breaths through her nose, willing her heartbeat to calm. It would be no use, of course. Darius would hear the blood coursing through her veins. Like any good predator.

She came to the final bend before the steps would spill her out into the open chamber and paused. A low murmuring chant, rhythmic and almost hypnotic, came from the room beyond. A woman's voice.

Phoenix was picturing the layout of the chamber, trying to wrack her memory for any possible cover, when Darius's warm voice broke through her thoughts. "Phoenix, darling, how good of you to join us."

Chills swept across her skin and she held herself frozen on the spot. Was he bluffing? A heartbeat. And then the sound of metal scraping against stone. Followed by a low whimper.

"Don't you want to see your friend?" he asked, his voice projecting an almost amicable curiosity.

At the mention of Abi, her gut lurched. She took the last few steps that would bring her into view of the open chamber, fearing the sight that would greet her.

The flickering flame of candlelight cast ominous shadows around the already dark chamber. Phoenix's eyes were immediately drawn to the stone altar where a woman stood, head bowed, arms extended towards the earth. It was from her that the chanting came, and from around her, the heaviest aura of magic seemed to fall.

Phoenix felt a brief flash of relief when she saw the altar empty, but the relief was short lived. As she cast her gaze around the chamber, she found her friend hanging by thick metal chains from the wall furthest away. Abi's head was slumped forward. Her long hair was ragged with sweat and obscured the view of her face.

She could sense, almost better than she could see, the rise and fall of Abi's chest as her heart frantically pumped blood around her body. And though her mind tried to shut out the implications, Phoenix could make out a number of tears in her friend's clothes, flashes of pale skin shining in contrast to the dark clothing.

Darius stood next to Abi. His posture was friendly and relaxed, even as his fingers gently caressed the knives gleaming on a small folding table beside him. He smiled in welcome at her as she stepped into the room, but made no move in her direction.

The image was so disconcerting that for a moment Phoenix wanted to weep. He looked so like the man she'd known as a child that her mind struggled to comprehend the new reality she'd found herself in. So many memories from her childhood – all lies.

"Abi are you okay?"

She was proud of how steady her voice sounded. Darius would be able to sense her fear, but for her own sake, she needed to at least maintain the illusion of being calm.

"Oh, she's fine." Darius waved a hand dismissively, the reassuring sentiment somewhat lost by the fact that the hand held a long, gleaming knife.

Beside him, Abi raised her head. Slowly. As if the simple movement took all of her energy. Her face was pale and beads of sweat ran a trail down her forehead, but her eyes were a flame of blue defiance. Phoenix could feel the anger behind her friend's glare and even through the darkness, she could see the implied order: leave.

Ignoring the burning glare – and the order – she edged cautiously into the chamber, assessing her surroundings for any hidden surprises.

"So, why did you call me here, Darius?"

The smile he turned on her was worse than any of

the lethal blades he had close at hand. It was so reminiscent of the man she'd known and loved that her steps faltered yet again.

"Can't a man just want to catch up with his favourite niece?"

Swallowing past the lump in her throat, she shook her head sadly. "If you'd said that a couple of days ago, I'd probably have believed you … I've learned a lot since then, Uncle D."

He tilted his head in acknowledgement and an almost rueful expression replaced the smile on his face. "I guess so."

She pushed away the grief of acceptance and tried to focus on her surroundings. She needed a weapon, something that might give her even a fighting chance. Losing was inevitable, but she would damn sure cause some damage before she did. She was vaguely aware that Darius was still talking – something about Raphael overstepping his orders – when a glint against the wall caught her eye.

Almost hidden by the dark shadows of the chamber, she could just make out the curved blades that leaned against the stone wall barely ten feet from where Abi hung. It left her little room for error with Darius standing so close, but the options weren't really stacked in her favour anyway, and there was something about the blades that drew her attention.

Needing to keep him distracted – that's what they did in the movies, right? – she asked the question that was eating away at her. "Why did you do it, Uncle D? My parents trusted you."

"They found out about the prophecy. They would have gotten in the way." His tone was so matter of fact that the shock of it brought her to a complete stop.

"But why? Why do you want the prophecy fulfilled?"

The blade closest to her, a short sword with a curved edge made of a dark metal, was almost within reaching distance. But she didn't move. Because on some soul deep level, Darius's answer was more important than the weapon.

His expression changed to one of genuine surprise, as if the answer should've been obvious. "Have I taught you nothing, Phoenix? For power, of course."

He actually seemed disappointed as he looked at her, and for a brief moment she was a child again, wanting desperately to make him proud. A stupid notion given she was obviously talking to a psychopath, but some habits were hard to break.

"This is not how it was," he continued, staring vacantly at the altar. "Not how it should be. We were once worshipped as Gods. And now, we will be again."

With a shake of his head, Darius turned his attention back to her, seeming to regroup. "Thanks to you we will regain our rightful place. The people who rejected you will bow down at your feet. Think about it, Phoenix."

A shiver of apprehension ran down her spine. Whether from his words, or the growing fervour in his eyes, she wasn't sure.

"You're insane."

Anger flashed in his eyes, and she knew she had to do something. Pushing her abilities to their limits, she moved faster than she even believed herself capable of. As she grabbed the dark, curved blade closest to her, she lunged forward to place herself between Abi and Darius. Phoenix had a bare fraction of a second to register Darius's lack of concern for her attack before the strangest thing happened. She froze.

Confusion hit her, followed swiftly by terror.

She couldn't move. At all.

Her brain was screaming at her limbs, but there was just … nothing. Her muscles failed to contract, and her joints remained locked in position. Her hand clung desperately – and uselessly – to the blade it held. Darius's laughter washed over her like ice as she looked up to meet his black gaze.

"You always did have so much spunk." A tilt of his head and the laughter faded. "Did you really think I'd be that foolish?"

"Well, a girl can dream," she said, relieved to find herself able to speak as she pulled her reflex for sarcasm around her like a comfort blanket.

"I think it would be best if you drop the knife now, Phoenix."

Just like that, the blade fell from her grasp and hit the ground with a clatter. There'd been no change in the grip of her hand. How had the knife fallen? She gritted her teeth and tried to push through the inertia, but everything from the neck down remained still. Panic began to build to such an overwhelming degree that she almost missed it – the heavy weight of witchcraft, wrapping itself around her like a snake.

And she knew she was truly in deep shit.

39

I let him trick me.

As the realisation dawned on Phoenix, her panic was temporarily overshadowed by anger. Anger at Darius for not being the man she looked up to. Anger at the witch for betraying her calling. Anger at fate for dealing her such a fucked-up hand. And mostly, anger at herself.

How could she help Abi when she couldn't even help herself?

With that thought, her attention was pulled back to the wall behind her. Testing the limitations of her movement, Phoenix twisted her head as far as she could while her body was held in stasis. The muscles protested, but still she strained, needing to see her friend.

Familiar blue eyes met hers, filled with a sorrow that made her want to weep. But there was no judgement, no anger. There should have been both.

"Abi ..." she whispered, but the word died on her lips as she grasped in vain for a way to convey how sorry she was.

Steel took the place of sorrow in her friend's eyes as Abi shook her head firmly, shutting down anything more she might say.

The sound of scraping metal made Phoenix's heart jump, and she quickly shifted her gaze back to Darius. There was no time left for self-indulgent pity.

He seemed momentarily oblivious of her as he sharpened a roughly hewn blade on the edge of a jagged stone. The metal of the blade was dull and any real sense of craftmanship was missing, but it appeared well-used, and there was very little question of the damage it could cause.

Darius looked up as she watched him in silence, his black gaze meeting hers briefly before flicking back to admire the sharp edge.

"Your mother was fond of this blade," he said. "She could refrain from screaming for so many of my other toys. But this one" – he turned the blade slowly from side to side – "this one she screamed for."

Phoenix clenched her jaw so tight it made her teeth ache. Anger turned her blood to molten lava, but she forced herself to remain quiet.

"It's strange really," Darius continued, unperturbed. "It's not even made of iron. In fact, I'm not really sure what it's made of, just that it's very old. It was my Master's favourite toy."

He moved towards her with slow, deliberate steps, while his fingers played along the edge of the blade. As he stopped in front of her, she looked up and found herself face to face with a complete stranger. There was no sense of recognition, no affection remaining in his eyes, just a strange luminescence that leant itself to the semblance of crazy.

Slowly, he trailed the flat edge of the blade down her cheek; the cold metal unlike anything she'd ever felt before. Like ice, it scalded her wherever it touched. Phoenix held her breath and waited for the sharp sting to follow, but Darius merely continued talking as he ran the blade almost absently down the line of her jaw, burning a path down her neck.

"Your father stopped screaming far too early for my liking. He really was no fun at all."

Phoenix felt her breath freeze in her chest.

"I really thought he'd give in." Darius's brow furrowed in confusion. "I was so sure he couldn't resist forever. Not when her sweet blood was so close."

Realisation hit like a forty-foot truck, and suddenly Phoenix knew. Knew what her mother had kept from her. Knew that if Darius had succeeded, it would've been a fate worse than death for her father.

"You starved him." The words left her mouth in a

whisper of disbelief. The horror she felt was so vast that she couldn't even find words to describe it.

He looked at her in surprise. "Well, of course. Although, I guess it's really a matter of perspective since he had such a tasty food source so close at hand."

The ice that had begun to fill her veins at the touch of his blade, turned to flames, burning through her like wildfire. She struggled with everything she had against the magic that held her, but even her rage was not enough to break the invisible bonds.

"I swear to you, Darius, on my very life, that I will find a way to make you pay."

Cold laughter filled the chamber. "Oh, don't worry, Phoenix, dear, I don't require your life just yet."

And with that, he slashed the blade downwards.

For a moment confusion was the only thing Phoenix felt, then a searing pain tore up her left arm. She was dimly aware of Abi's screams as she looked down to see a thin line of blood trickle down her arm. Funny, it hurt so much more than it should for such a shallow cut.

Darius stared at the blood, mesmerised, and she could almost feel the force of the hunger coming off him. "So much power," he muttered, as he reached for a dull metal bowl on the table beside him.

He held the bowl under her wrist, watching as the blood drew a path down towards her fingers, and slowly dripped into the waiting container. A sense of dread purer than anything she'd ever felt before swept through her, and she twisted her head once more to focus on her friend.

The look of terror on Abi's face grounded her in a way that nothing else could. She committed every line of Abi's face to memory and swore to herself that her friend would not die here with her. Not like this. She closed her eyes and tried to focus deep inside herself for any thread of power she could grasp.

All of a sudden, the chamber around her was filled with silence, and it took her a moment to realise that the low murmuring chant of the witch had stopped.

When she opened her eyes, she was surprised to find that Darius was no longer standing in front of her. It took her another precious few moments to realise that the indescribable heaviness had also lifted from her. And when she tried once more to move her fingers, they miraculously responded. Aware that her window of opportunity was narrow at best, she dived for the blade Darius had discarded on the table in exchange for the bowl.

His rich laughter filled the silence around her, skittering over her skin. "Oh, Phoenix, have we not already established how futile it is for you to fight me?"

He was right of course. She wasn't strong enough to beat him, but that didn't mean she would stop trying. She clung desperately to the blade and wracked her brain for any kind of plan that would get Abi free. Suddenly,

Darius's words came back to her. *I don't require your life just yet.*

He may not require it, but he wouldn't keep her alive if he didn't need to. Would he?

Turning to face Darius once more, Phoenix flipped the blade towards herself, the sharpened tip poised directly over her thumping heart as her eyes met his defiantly. His flinch was so fleeting, the mask so quickly back in place, that if she hadn't been watching for a reaction, she'd have missed it.

"You have what you want now, Darius. Let Abi go. This has nothing to do with her."

He laughed again, but something in his tone rang so much hollower this time. "Now why would I let my leverage go?"

"I'll make this very simple." She pressed the icy edge of the blade closer and felt the cold seep through to her very soul as the blade met the resistance of her chest. "Let her go or I will end this, and you'll never see your precious prophecy fulfilled."

The eyes that stared back at her blazed with a fury unlike any she'd ever seen, and for a moment Phoenix felt true fear. But instinct told her that her assumption had been right, and that knowledge brought with it a strange sense of calm.

She wasn't afraid to die. Not if it meant Abi would live.

For an eternity Darius simply watched her, as if trying to read her thoughts and decide if she was bluffing.

She wasn't.

As if coming to the same conclusion, he shrugged nonchalantly. "If you're going to make a big deal of it, the human can go. She really is of no interest to me now that she has served her purpose. Humans are far too ... breakable."

Abi struggled against her restraints, stretching towards Phoenix with muffled protests. Blue eyes blazed their anger and she shook her head, pointlessly refuting the trade that had been made.

With effort, Phoenix ignored her friend, keeping her emotions in check and her gaze firmly locked on Darius. She nodded for him to unlock the chains and held her breath as she waited for the slightest twitch that might indicate betrayal.

He reached one hand slowly towards the key hanging on the wall to the right of Abi. His other hand was slightly hidden from sight. A split-second flash of fangs was her only clue, and knowing she'd never reach Abi in time, Phoenix turned the blade from her chest and flung it towards Darius's head in blind panic.

The blade missed by millimetres, lodging in the stone wall with a thud.

Darius smiled at her, a victorious glint in his eyes. As he stalked towards her, Phoenix heard it – a loud inhuman roar, followed by a commotion that could only mean one thing. Help had arrived.

40

The sight that met Ethan's eyes as he forced his way into the chamber made his blood run cold and his vision cloud red. Phoenix was on the opposite side of the room, about as far from him as it was possible to be. A vampire he could only assume to be Darius stood facing her, much too close for comfort.

Even across the space he could smell the blood that dripped down her arm, and the scent caused his wolf to roar as it crashed against his mental barriers, years of control eroded by the simple knowledge that she'd been hurt.

Behind him, Nate, Shade, Lily, Aria and Marcus pushed their way into the chamber, followed closely by the remaining vampire guards as their fighting spilled into the large stone room. He had to trust the others had it under control, because the only thing he could focus on was the vampire and Phoenix.

Unleashing control of the wolf, he gave himself over to instinct. The wolf's speed enabled him to close the distance in fractions of a second and his razor-sharp claws tore free of his skin as he moved.

Ethan lashed out and felt the warm gush of blood over his hand, but his vampire target seemed to simply disappear, as if he'd never been there.

The faintest of breezes caressed the back of his neck, and he spun around in time to see the glint of silver move towards his throat. Instinct drove his body back from the blade, just enough that it lightly grazed his neck, the silver leaving a burning trail in its wake. But the sudden shift threw him off balance, and it was all he could do to avoid the blade a second time as he fell.

Darius's attack was relentless, the slashes becoming little more than a blur. Even with the speed of his wolf, Ethan was no match for a vampire of Darius's age, and the lethal edge of silver came closer and closer as he fought to get up from the floor.

It was only the brief flash of red that gave away Phoenix's movement as she attacked Darius from behind, giving Ethan the precious seconds needed to lunge to his feet.

He used the temporary distraction to launch a second attack at Darius, forcing the vampire to divide his attention between both of them. Weeks of training

303

together allowed him to fall into an easy rhythm with Phoenix as he complemented her movements with his own. But Darius was too quick. Each fist merely glanced off the intended target and each claw merely grazed.

Ethan's wolf pushed against the final restraints that bound it, but he fought back. They needed to find a weakness, and he needed to think clearly. He was slowly pulling back from the haze of animal instinct when his concentration was shattered by a high-pitched scream of terror.

Lily.

Spinning out of the way of Darius's fist, he used the momentum to pivot so he could seek out the young witch in the chaos that surrounded him. His eyes found her, little more than ten feet to his left where she was pinned to the ground with a stocky, blonde vampire looming over her. Ethan could tell by the frantic movement of her lips that she was trying to cast a spell, but the vampire was twice her size, and was easily overwhelming her.

Torn between the need to save Lily, and his wolf's instinct to protect Phoenix, he hesitated.

"Go!" Phoenix yelled as she shoved him insistently.

Lily screamed again as the blonde vampire reared back to lunge for her throat, effectively cutting off any further argument.

Ethan propelled himself to the side, sending his full weight barrelling into the vampire and knocking him away from Lily; leaving Phoenix to once more face Darius alone.

⬥⬥⬥

Phoenix's heart thudded in her chest. The terror she felt for Abi now extended to each and every person that had come to fight by her side. People that were willing to risk their lives for her.

Darius waited patiently for her to make a move. The smile that graced his face was one of complete arrogance, filled with the surety that he was faster and stronger.

He was. But it changed nothing.

They had come for her, and she would fight.

Drawing on every ounce of resolve and strength she had, Phoenix moved in a blur of speed, trusting her instincts to guide her strikes. For each blow Darius evaded, she followed with another from a different angle.

Another scream tore through the air, coming from Ethan and Lily's direction. The momentary fear she felt for them distracted Phoenix long enough that she failed to see the glittering blade swinging towards her in time. She threw up her arms in defence, but a blaze of fire burnt through her left shoulder as the blade struck.

Pain blackened her vision momentarily until there was only numbness. The arm fell limply to her side, useless and unmoving.

Darius's blade dripped with blood, and a look of

satisfaction filled his cold stare as he stalked towards her. He slowly ran his tongue along the blade, shivering with undisguised ecstasy.

Disgust and terror washed over her in equal measures.

Backing away from his advancing form, she abruptly hit a cold, hard surface with a thud. The jagged wall dug into her sweat-soaked back, effectively cutting off one avenue of escape. The smile on Darius's face widened as he looked to her right and his shoulders appeared to relax ever so slightly.

Every instinct told her not to take her eyes off the snake in the grass, but she needed to know what could've possibly made him even more sure of himself. Tentatively, she reached her only working hand out to the side to blindly feel along the wall until it hit something. The rattle of cold iron made her stomach drop.

How many bloody chains are there in this place?

A frantic urgency clouded her thoughts, but she pushed it back forcefully. She needed to get away from the wall. If he managed to chain her, she'd be at his mercy.

Just like her parents.

The thought brought with it a desperate need to act, and Phoenix shoved forcefully away from the wall before lunging to the right. In less than a blink, Darius was there, his body an unmoving barrier as she barrelled into him, damaged shoulder first.

The impact brought a burst of pain that caused her vision to go black again, followed immediately by a flare of colour behind her eyes.

Darius's chilling laugh filled her ears as she fought to regain her orientation. His empty black eyes swam in and out of focus, mere inches from her face, and his hot breath brushed against her skin as he placed an almost tender palm against her cheek.

The burning itch in her palm was so unexpected that for a moment Phoenix thought her bruised consciousness was causing her to hallucinate. An instinctive desire to pull back from the feeling caused her gut to clench. With a surge of hope, she did something she'd never truly done before – she embraced it.

She grasped the infant thread of power and held it for all she was worth. Letting go of all doubts, she urged the burning to grow, to expand, to take on a life of its own.

Darius leaned closer, his fangs extending as his hand moved down to her neck. "Maybe one more taste …"

Her body rigid, Phoenix fought to stay controlled, to encourage and nurture the heat that continued to rise in her palm, even though all she really wanted to do was scream and fight back.

She waited until she felt the first sharp scratch of his fangs before placing her hand on his chest. And finally, she let go.

The light left her body in a blinding explosion of white. Brighter than anything she'd ever before called to her.

When she could finally see again, she found the space in front of her empty. Darius lay slumped against a wall almost twenty feet from where she stood, and spiderweb cracks began to spread through the stone behind him.

Slowly, he began to rise to his feet. He looked so much like something from a horror movie that Phoenix felt a strange urge to laugh hysterically. Charred skin covered his face and hands. Patches of glistening red showed through as blood oozed down his cheek. White fangs glowed in contrast to the blackened flesh surrounding them. And the rage in his eyes was clearly visible even at a distance.

Desperately, she began to call the light to her again, pushing her untrained abilities to their limits as her hand shook and sweat ran down the back of her neck. Her vision faltered and the pain in her head grew, but still she raised a trembling hand.

A slim, pale hand wrapped itself around hers, squeezing gently. The warm, comforting scent of the sun filled her senses, and her trembling hand steadied. Phoenix looked into her mother's green eyes, and the pride she saw there made her breath catch in her chest.

She wasn't alone.

Marcus came to stand on the other side of her, a

similar look of pride in his eyes. He placed a large hand on her injured shoulder, and warmth spread through her arm, chasing away the chilling numbness.

Together, they turned to face the vampire before them. The man that had betrayed their family.

41

Phoenix saw the surprise register on Darius's face. Rage filled his eyes at the sight of her parents standing whole and healthy by her side, and he snarled.

"Hello, old friend," Marcus said softly, moving forward to place himself in front of his wife and child.

She moved to protest, but Aria squeezed her hand once more, giving an almost imperceptible shake of her head before pointedly closing her eyes. Reluctantly, she followed her mother's lead and tried to slow her breathing by blocking out the sound of fighting.

A strange pulsing sensation began in the palm Aria held, and Phoenix's eyes flew open with a gasp. Each little pulse felt like a mild electric shock, an oddly comforting electric shock that began to gradually build in heat.

Aria threw her a wicked smile, and as if on command, Marcus launched himself at Darius, moving so quickly he became an indiscernible blur. Phoenix tried to pull her hand free of her mother's grip; fear for her father's safety demanding action. But Aria held fast, her green eyes urging Phoenix to trust her.

The recent infusion of werewolf blood seemed to give Marcus an edge the other vampire didn't possess. He matched Darius blow for blow and more wounds appeared between the charred patches of skin as Marcus's strikes landed true.

When a well-timed throw sent Darius flying in their direction, Aria squeezed her hand tightly and yelled, "Now!"

The flash of light was effortless this time. Controlled and beautiful in its simplicity, it struck its intended target, causing Darius to roar in pain.

Aria moved forward and Phoenix realised her mother had finally released her hand. She watched in shock as the gentle woman she called mother viciously kicked the fallen vampire in the gut. Blood and spit flew from Darius's mouth with the blow, but he remained on the ground.

A second kick to the head lifted his body clean in the air, causing him to land a couple of feet away on his back. His body started to shudder. It took Phoenix a moment to realise he was laughing; full-bodied, soul-deep laughter.

Aria stalked towards him, her green eyes flashing with barely contained wrath. Her pale skin began to glow with a white light that emanated into the darkness of the chamber.

Darius rolled to his side, and Phoenix had just enough time to register the blade in his hand before it was flying through the air towards her mother. A silent scream froze in Phoenix's throat and her heart stopped beating as Marcus threw himself in front of Aria, knocking her to the ground.

In an instant, she found herself standing between her parents and Darius, unsure quite how she got there. The scent of her father's blood filled her senses as she faced the other vampire.

"Mam?"

"We're okay, Phoenix."

The sound of shuffling followed the muffled response and Marcus's pained voice concurred, "Just a scratch."

Darius snarled and spit blood as he slowly rose to his feet. She noticed with surprise that he wasn't healing, at least not like a vampire normally would. The parts of skin that had been burned by their fae powers remained exposed and oozed blood.

As if he had been burned by the sun.

Realising this, Phoenix encouraged her still fledgling heat to grow once more. She fuelled it with all the fear and anger she felt as she walked towards Darius.

A single tear ran down her cheek as she placed her

palm to his cheek.

In a vague recess of her mind, she wondered why he didn't stop her and felt an uneasy confusion at the victorious look in his eyes. But then her only thought was of the sun. The bright heat and the warmth of it on her skin.

This time the light was not as strong, but it came. Bringing with it the acrid smell of burning skin, screams of agony, and a headache unlike anything Phoenix had felt before.

She pulled her hand away and stumbled backwards as she grasped her head to keep her brain from leaking out with the pain.

Then everything went completely black.

Time seemed to hold its breath. A silence so complete and a darkness so never-ending filled the entire chamber. With it came a whole new level of fear.

And then, on an exhale, it was gone.

Phoenix looked immediately towards Darius, expecting some form of attack. But there was nothing. No attack. And no Darius.

The floor was covered in a pool of blood that almost appeared black in the dim light of the chamber, but no other signs remained of the vampire.

"Where is …"

Her own scepticism was met with similar perplexed expressions from her parents as she turned a slow circle and waited for the shadows to attack.

Guards littered the floor around her. Many lying motionless, some even missing their heads and beginning to fade. Blood soaked the walls and seemed to pulse with life as it seeped back into the earth. The remaining vampires were swiftly retreating, leaving Phoenix to stare in confusion.

A cold breeze began to fill the chamber, and the skin on her arms pebbled with goose bumps that had little to do with the chill of the wind. Electricity charged the space around her, and the air became heavy, like the weight just before a storm. Every cell in her body screamed danger. She held her breath and waited.

A shuffling sound to her left caused her heart to leap into her throat. Relief flooded through her as she saw Ethan moving towards her, holding Lily. Phoenix ran to him and added her support as she wrapped her arm around Lily's waist. The knot in her stomach eased somewhat as she looked at him.

The young witch appeared to be limping, and blood dripped from a number of cuts along Ethan's forehead and chest, but both were alive. A further look around the chamber and she found Nate and Shade, both in a similar state of disrepair. Nate's cocky grin as he flipped a long knife in his hand told her that he had sustained no serious damage. Shade's trademark scowl could have indicated he was at death's door and she'd have been none the wiser.

Finally, her eyes fell on Abi.

Her friend hung limply from her chains, no longer conscious, but breathing.

Without a word from her, Aria and Marcus rushed to unlock the chains, gently lowering her friend to the ground. Even as the wind picked up, blowing strands of red hair into her damp eyes, relief wrenched a sob from her throat. She'd been so afraid. So afraid they would die because of her. Her friends. Her family.

A sharp cackle echoed around the chamber and Phoenix whipped her head around, her adrenaline spiking once more. Everyone stood to attention with weapons drawn, waiting for the next threat to make itself known. But for a moment there was just silence, and the wind.

The cackle came once more, changing to a gurgling cough that choked off abruptly.

Phoenix followed the sound, ignoring Ethan's attempt to pull her back as she walked slowly towards the stone altar. The shadows seemed deeper somehow, more complete, but she could just about make out a woman's form lying hidden from view.

The witch.

Cursing the stupidity that allowed her to forget such a dangerous foe, Phoenix picked up a long, black blade that lay on the altar. Slowly, and deliberately, she made her way towards the woman that, not long before, had held her completely defenceless at Darius's mercy.

42

Even in the shadows Phoenix could see the dark stain that surrounded the witch. It slowly expanded as the blood continued to flow. A quick glance showed a jagged object protruding from the witch's chest that shuddered with each wracking cough. The dagger in Phoenix's hand suddenly seemed unnecessary.

"Kill me if you want, hybrid. It won't change anything." The witch's words wheezed out and were quickly followed by a coughing fit that brought up more than just phlegm.

In a blink, Ethan was by her side, extended claws gripping the witch's throat. Phoenix wasn't ashamed to admit that a large part of her felt satisfaction at the shift in power. She could easily turn her back and let the woman die. If she was so inclined. But something about the shrewd gaze that met hers made her hesitate.

"Ethan, wait."

She held out a hand towards him, as if the gesture alone would stop him if he decided to rip out the witch's throat.

"Let her speak."

Dark eyes met hers from the floor, assessing and calculating, even as the life force behind them seeped out onto the floor.

"Your friends may have saved you, child, but it's too late."

"Speak plainly, witch," Ethan growled, and his fist tightened on the pale throat beneath his grip. "Or I will gladly end your suffering."

"Nothing you can do will change my fate now, wolf." The witch's eyes briefly flicked towards his face before their heavy weight fell once more on Phoenix. "The spell was complete. The prophecy will be fulfilled tonight."

Phoenix felt her stomach drop as the tension she'd been holding left her body in a gasp. She had known. It had been too easy. Some part of her knew there was more to come.

Around her, everyone began to speak at once, but it was only noise. Her mind was unable to focus on anything besides the witch's words, repeating themselves over and over again in her head.

"Unless ..." The witch spoke in little more than a whisper, but it brought the noise to a sudden and complete halt, all eyes falling on her.

"Unless what?" Ethan shook her impatiently.

The witch glared at him even as another choking fit took hold of her failing body. When she'd caught her breath, the weight of her gaze landed on Phoenix and it softened as something akin to pity settled in the dark depths of her eyes.

"By your bloodline this was started," the voice that came out of the witch's mouth changed, becoming deeper as the wind began to whip around them with more force. "By your bloodline it may end."

Phoenix looked around nervously as confused murmurings echoed her own thoughts. The wind was picking up speed, and strands of red hair blew across her face, blurring her vision as it grew in strength.

Pushing the hair roughly from her face, she turned back to voice the multitude of questions flying around her head, only to find a lifeless form lying on the ground in front of her, shrewd eyes now staring blankly at the ceiling.

She glanced towards Ethan and the look he gave her mirrored the feeling of dread that was beginning to rise from the empty pit of her stomach.

"What the hell ..." Nate's voice drew everyone's attention as he pointed a shaky finger at a small vortex that was forming from the wind above the altar.

The centre of the vortex was growing darker by the

second, as if sucking away what little light filled the chamber.

A sharp intake of breath drew Phoenix's attention to her mother, who stood ghostly pale and stared at the blackness forming.

Phoenix rushed to Aria's side and grabbed her arm. "Mam? What is it?"

"He's done it," Aria said, haunted eyes turning to look at her daughter. "He's torn the fabric."

An icy fear washed over Phoenix, but her mind struggled to make sense of what she was seeing, and she felt a growing sense of hysteria. "I don't understand. What do you mean he's torn the fabric? He can't have torn the fabric."

Ethan came to her side and placed a gentle hand on her back, almost as if he needed to touch her. "The talisman." He looked at Aria for confirmation. "He's found a way to speed up the prophecy. And when the fabric becomes weak enough, they'll be able to get through."

"They –" Phoenix stopped suddenly, memories of a night not so long ago flashing through her mind. "Demons."

"Not just any demons," Aria said, her voice little more than a whisper. "Darius was planning on bringing through the Horsemen."

Phoenix backed away, shaking her head. Her

knowledge of the supernatural may have been sorely lacking, but every Supe knew of the Horsemen. They were the things that even the strongest supernatural feared; the bringers of death and destruction to all.

The voices around them raised, panic-filled questions that blurred into one.

"How long?"

"What happens if they get through?"

"How do we stop it?"

Phoenix knew the answer because the witch had told them. Her bloodline had started this, and only her bloodline could stop it. She looked around at the people who had risked their lives to save her. People that had become her friends. Family she'd only just gotten back. The thought of something happening to them hurt her heart. The knowledge that it would be her fault almost brought her to her knees.

But she could stop it. That was what the witch had been saying. She was the key.

Phoenix walked closer to the blackness. Her movements went unnoticed amongst the panic. As she watched, it pulsated and expanded. What had started as small as the narrow gash on her arm, now stretched almost three feet in length, suspended in nothingness.

The closer she got to it, the more she could feel its inexplicable pull. Darius had only used a small bit of her blood to complete the spell, but the darkness wanted more. Somehow, she knew it would take a much larger sacrifice to undo the wheels that had been set in motion.

Tears pricked the back of her eyes as she looked around again. She wasn't ready to say goodbye. For the first time in a very long time, she had more to lose than just Abi. But even that would've been enough. She wouldn't let these people die for her.

And with that thought clear in her mind, she stepped towards the void.

43

"Phoenix, no!"

Ethan grabbed her just in time. His heart raced like a freight train in his chest as the blackness reached eager tendrils towards its willing victim. She turned to look at him, a single tear rolling down her cheek, even as she resisted his pull.

"It's the only way, Ethan. You have to let me go."

He shook his head vehemently, unable to form the words as he pulled her forcefully away from the void and into his arms. For a moment, Phoenix resisted, but then he felt her body soften and she wrapped her arms around him, laying her head on his chest.

"It's the only way," she repeated, words muffled against the remnants of his torn shirt.

Ignoring her words, he held her closer and focused only on the heat of her body next to his. There had to be another way; there just had to. As the thought formed in his head, the wind began to pick up speed. A strange murky smoke trailed from the bottom of the gaping black hole, and as he watched, the edges pulsated and stretched. The smell of sulphur drifted up from the smoke that was settling on the ground around their feet. Ethan cast a worried glance towards Aria to find a similar look of concern filling her green eyes.

"Em ..." Nate cleared his throat awkwardly, "not to break up a touching moment and all that, but can I make a suggestion?"

Reluctantly, Ethan relaxed his hold on Phoenix as she twisted in his arms to look at Nate.

"Couldn't we just destroy the talisman?" Nate eyed the tear warily. "The Ouroboros. I'm assuming this was why they needed it?" He waved a hand towards the growing void.

A terrifying thread of hope surged through Ethan, but he cautiously held it in check. "Could it work?" he asked, directing the question to Lily, who stood looking uncomfortable by the stone altar.

She fidgeted nervously, averting her gaze from his as her shoulders dropped. "I already searched the witch. I couldn't find the talisman." Her soft-spoken words drove home like a knife, and Ethan felt the whisper of hope bleed from him.

"Do you mind if I check?" Aria looked in askance to

Lily before moving to crouch by the witch's frozen form.

As she rustled about, searching every inch of the witch and the surrounding area, the smoke began to thicken. The blackness that had seemed so complete only moments before, formed shadows that brought with them terrifying possibilities.

The bottom edge of the tear pulsed. Once. Twice. Three times. Then a black ink-like substance began to pour over the rim. It flowed and morphed in such a way that no one particular form could be discerned. He heard Phoenix's gasp as she too noticed the movement and her grip on him tightened involuntarily.

"Aria," he said, urgency biting at the edges of his tone. "I don't mean to rush you, but we seem to have a situation here."

A blade flew through the air, flipping handle over tip, and abruptly sliced through the inky mass, causing it to pool motionless on the ground.

"Not anymore we don't." Shade shrugged nonchalantly and spat on the ground.

But the blackness pulsed again, and yet more shadows began to slowly seep from its depths. Sinuous tendons reached out, searching the possibilities of their new surroundings.

Aria's face was sombre as she met his questioning look with a silent shake of her head and she looked longingly towards her daughter. Everyone began to speak over each other again, and he could feel Phoenix's deep breath as she stared intently at the hole that was now almost five foot long.

She'd do it. Despite her fear, and the unknown terrors beyond that void, she would sacrifice herself if there was no other way. Ethan looked around desperately. There had to be something he could do, someone he could kill. Instead, he found Marcus staring at him intently.

It was then he noticed the subtle prodding in his mind. Almost like a politely cautious knock on the door. Something told Ethan he could choose to answer the call or not, but the sadness and regret he saw in Marcus's eyes made him lower his defences.

I'm sorry, Ethan, I would never use your gift like this if I had a choice, but we're running out of time.

Marcus's words, although only in his head, were so clear that Ethan looked around to see if anyone else acknowledged the vampire's statement.

They didn't.

He looked back to Marcus in surprise, realising immediately what gift he was referring to. His blood had created a link with the vampire, however temporary, allowing Marcus to speak to him in a manner far more intimate than was comfortable.

The witch said bloodline, Ethan. Her bloodline *is the key.*

326

The words registered, but it took Ethan a moment to truly understand them. He had to stop himself before he spoke aloud, suddenly conscious once more of Phoenix's warm body still held in his arms.

No, he thought fervently, *she'll never let you do it.*

Dark eyes met his, filled with a sadness that had no words. *I know. That's why I need your help.*

Moving silently through the shadows, Marcus grabbed a small knife and stepped closer to the tear. Ethan tensed, preparing to shout his objection, when a light touch on his shoulder turned his focus to Aria, who now stood by his side. The shake of her head was barely perceptible, but the look in her eyes spoke volumes.

He hesitated, torn between protecting the woman in his arms and the truth that was staring them all in the face. The prophecy was coming, and if they didn't find a way to stop it, everyone would suffer. Conflicted, he watched silently as Marcus ran the blade along the palm of his hand. Blood flowed from the wound and dripped down towards the tendrils that were eagerly pulling themselves out of the black void.

The thick, viscous liquid hit the inky mass with a hiss, and the tendrils recoiled. Clumps fell to the ground, disintegrating in a cloud of sulphur. Marcus met his gaze for a brief moment, before turning to look at Aria. The look they shared was so full of love that Ethan almost felt like he was intruding on a private moment just by being in the same room.

We've had our time, Ethan. Marcus's voice came once more, steady and sure. *It's her time now.*

Phoenix chose that very moment to pull back from him. She squared her shoulders as she turned to face the others, oblivious to the panic that was constricting his chest.

She will never forgive me. He clenched his fists, wanting to reach out and pull her back to him.

The look Marcus gave him was sympathetic, but unwavering.

She will forgive you. And in time she will understand.

44

Phoenix's throat was achingly tight as she pulled back from the comforting warmth of Ethan's arms. The feeling of safety was just an illusion, but damn if she didn't want to cling to it. Which was why she had to move now. Before she lost her nerve.

Looking around, she was once again struck by the knowledge that these people had risked their lives to come for her. They knew who – and what – she was, yet they still came. She held that thought close to her and pointedly ignored the creeping tendrils and cloying smoke, turning first towards Nate.

The sparkling humour that seemed to show in his eyes no matter how dire the situation acted as a balm to her soul and allowed her to smile past the tightness in her chest as she hugged him. Phoenix couldn't tell if his eyes seemed just a little bit duller when she pulled back, but she quickly blocked the thought.

Lily was next to him, still slumped against the altar. She looked as dejected and broken as the night they first met. Phoenix wanted so much to wrap the young girl in her arms and tell her it would be okay.

But that would be a lie.

The best she could do was hug her tightly and pray to whatever god or goddess might be listening to watch over the young witch.

There was no hugging when it came to Shade. He simply paused his ongoing knife attack on the inky tendrils, looked her in the eye, and gave a single nod; the small gesture meaning more than words ever could.

Her heart shattered as she turned to look at Abi, still lying unconscious against the wall. She'd never get to tell her friend how sorry she was. Never get to tell her how much her friendship meant. Kneeling by her side, Phoenix gently brushed the hair back from Abi's sweat-soaked face. She let her forehead rest against Abi's cheek for a brief moment, and whispered, "I love you," before giving herself a brisk shake and rising to stand once more.

Phoenix took a deep breath and turned to face her parents, who were now standing side by side at the altar. Tears threatened to break free of the prison that had held them for ten long years. Memories of laughter and childhood innocence brought with them a yearning so strong she almost doubled over.

"At least this time we get to say goodbye," she said, attempting a weak smile.

The returning smile her mother gave her was so full of love and pride that it was almost painful to look at. She let herself fall into Aria's open arms as a sob of pure, raw grief broke free from her throat.

Her mother held her close, gently rocking her as Phoenix breathed in the warm scent that reminded her so much of happier times. Another set of arms surrounded them both. Broader. Stronger. She knew without looking that it was her father, and even with what was to come, she felt safe.

"We're so proud of you, sweetheart." Her father smoothed back her hair and his warm voice became deeper as it strained with emotion. "So proud of the woman you've become."

At his words, the tears came. She shook her head and pressed her forehead against her mother's shoulder as she fought to stay strong for a little longer.

Just a little longer.

"I failed, Dad. I couldn't stop him."

Marcus turned her firmly towards him and lifted her chin to ensure she was looking him in the eye. "It wasn't your job to stop him, Phoenix. We should've protected you better. We should've prepared you better."

His dark brown eyes were full of such sadness that all she could do was hug him tightly.

Eventually he pulled back, took a deep breath, and smiled as he held her at arms-length. For a moment, he seemed to be taking in her every feature, then he turned her with a knowing nod and gentle push towards Ethan.

The look of raw pain that met her as she raised her eyes to meet Ethan's stole her breath away and brought the tightness back to her chest tenfold. She searched in vain for something to say, some way to let him know how much it meant that he'd come for her, but she couldn't find the right words. She didn't even know where to start.

His strong arms reached for her and pulled her against the warmth of his chest. She felt small in his embrace, and for a moment, she let herself revel in the safety of the solid muscle that seemed almost contradictory in its welcoming softness.

"I'm sorry. I'm so sorry. Please forgive me," he whispered desperately, lips pressed into her hair.

The words registered with her, but they didn't make sense. Why was he apologising? Phoenix moved to pull away. She needed to tell him it wasn't his fault, but as she tried to pull back, his arms locked tighter around her.

A mild sense of panic washed over her as she pushed against the restriction, but she fought it back, understanding his desire to protect her. However pointless it might be.

He needs to let me go. There's no other way.

She raised her head, ready to reason with him – plead

with him, if necessary – so that he wouldn't make this harder than it already was, but the look in his eyes stopped the words before they even left her mouth. The earlier sadness was there, but now it was overshadowed by a resolve unlike anything she'd ever seen in those rich brown eyes.

And he wasn't looking at her.

It was then that Phoenix realised she'd missed something. Something important. Panic overwhelmed her as she began to struggle in earnest, twisting her neck to follow his gaze towards her parents. They stood together holding hands, looking at her with eyes filled with so much love she almost missed the subtle shadow of regret. As she watched, they stepped closer to the blackness, and the inky tendrils grasped for their legs.

A wordless scream clawed its way up her throat as she wrenched against Ethan's arms, her hand reaching for them. Willing them to step back towards her. Praying the look on their faces meant something other than what she feared.

Her mother smiled, her face peaceful. "I'm so grateful we got to see you one last time, sweetheart. It was more than I ever hoped for."

Marcus put one arm around his wife's shoulders and tucked her close to his side. His other hand reached out, revealing a folded piece of paper with tattered and torn edges.

The banshee wail began before they even moved. The sorrowful keening filled the chamber and ripped her aching soul to shreds.

"We love you so much. Don't ever forget that."

With that, they turned as one and stepped into the void.

Her scream was swallowed in a flash of blinding light as the folded paper fell to the ground.

45

Flashes of light. Snippets of conversations. It was all a blur. Phoenix had no idea how much time had passed. For all she knew, the fabric could have torn and the black void swallowed them whole.

For all she cared.

As the sounds started slowly filtering into her consciousness, she looked around in a daze. It seemed as if everything was moving in slow motion. The image was made even more surreal by the smoke that filled the chamber.

She was dimly aware that Ethan's arms still surrounded her, but she couldn't hear any of the words he spoke. They didn't matter anyway. There was no sign of the tear, no sign of any demons. And no sign of her parents.

They were gone.

A strange numbness filled her body from the knowledge, providing a detachment that was almost comforting. It was all just a sick joke. Or a bad dream. Maybe she'd never really found her parents again, and everything to this point had been the wishful imagination of a lost child.

A fluttering movement on the ground caught her eye and pulled her out of her rambling thoughts, drawing her attention to the spot she last imagined her father standing. On shaky legs, she pushed away from Ethan. This time he let her go.

The floor rushed up to meet her as she stumbled and fell to her knees. She pushed an unsteady hand out to grasp the yellowing piece of paper that lay on the ground. Some part of her consciousness told her it was important, but her thoughts were so jumbled that the dots weren't connecting.

The paper was old, edges fraying, with dark splattered stains marring the surface. In the far recesses of her mind, she recognised the shiny surface of a photograph, and she was overcome with a sudden need to see what secrets it held.

Her fingers fumbled ineptly, shaking so badly she was terrified she'd rip it. Ethan's large hand appeared before her, and she hesitated for a second before handing it over. She watched him unfold it, gently, as if it was the most fragile thing in the world.

The picture revealed itself and her breath left her completely. The smiling green eyes of an innocent child and the loving gaze of two adoring parents. The scene burned itself into her mind, searing open old wounds even as new, deeper scars were forming.

So many memories. So much happiness. All buried deep in order for that innocent child to survive.

A scream of anguish left her throat raw.

Strong arms enveloped her as the tears began to fall in earnest, blurring her vision. They tried to pull her close, but she resisted, recognising his scent. Recognising the arms that had restrained her while her parents sacrificed themselves.

With a cry of fury, she beat her fists against the solid wall of Ethan's chest. She wanted to hurt him. She wanted to make him feel even a fraction of the pain that was shredding her apart.

But he didn't budge. He stood before her, making no move to stop the blows, arms ready and waiting to hold her.

Eventually the sobbing slowed and a bone-aching weariness washed over her. She slumped against him, empty and shivering. The heat that burned through his blood-soaked t-shirt did nothing to chase the chill away.

"It should have been me."

Ethan's body tensed at her whispered words, and he pulled back so suddenly Phoenix almost fell over. He grabbed her shoulders in a bruising grip as fire blazed in his brown eyes.

"Don't you dare say that."

Anger wrapped around her like a familiar blanket and she clung to it eagerly.

"It should have been me! My blood, Ethan. It should have been my blood that closed the tear. And you stopped me."

"Dammit, Phoenix. Don't you get it?" Ethan yelled, his voice cracking. "I had to do it. I couldn't lose you."

He pulled her forcefully to him. His lips crushed hers and stopped her anger in its tracks. His hands were like fire as they pressed against her back, pulling her tight against him. The fierce eagerness of his mouth created a luscious contrast to the softness of his lips and her head swam with the muskiness of his scent.

She couldn't think straight. The cold that had overtaken her body shifted to molten lava as shock was replaced by an almost primal need. She gave herself over to the sensations, and for a moment, the world became little more than lips, and teeth, and hands.

And then once again the world was empty.

Ethan stood away from her, breathing ragged with an uncertain look in his eyes. His hands clenched into fists by his sides, almost as if he needed to stop himself from reaching out for her.

The silence in the chamber was deafening.

Her heartbeat roared in her ears, and her lips burned with the memory of him. She was suddenly acutely aware of all the eyes that watched them.

"We need to get out of here." Shade's voice was cold as he pushed past her on his way to the stairs.

46

Phoenix hovered by the bedroom door, nervously twining the platinum medallion around her fingers. For the first time since she'd come to the pub, she was unsure of her welcome.

She'd stayed away for twenty-four hours, but even with Lily's assurances, she needed to see for herself that Abi was okay. And she needed to say goodbye.

Ignoring the sickening twist of her stomach, she pushed open the door and peeked hesitantly into Abi's bedroom.

"I was wondering how long you were planning on loitering outside the door." Abi smiled up at her from the bed where she lay engulfed by soft, fluffy cushions spanning the colours of the rainbow.

Her naturally pale skin held a deathly hue that made her seem almost green. Fortunately, the shade nicely accentuated the mottled bruising which formed a patchwork over her cheek. Her arm was held tight against her body in a sling. Much of the damage had been minor or superficial, thankfully. But psychological damage was always harder to quantify.

That had been Darius's pleasure – psychological torture. It could last so much longer than mere physical pain, and hurt in so many ways the body couldn't.

"You're awake." Phoenix fidgeted nervously. "I wasn't sure you would be."

The attempt at casual sounded pathetic even to her own ears, but for the first time, she didn't know quite what to say to her best friend.

Sorry I've lied to you for all these years?

Or, how about, sorry that lie almost got you killed?

"Would you come sit on the bloody bed. You're making me feel like I've got the plague." Abi's tone was light and teasing as she scooted over awkwardly, but her eyes were serious as she watched her friend.

Phoenix stepped fully into the room and steeled herself for what was to come as she shut the door behind her. She deserved whatever Abi threw at her.

She perched on the edge of the bed, itching to reach out and take her friend's hand. To apologise. To find any way that might make her understand. But she kept her hands clasped firmly in her lap.

"I should have told you –"

"Yes, you should have." Abi's blue eyes turned to steel.

Phoenix looked down at her hands, unable to face the anger that blazed behind those eyes. "I wanted to apologise. I don't expect you to ever forgive me, but I needed you to know how sorry I am before I left."

"You're leaving?" Abi sat bolt upright, only just managing to disguise the wince of pain.

"I didn't think you'd want me around after –"

"Phoenix," Abi said firmly, "Phoenix, look at me."

The hand that grabbed her arm looked so frail and pale, yet it held an unexpected strength as Abi demanded her attention. "I'm not angry that I got hurt – well okay, I am, but not at you – I'm angry that you didn't trust me."

The words registered, but they didn't make sense. Confused, Phoenix raised her gaze to meet blue eyes that had softened considerably, but still held firm with resolve.

"Phoenix, I don't care if you're a vampire, or whatever the hell you are –" Abi stopped for a second, a confused look on her face. "Actually, what are you?"

"I –"

"No, no," Abi shook her head, waving the thought away with her hands, "it doesn't matter. You can tell me later."

It was Phoenix's turn to shake her head as her confusion increased by the minute. "Abi, what do you mean it doesn't matter? Of course it matters."

"Why? I know who you are, Phoenix. You're my best friend. Sure, you're irritating and stubborn as hell, but how does any of that change?"

You're my best friend? Present tense?

Phoenix stared at Abi in complete and utter disbelief, the tears that burned the back of her eyes coming on so suddenly she had to swallow hard to hold them back. But Abi wasn't planning to let her off the hook that easily.

"That doesn't change the fact that you should have told me." The stern look was back, chastising her like a bold child that had just written all over the newly painted white walls. "You should have trusted me."

There was nothing Phoenix could say in her defence. How could she explain to Abi that she'd grown so used to the idea of being rejected that it never even occurred to her to try? Of course, with Abi being a human, it was slightly different, but that didn't make it right.

As Abi continued to berate her, Phoenix watched her friend silently. There were so many things she wanted to share with this wonderful human being. A huge part of her wanted to embrace the acceptance and forget everything else. But she couldn't. And Abi wasn't going to like what she had to say next.

"He's still out there," Phoenix said softly. "Darius. He's out there and he's dangerous."

Tentatively, she took Abi's hand in hers and allowed, for once, the full force of her fear to show on her face. No more hiding. "He's not going to stop until he gets what he wants. And now he knows he can get to me through you."

Abi squeezed her hand tightly. "What are you trying to say, Phoenix?"

"Ethan knows a place, a safe house you can go to. It's run by shifters. They can protect you there. He won't be able to find you."

"No." Abi pulled her hand away and sat further up in the bed. "I have a life here. A business. I'm not going to run scared."

"Dammit, Abi. You could have been killed!"

"Don't you think I know that? I was there, remember."

"This isn't your fight."

"Yes, it is."

Abi relaxed against the headboard of the bed with a look of utter surety settling over her features. "I know what he's planning, Phoenix. You can't tell me this isn't my fight. It's humans that will suffer if he succeeds. We have more right to be counted in this than anyone."

And just like that, every argument Phoenix had was taken from her. Because Abi was right. "I can't watch you die too," she whispered as the tears began to fall for what felt like the umpteenth time in the past twenty-four hours.

Abi smiled as she wiped a tear from her cheek. "Then

you'll have to teach me how to kick some serious ass."

Phoenix laughed, her first genuine laugh in what felt like a very long time.

The gentle smile on her friend's face turned devilish.

"So, when are we going to talk about that kiss?"

*****

Not ready for it to end?
Find out how it all began …

Join Phoenix in a FREE bonus short story exploring her life in the lead up to her parent's disappearance and her residency with the Dublin vampire clan.

Get your copy at <u>pages.lmhatchell.com/3mm</u>

Author Note

Thank you for joining me on this new adventure through Ireland's hidden supernatural world. If you enjoyed this book, I would be very grateful if you could leave a brief review (it can be as short as you like) on the site where you purchased your copy.

As an author, reviews are the most powerful tools in my arsenal when it comes to getting attention for my books. Honest feedback goes a long way in increasing visibility and helping me to reach other readers like you, so thank you in advance!

A Quick Thanks

I'm sure most readers will skip this section, but I couldn't finish the book without saying thank you to the people who are most important to me. I'll keep it short and sweet, so no one can accuse me of getting too mushy.

For my Mam, who instilled a love of books in me from as far back as I can remember, and will read this book from front to back even though she has zero interest in urban fantasy. And my Dad, who probably won't read a word of it but will be proud of me nonetheless.

For my partner and my baby girl, who support me in everything I do (well the baby doesn't really have a choice, but she's adorable so she has to get a mention). I hope I make you proud.

And for Sandra, who I can always count on to be my cheerleader. Thank you for being the best sounding board through this process.

WHERE TO FIND ME ONLINE

LMHatchell.com

Facebook.com/LMHatchell

Just want to be notified when I've a new release?

Follow me on:

Bookbub

Amazon Author Central

Made in the USA
Monee, IL
29 January 2022

90278481R00208